The Chilling Zone

Morgan Duran

Cover illustration by Teja Arboleda

For more information on the author please visit:
www.Morgan-Duran.com

Entertaining Diversity Press is a subsidiary of
Entertaining Diversity, Inc.
www.EntertainingDiversity.com

ISBN: 0692756183
ISBN-13: 978-0692756188

DEDICATION

Dedicated to Mr. Rodman, my 10th grade English teacher. He read my first "novel" and actually managed to give me serious feedback, while keeping a straight face. "Never be afraid to let something end up completely different than you thought it would be when you started."

ACKNOWLEDGMENTS

This book has been a long time in coming and I've had amazing support from so many people. First, I would like to thank my husband for believing in this project, reviewing drafts and encouraging me forward even when I was feeling far from my goal. I also owe a debt of gratitude to those who gave of their time reading various early drafts and providing me with important feedback and suggestions. They include Pamela McCarthy, Will Hines, Dana Moreshead, and Marlis Joergensen Arboleda. Special thanks also to my daughter Katie for brainstorming with me on futuristic brand names. Of course no book would be complete without the ministrations of a good copyeditor. I'd like to thank Cyrena Musset for her steady attention and suggestions in the final preparation of this manuscript. Thank you also to Meghan Corbett for introducing me to Cyrena.

THE CHILLING ZONE

Year: 2062
The Chilling Zone: Boston, Massachusetts

She had ten perfect little fingers, ten perfect little toes, and a blank neural network of flexi-wired etchable silicon plate. Daddy was very proud of her, premature as she was. He emptied the third and final injection of insulin-transported Amino-Enzymatic Accelerant into her abdomen and vowed to watch over her more carefully than he did the last time. Daddy was very attached to this little girl. He wouldn't leave at all...except now his work was done. All she needed was her name. When it arrived, the Governess would bring her unique magic to the sacred circle of the Chilling Zone—and she worked strictly alone.

Daddy looked up to stretch his eyes and caught his reflection in the mirrored surface of the refrigerated storage locker above the one containing this precious girl. He was grayer now than he used to be; not just his hair, but his skin. His shoulders sagged perpetually bunched toward each other across his concave chest. *Who are you,* he asked himself. One course segment of his hair reached for the sky from over the right arm of his thick black plastic glasses. His brown eyes were creased into a perpetual expression of concern. The collar of his white button-down shirt lay half in and half out of his lab coat.

Daddy looked down again at the helpless female form, known for the time being only as F-03. Female number three. There were two failed females before her and three failed males. Staring at the closed eyelids and placid expression of his latest design, he remembered the terrifying disintegration of the last trial and felt his stomach curl into itself. That was three years ago. The Morbidity and Mortality team determined that the neural interface itself was unstable. So the programming committee was sent on retreat to the Caymen Islands while the hardware Research & Development team stayed at home playing with rat neurons. He was cloistered in the lab to seed the next batch of cell clusters, a precise but not mentally challenging task.

Maybe if he'd gone with the programmers the doubts that now consumed him would never have rooted. He could have spent two weeks buried in schematics and pontificating about null DNA strings ten hours a day, taking breaks only to sip margaritas on the beach at lunchtime. Instead, he was juggling eyedroppers and Bunsen burners in the lab with nothing to do but think.

Daddy struggled to comprehend how naïve he had been when he signed on to the Transformation Protocol project six years earlier. Dubbed T-Col for short, the Protocol was the brainchild of Dr. Alexander Imitri. Daddy was recruited straight out of his fellowship by Dr. Imitri himself. The ink was barely dry on his board certification in Hybrid Maintenance Medicine before he was sucked into the vortex of power and politics that was the Transformation Protocol.

The HMM specialty was a new offshoot of Internal Medicine combining general care, genetics, and neurology. This cutting edge combination grew out of the need for specialists to care for the genetically enhanced clone workforce that had been licensed for use in highly hazardous industries. The clone workers were implemented after a number of landfill miners suffered from toxic exposure to mercury that had been buried in the late twentieth century. Daddy had been fascinated by the processes used to tinker with the inner workings of the immune system, and also in the maintenance of the neural interfaces used to implant the specialized tools and prostheses the workers needed in order to fulfill their functions. He already had three offers on the table and was about to sign on with a mining company in Pennsylvania when he met Dr. Imitri.

From the moment of their first discussion, the mere concept of T-Col excited him. The government was disappointed in the performance of their current mode of memory filtering. "Associative Filtering" had been designed to wipe select memories from the minds of insurgents and compromised secret agents for the past ten years. The incidence of tracer memories triggering a cascade of reconnection of the neurons involved in the filtered memory was too high, resulting in the need for termination of subjects on a regular basis. The Integrationist party, which had been gaining support as the depth of the economic recession increased, was beginning to take note of the disappearance of their operatives. Exposure by the Integrationists, who were willing to do anything to bring the United States back into the world economy, would have threatened the secrecy of the entire anti-terrorism strategy of the Office of Civilian Defense. The OCD was adamant that the success rate for elimination of unwanted knowledge be improved.

The basic concept of T-Col was elegant but complex. Dr. Imitri postulated that an interweaving of cloning technology, associative filtering techniques, and gene therapy could be used to transfer the consciousness and DNA template of a target into a blank clone template. He asserted, that the risk of the unwanted residual memories called "tracers" would be low, given that the template brain would never before have been exposed to the information. Logic dictated that one can't retrieve a memory that never existed. President Andrew Fein, concerned as he was about the rise in internal terrorist attacks approved the project and it's extensive budget without even informing the Central Senate.

Daddy fit the profile of the idealistic patriot that the project needed precisely. His skills in the relatively new field of Hybrid Maintenance Medicine were essential to construct a stable template onto which a Primary personality could be imposed. He was full of spit and fire against the Integrationists who themselves had been run out of power after they were accused of organizing the bombing of Atlanta General Hospital. Daddy's father, a brilliant surgeon and a supportive father, had been killed in the Atlanta bombing. Daddy learned of his death two months before his own graduation from medical school.

Common knowledge had it that the Integrationists thought they could gain support for their policies by blaming the attack on extremist elements of the isolationist and authoritarian Home Trust party. Instead, the Integrationist President and his entire cabinet had been jailed and Home Trust party leader Andrew Fein assumed control of the government, vowing to root out treason from every corner in which it was hidden.

Given the opportunity to expose the Integrationist insurgents responsible for the continued destruction of so many families like his own, Daddy committed himself thoroughly to T-Col. He felt like a bold protector of the country's citizenry. His template forms were flawless. The assimilation of DNA introduced was almost one hundred per cent. The likenesses they created of various volunteer DNA donors were indistinguishable from their Primaries. In the initial tests, however, brain function was missing and the inert copies were destroyed after each test run.

Even the first two or three memory transfer failures had not deflated Daddy's belief in the importance of the Transformation Protocol. One male and one female had simply never integrated a cognitive pattern and remained inert. Another male accepted a cognitive pattern, but old memories slid out as new ones developed and the team found it impossible to communicate with the neural implant. He never gained consciousness. The other male retained a greater percentage of the memories introduced, but the communication problem remained. While disappointing, these failures were benign—just part of the process. It was the memory of the second female failure that haunted him.

The Primary in that case had been convicted at a closed Office of Civilian Defense tribunal of transferring capital out of the country for the purpose of supporting the remnants of the old Integrationist administration. The Integrationists still considered themselves to be the true government of the United States of America. The convicted woman was a financial strategist who had extensive knowledge of the secret hermit lines that routed around the data seals of the embargo barriers erected by the Federal International Organization to enforce US isolation. The OCD wanted that information at their disposal. Her politics made her an enemy of the State, but her knowledge was worth saving.

The tech team didn't think to warn Daddy before the procedure that their revised technique would eliminate the sedation process for the Primary in order to apply their new direct patterning solution. Daddy watched in horror as she spasmed and writhed. *My God! She can feel everything!*

Daddy closed his eyes and shook his head to bury the memories in the sand of his subconscious once again. The thought and movement combination triggered the beginnings of a migraine behind his eyes. At first, he'd briefly considered having the memory filtered, conventionally of course, but he decided that he didn't want to forget the lesson in humility that the experience had taught him.

The migraine bloomed from front to back in Daddy's head and his peripheral vision blurred. Clearly he'd been working too hard. At least that's what he told himself when he took off his examination gloves and crouched next to F-03's storage platform. He felt the tops of his plastic safety clogs bite into the joints of his toes as he lowered himself to face her. Just the smallest nubs of what would be hair peeked out of her pristine scalp. Wasn't there yesterday. Even in his current mindset, he maintained a horrified fascination with these featureless hybrid clones, but this was now blended with a sad compassion. He stroked her head with his bare hand. The hair follicles were stiff and sharp.

He was crossing all boundaries by not closing her away and walking sternly out of that room. Some part of him, however, was pushing at a limit—he didn't even know of what—and he had to stay. He stroked her cheek. It felt like the skin of an infant, as did the skin of her slightly rounded breasts and the surface of her arm. The toenails on her feet remained undifferentiated. When she had a name, their final shape would take form along with the contours of her face and her mind. "You're going to make it," he promised, more to assure himself than the unhearing clone. "I promise, I won't let anything happen to you. Everything's going to be all right."

Daddy slid the drawer shut just as his assistant poked his head through the partially open sliding glass door. "Dr. Ames, the Director's on line one."

"Thank you, John. I'll be right there."

John scooted back through the anteroom and into the hall. Daddy followed shortly thereafter, with a pause and a prayer for the forms contained in the six additional drawers across from him. *God save our souls.*

Total Wire News Service – Manhattan Bureau: New York, New York

Jessica Butler spun around in the cradle of her Wire station, smirking gleefully. *I'm such a fucking genius,* she thought. She turned back to her interface hub and placed the glowing rose-colored floaters back over her eyes just in time to see her news feed go live. Connected to the TWNS nexus as they were, the lightweight glasses were capable of displaying both the public feed and the Service's internal reaction monitoring system simultaneously. Virtual impressions of her hands and arms played across her sightline as she tidied up her virtual workspace.

Jessica pictured millions of individuals in their homes, offices and Porters—hopefully on autopilot—being simultaneously informed of the dangers of the armies of bacteria being harbored in their upholstered furniture. From the day the hybrid interactive virtual reality modules, called neuro-diode consoles, were added to the public's entertainment systems the power of the media to incite public reaction was increased tenfold.

She considered the cascading effects of her current story. Twenty percent of viewers will stand and make casual excuses as to why they have to sit in old wooden chairs. Five percent will panic and run to their bathroom to take a shower. Ten percent will be asleep in front of or immersed in the virtual reality functions of their consoles, some of them poking at and manipulating magnified images of the various "dangerous" critters as they appear in their view space. About eight percent just won't give a shit.

It was the other fifty-seven percent her sponsor was interested in, those people who will quietly absorb the information, maybe even think it's absurd at first. This group will carry her story around with them until the next time they pass a furniture store. Then the seed of doubt will grow. *Maybe it is time to update the décor.* They'll think. Then will come the justification. *Hey, the news said I could stay healthier by buying new furniture every three to five years.* That seed of doubt is the one that will make them take out their wallets and hand them to her sponsor without blinking. *God and country, folks. Gotta perteckt the family—ah yup.*

Jessica locked up her clips and files before shutting down and pulling the copper colored lightweight dedo controllers off her hands. She was glad she upgraded, some days she almost forgot the dedos were there as she clicked away on the virtual interface driver. They moved seamlessly with her fingers. Form-fitting without being restrictive. No more gloves attached to the new set, just the activators and their slightly fuzzy, lined cabling running from her wrists across her palms and fingers. The freedom of ditching the old hardware interface made this part of her job doable. Of course, some days it was harder than others to keep up the front. *Jessica*

Butler, hard-hitting news reporter, bringing you everything that's important in your miniscule, tedious world.

Jessica applied carnation pink lipstick while fumbling through her shoulder bag, looking for her Mini-Mate net interface. A strand of her blunt cut jet black hair fell over her eye as she leaned in. Finally her fingers felt the curved edges of the portable computer and she pulled it out. She tossed the lipstick carelessly into the jumble of tools and electronica she carried wherever she went. She signed on to the Mate and dropped into her private Parlor on the public nucleus. Jessica's home base in the interactive universe was functional, but not unattractive. The space reflected Jessica's ironic salute to the common name for each person's virtual access to the net. Like a real-world parlor, it is where one was to enter and exit and accept communications and visitors. Today she didn't bother to recline on the spongy black sofa or even flick on the tiffany floor lamp that would illuminate the peach-colored walls.

Three messages awaited her attention. Richard. *Euw!* He was the new guy in the graphics department who liked to croon over how exotic it was that she was half Japanese. He kept staring at her eyes and trying to stroke her hair. *If I wasn't undercover...* she thought. [Delete]

Moving on. Automated message from her Scrubbie Mabel. [Read] "Reminder: get milk for coffee. Yes. You need for morning. Yes. Mabel." Jessica could never get over the strange grammatical structure the engineers programmed into the Scrubbies. *Yes, we get it. They're not human. They're robots. Can we get over it now, please? God!* [Delete]

Last message. It was from Delph. *Finally!* [Read] "Ready to rock. The Wolf is bustin' its leash. 593 Park Drive West. 1pm. Same room." Jessica relaxed a little now. The pieces were in place. She smiled at Delph's pet-name for the customized mobile nucleus he used to rule whatever corner of the net he chose to focus on. *Life is good.* [Secure Delete]

Jessica spent the walk to the porter platform contemplating her dinner options. Chinese? No. Indian! Yes! She rotated the navigator and plugged in the address of her favorite takeout, then leaned back in her seat and looked out the sun roof as the porter engaged and slipped out of the platform bay.

As the she neared the secure exit of the Newswire complex, Jessica languidly reached her left arm out the window and passed her Express Access Subdermal chip under the scanner. *Bleep! It's so EASy!* Jessica thought, aping the ubiquitous advertising phrase currently in use to lure the general population into implanting their most intimate personal information and financial access codes into the EASy chips in their arms. It was a difficult transition for those who still suffered under the delusion that privacy existed. Somewhere in the wirespace nuclei of the security company and her bank, two computers shook hands, introduced themselves and decided that she was in fact who she said she was. The appropriate parking fee was subtracted from her account and the gate swung open, freeing her to leave. The front-end sensors on the porter's navigation system detected the removal of the barrier and she slid forward into the street.

Entering traffic, the porter turned left and paused at a traffic light. A team of the city's Scrubbie clean up crew crossed in front of them and began vacuuming the sidewalk and polishing the parking meters. Their brushed aluminum limbs and square faces reminded her of some archival footage she's seen of an old cartoon. *What was that called again?*

The janitor's union had caused quite a ruckus during the transition to the automated force. There were even rumors that they had sabotaged a group of Scrubbies near a grammar school, reprogramming them to spray profanities onto the sidewalk with foaming cleanser. Let's just say those responsible won't be seen for quite some time.

The light turned and Jessica's porter glided ahead toward midtown. She sighed and shifted in her seat. Two people scurried into the subway station at 14th Street. She had her boss Tripp to thank for the unlimited Central Region permit that allowed her to drive anywhere in the city at any time without paying a fee. It was part of her benefits package for leading a double life. Yes, she was an innocuous, if pestering, reporter by day; secret agent for the Office of Civilian Defense by—well also by day—and by night too. It was amazing she ever found time to sleep. *Oh, that reminds me…* she made a mental note to pick up a bottle of Prolert before heading home.

Passing under the bridge near the entrance to the Lincoln tunnel, she admired the new billboard, reminding young people of their military obligation. "TWO YEARS OF SERVICE—A LIFETIME OF PRIDE." The graphic showed a small cluster of well-armed young people seizing unauthorized produce at the US Border. Below and to the right of that, a thankful family sat around a chrome table, saying grace to their abundant and safe, legal food.

In the two-dozen years since reinstitution of the draft, most people had gotten used to the idea of forestalling their career ambitions long enough to complete their service or get killed, whichever came first. Jessica herself, thought she probably would have been sent to the Canadian border instead of the Mexican front, given her lack of insight at the time of her graduation from college. Of course, her current choice of profession counted as her service. So, she was saved from the tedium.

As she curved around the private drive of her condo complex, Jessica pinged Mabel remotely to open the door for her. "Jessica. Welcome home. Yes? I take the packages. Yes."

Jessica stepped into her sparse entryway and handed over her bags of tandoori and palak paneer. She upended the Duane Reade bag, dumping the small box of Prolert on the counter and made short work of opening the safety seals. She had a lot to do tonight and couldn't afford to fall asleep. "Mabel. Food. On plates. Yes?"

"Yes." The Scrubbie flustered toward the cabinet.

Mabel was Jessica's first large purchase after landing the job at TWNS and was still the best investment she'd had made for her home. Mabel's initial programming was flawless and she'd learned Jessica's preferences in the first two weeks. In the time Mabel had been sharing the condo, Jessica's bedroom had been transformed from a clothing graveyard, to an oasis for relaxation. Mabel even independently discarded the items Jessica had not worn in more than a year. Jessica had grown accustomed to calling in her dinner request an hour before coming home for the night and Mabel's even voice was a much less jarring wake up call in the morning than the shrill beeping of her old alarm clock.

Jessica began to wonder if she'd been wise to buy a model with that purplish hue. She thought she might get sick of it soon. Maybe if she bought Mabel one of those little ruffly hats...She crinkled up the corner of her mouth before downing two Prolerts with the glass of water Mabel delivered without Jessica needing to request it. *Too much programming to waste though. I'll live with it.*

The Golden Pilsner Pub: Washington, District of Columbia

The patrons of the Golden Pilsner were in a peculiar state of elatedness tonight, which suited Evan Marcelo just fine. It was all the better for a private conversation. He craned his neck to check the doorway again. He leaned back into the shadows, flexing and unflexing his hands and tapping his feet restlessly. He felt claustrophobic folding his six-foot two frame into the tiny corner booth. The dark stain of the wooden wainscoting made the space feel even smaller. Marcelo lifted the small cocktail menu from the middle of the table and began fanning himself. *Damn stuffy in here. Where the hell is he?*

The waitress came by with his second whiskey sour. He tipped her well. She called him "sir", but her eyes lingered longer than they should have, draping themselves across his well-muscled arms and over his tawny complexion. Lately there'd been a sudden outburst of jungle fever in this town for Native men. It started with that damn documentary. Ordinarily, he'd be happy to attract the attention of a little skirt like this. Just not tonight. Not in this place. "Is there anything else I can do for you, sir?"

"No," he replied sternly.

"Well, you just let me know." She sauntered away, swaying more than she was naturally designed to.

Soon afterward, Central Senate Leader David Marks slid into the seat across from him. Always well-pressed in public, he pulled his burgundy tie loosely askew as he greeted Marcelo. "Sorry. I was stuck in a committee meeting."

"Anything interesting?"

"Nothing I can talk about without having you killed." He raised his hand for the waitress. His gold Rolex gleamed against his chocolate brown skin.

"Then you might as well tell me, cause it could all be moot by tomorrow any way."

"Stop being cynical. You're a professional."

"That's why I'm cynical."

Marks glanced at Marcelo sideways and ordered his scotch. Neat, of course. He turned back to Marcelo. "Going underground is the best you can do right now. You'll have more freedom of movement. Your accounts and identities are all secured. I even have a lead on an insider with the OCD. An informant should be in the loop soon."

"You don't think they'll be looking out for spies?"

Marks feigned insult. "Sir, I'm insulted that you would imply such a thing. I'm the Leader of the Central Senate."

Marcelo smirked and huffed a half-laugh. His foot began tapping again.

"And as of Friday I control the OCD budget too." Marks handed Marcelo a package. There's everything you need. You'll find I've been very thorough about your routes of egress." The Senator's drink arrived promptly and with an unexpected additional whiskey sour for Marcelo. Marks reached into his coat pocket and pulled out a small foil packet. He unfolded the top and offered it to Marcelo. "Nothing like a little Polythanidone to calm the beasts of doubt within, huh?"

Marcelo took two of the small orange tablets and dropped them into his drink. They were still fizzing when he gulped them down. He felt the effervescent tingle down the length of his esophagus and the spread of warmth through his stomach, his chest, his arms and legs. His heart slowed and his jaw loosened. *Relief.* It was just what he needed. Senator Marks was lowering his glass from his lips and exhaling contentedly when Marcelo looked up again. "They say the Central Senate will eventually make Pollie illegal."

"Not a chance." Marks said with finality, leaning his head against the high back of the chair and closing his eyes.

Jessica Butler's Condominium – Amsterdam and 61st Street: New York, New York

In mid-town Manhattan the twentieth century block apartment buildings and drab stores with dusty plate glass windows and metal-framed doors had been replaced with sleek multi-block high rise gated communities. Jessica's unit looked over the now private block of 61st Street. The road had been lined with a garden of tropical flowers that were warmed by discrete full spectrum heat lamps built into the landscaping. The poor schmucks overlooking Amsterdam had to watch the daily parade of underemployed who gathered around a city garbage can, waiting to be chosen for odd day jobs. Jessica saw enough of the underbelly of humanity at work. She paid an extra 30,000 credits to avoid the unsightly distraction.

Comfortably changed into royal blue silk pajamas, Jessica scuffed down the hallway feeling the nap of the carpet drag through her toes. The expanse of the almond colored walls was undefiled with the exception of several photographs of herself with her boss Tripp and some dignitary or other. She lifted her Mate pocket interface from the breakfast bar on her way to the living room.

The two-bedroom single-floor unit was sparse, but comfortable. Two years before, Jessica had splurged on an interior decorator. He read Jessica well, opening up the floor plan between the narrow kitchen and the living room. The color scheme featured a varied palate of natural solids and thick fabrics. The picture window in the living room was draped in frosted brown, reaching elegantly toward sand plush carpeting. The sofa and chaise lounge were forest green.

Mabel had already finished putting away the leftovers and making the kitchen sparkle. When she was done, she'd stowed herself in her cubbie-charger, so the room was quiet. As she turned toward the couch, Jessica's elbow jabbed the marble corner of the counter. She didn't feel anything.

Jessica sank into the soft cushions and stretched her feet out on the wrought iron coffee table in front of her. She jacked her Mate into the dock on the projection console, tuned in to some sit-com she didn't recognize, and connected to the OCD nucleus. Canned laughter rewarded the lead actor's most recent pratfall as she keyed through several deeper layers of security. Finally, she found the mission document she was looking for and flipped straight to the Psychological Review section.

Tomorrow's protest was being organized by the "I's Have It!", a bunch of Integrationist party crazies still angry about the suspension of Presidential election privileges ten years ago. *For God's sake, get over it.* Jessica knew the whole fuss was simply a metaphor for the average person's frustration with the ongoing recession that had gripped the country since the initiation of the international embargo in 2053, which left the United States with no trading partners and no foreign investment. Now these dullards had been duped into becoming shills for the old administration, the remnants of which had scattered to Canada and various other countries after they were ousted from power in 2049.

Jessica couldn't blame President Fein for his caution. The Integrationists had threatened violence if their party was not allowed to put a candidate on the 2052 ballot. He couldn't risk letting proven traitors gain a foothold in the new administration. Fein's subsequent consolidation of the US Legislature into the Central Senate finished the job of cleaning out the old regime. People—certain people—pissed and moaned again. *What, 30% of people would vote if they could any way. Who gives a rat's ass?*

Jessica tapped the photo file of the "I's Have It" leader, Evan Marcelo. *My, my...Isn't he fine.* A list opened up beneath the photo detailing the crimes of which Marcelo was suspected. *Assault and battery, transport of illegal weaponry by a civilian, financial piracy. Impressive.* She'd be interested if she didn't know he'd be dead in twenty-four hours.

Jessica closed her eyes and imagined the angry, self-righteous hysteria she would be walking into tomorrow. *Blend and blam! Yup. I can do that.*

Wirespace: An Independent Nucleus in the Non-Aligned Territory

Damn! Senator Marks started sweating as his sensory system was dumped from his personal Parlor into the soundless gray environment of the illicit hermit line connection to the international darknet. Disoriented, he reached out for the fingerprint scanner that would allow him to be pulled into the British Prime Minister's private Parlor in a hidden nucleus. *Come on!* He cursed when he failed to find the controller on the first three tries. He was getting dizzy from floating around the empty space between nodes. He found the complete loss of visual and auditory stimuli to be oppressive. One more error would cause the sequence to reinitiate, increasing his likelihood of being detected. It would be embarrassing to say he missed his meeting with the British Prime Minister simply because he passed out before he could find the entry key pad.

Finally his hand found something solid. He pressed his palm to the center of the gel reader and curled his hand into a spread-fingered "C", compressing the gel to activate the scan. A vertical red bar appeared and separated into a doorway. Marks advanced his avatar into the room that appeared. The Prime Minister had certainly spared no expense in creating a proper meeting area for his Wirespace acquaintances. The walls were dark green with white trim. Large windows opened onto sunswept gardens of roses and marine-themed topiary. The furniture was formal, but welcoming. Small cushioned chairs were set up in two conversational clusters, each surrounding a table that doubled as a neuro-diode console and data dock.

Still aware of his body resting comfortably in his home-cradle in Alexandria, Virginia, the Senator neither sat, nor wandered the room that enveloped his vision. Somehow, he never became as consumed by virtual reality as others seemed to. He had a strong connection to his body and always knew where it was and what it was really doing. After a few moments, Tyler Grey blinked into view.

"Senator Marks. So nice to meet you at last." Prime Minister Grey extended his hand in greeting. Marks shook it, uncomfortably aware of the absurdness of pretending their hands were in real contact with each other. "Please have a seat."

Marks complied. "You're taking great risks in meeting with me, Minister Grey. I appreciate your assistance."

"The United States and Britain have a long, if not completely smooth, history of alliance with one another. I can't watch your country become consumed by its own paranoia without at least trying to effect some sort of change in direction." Grey paused to smile. Marks nodded. "I understand some congratulations are in order, Senator, or rather shall I say President Marks."

"It's a title written on air, right now, Minister Grey. Nothing more." Marks turned his face away from Grey, unsure of what the Minister could read in this space.

"Nonetheless, it is certainly a vote of confidence that the Integrationist party considers you to be their new President in exile. With your position in the Central Senate and your apparently close relationship with President Fein, you may be presented with certain opportunities others couldn't hope to take advantage of."

"That all depends on whether or not we can provide you with the evidence you need to expose what the Fein administration is doing to protect itself."

"Have there have been any successful cognitive transfers yet?" Grey asked, changing the subject.

"No. All failures. But they're close. I have a team looking into it. We're working as fast as we can, but if the FIO gives up on this before we have proof..."

Grey cut in. "The Federal International Organization can be kept busy for months arguing with Fein about his illegal annexation of Mexico and the amassing of troops at the Guatemalan border. In the end, they're just another group of politicians."

Marks quirked up the side of his mouth, "Like us?"

"I like to think of myself as a mediator, Senator. I can buy you time."

"They're no better than the United Nations was before it imploded. They can't even agree on what to buy for lunch - or what vendor to use. I don't know what the international community thinks it got out of pulling out of the UN and starting the same kind of organization all over again."

Grey leveled a firm gaze at Marks. "Escape from American hegemony, Senator. And a chance to expand human liberty instead of contracting it." Grey's avatar stood and wandered over to the window. "Which brings me to a very serious question and the real reason I brought you here today."

Marks had already guessed where this conversation was going. He reminded himself to appear casual. "Please, Prime Minister, I'm an open book."

Grey turned to face Marks again. "I have been curious as to your somewhat sudden change in loyalties. Until you contacted me last summer, I would have thought you were President Fein's right hand man. What happened?"

Marks felt his jaw lock and his neck become rigid. "I discovered that I had been lied to. I was the Marine commander in charge of rescue operations and investigation of the Atlanta General Hospital bombing. I was responsible for collecting the evidence damning former President Kessler and her cabinet as the perpetrators of the crime. It was the victory that raised my profile and resulted in me being elected to the new Central Senate."

"And that wasn't so?"

"Last May, I arrived early to my office. A cleaning woman was just exiting the door." When Grey didn't react, Marks sighed. "The cleaning staff only work in the *evening* hours." Grey cocked his head, curious. "I grabbed her before she could reach the elevator and pulled her back into my office, demanding to know what she had been doing there. She was so scared she was weeping, but she pointed to a manila envelope she had left on my chair. I made her open it." Marks spread his hands. "Inside were two data planks containing sealed images directly mined from the OCD nucleus. They proved that it was the Office of Civilian Defense, under the direction of Andrew Fein that organized and executed the attack." Grey raised his eyebrows in surprise. "Privately, I called in a data forensics specialist I trust to test the images. He used every technique at his disposal to ascertain whether the images were forged or altered in any way. Each time the answer was the same. The images were unaltered. Let's just say, I had a change of perspective after that."

Grey sighed. "There's nothing so painful as the betrayal of faith, is there?"

Marks was silent for a moment and nodded. "At least the summit in New York has people talking. I was pleasantly surprised that representatives from Singapore agreed to attend as long as it wasn't held in DC. If they can see the growing strength of the Integrationist movement, we may be able to win some trust."

"In truth, it's not going well. The Fein administration sent as many spin doctors as diplomats and they're dominating the conversation, making veiled threats and demands." Marks sighed. Grey continued, "The summit will end tomorrow afternoon, I'm certain of it."

Marks was surprised. "But you were scheduled to be in the country for two weeks at least. We can't possibly provide you with what you need by tomorrow afternoon."

"I know. I'll be back. I have my undersecretary working on a private meeting between Fein and myself. It may take several months."

"That's time I can use."

"Good. Use it well." Grey said. "Good night." He blinked out of sight.

Back in his Alexandria home, Senator Marks propped his floaters on top of his head and rubbed his eyes. *Showtime!* He thought morosely as he hoisted himself out of the cradle and dragged himself upstairs toward sleep.

Park Drive Hotel: New York, New York

At thirteen hundred hours, in a five-star hotel overlooking Central Assembly Square in Freedom Park, Jessica Butler was enjoying the pleasure of Delph Crane's company. The covers of the bed lay pushed to one side and on the floor. A hot breeze floated across their sweaty bodies from the open sliding glass door by the balcony. The room was painted in a swirl of aqua variants, which in combination with the filmy white curtains gave one the impression of floating in a Caribbean sea.

Jessica sat astride Delph, her compact frame angled provocatively over his face. She stretched, restraining his wrists above his head with her hands and smiled in mock challenge.

Delph was the sexiest geek she'd ever had the fortune of working with. He was a big-time footballer when he was abroad studying cryptology at some university in India that had a name she couldn't be bothered to pronounce. Somehow he managed to maintain his six-pack abs and solid calves despite his tendency to inhale half a pizza at every staff meeting. His long bangs fell over his left eye when he tipped his head. He had an unconscious habit of combing it behind his ear when he was concentrating, revealing the elaborate interlaced piercing around its edge. As she'd gotten to know him better, Jessica had enjoyed uncovering the other hidden piercings and body art he kept secret. She thought it was Christmas in July when Tripp introduced them three years ago and announced that they were going to be partners.

Delph was a brilliant technician. He was infinitely useful to her missions and she was lucky to have him at her side. That he also happened to be a very good lay was merely a bonus she discovered six months earlier on a mission to LA. She took advantage of this as often as he would allow, which was frequently.

In a surprise move, Delph's long-fingers entwined hers and he gained control, trapping Jessica's hands in his as he rolled her underneath him.

Three hundred yards down the street, a churning flock of limousines circled through the porter hub of the British Embassy. Secret Service personnel armed with the ironically named, wrist-mounted "Crowd Pleaser" pin-grenade launchers whispered into their earpieces, and adjusted the clips of ammo running up their forearms.

Across the street from the marble exteriors of both the Park Drive Hotel and the Embassy, a group of protesters assembled around a plywood stage. At first, the group was small, but it soon spread across the entire clearing of Freedom Park's Central Assembly Square.

Delph ran the tip of his tongue back and forth slowly along the inside of her upper lip. The ball of his pierced tongue sent waves of pleasure through her chest. She leaned down and nipped his ear.

When Jessica arrived earlier, she knew exactly where to go. She passed Registration without stopping and headed straight for room 1023. The room had a direct overhead view of Freedom Park and was their headquarters for their first mission together. *So sentimental,* she thought. *It's cute.*

Jessica and Delph now moved in synchrony. She leaned forward and rested her forehead against Delph's, before running her tongue along the length of his jawbone. He turned his face toward hers and bit her neck lightly.

At the Embassy, all vehicles and personnel had been cleared from the entryway, except for the Secret Service, who had by now fanned out into the street monitoring the wall separating Central Assembly Square from the roadway. All other traffic had been diverted to Freedom Park West and 66th Street. A bullet-shaped silver porter displaying the American flag at each end hummed through the empty street, straddling the yellow dividing line. The Secret Service alerted as it passed and came to rest in the porter hub.

The crowd in Central Assembly Square had now reached proportions that triggered a response from the Office of Civilian Defense. Automated Robotic Intelligent drones were dispatched from the nearest OCD facility in Hoboken. These "ARIels" were equipped with wide spectrum cameras and sophisticated facial recognition algorithms. The crowd reacted divergently when presented with the mosquito-like buzzing of the surveillance machinery. Some fought the inevitable with hats and scarves. Others looked right up into the lenses pointedly giving them the finger. Throughout the park though, the arrival of the ARIels signaled that this gathering was going to be noticed, a thought which both energized and frightened all in attendance.

On the tenth floor of the Park Drive Hotel, Delph held her head gently on each side. He turned her to face him eye to eye their noses almost touching. Jessica could feel her control slipping away, ordinarily not a good thing, but with Delph, somehow it was okay. This time, she didn't even close her eyes. Neither did he. She shuddered quietly then slipped easily to sleep.

An hour later, sleep drained quickly away and Jessica's eyes opened suddenly. The sun slanted in the open slider at a steep angle. She looked at the clock. Fourteen-thirty. *It's time.* She turned over and stood up, unraveling herself from the sheet quickly before retrieving her previously discarded panties. Grabbing her PhysiForm jeans and torso-clinging spandex crop top, she reviewed the plan in her head. "Delph. Get up."

He groaned and turned his face into the pillow.

There was a lot to do. She crossed to the closet and opened her gig bag. She pulled out four microcell detonation charges and stowed them in various shielded pockets in the seams of her jeans.

"Get up. It's time," she called out again.

Delph hoisted himself vertical and looked at her with a dark gaze. His close-cropped hair never needed combing, but two sheet marks crisscrossed his left cheek, making him look like a schoolboy who was late for the bus. He wandered to the bathroom while she popped a Prolert into her mouth and washed it down with a swig of flat cola. She hadn't slept more than an hour in two days. *Can't let that shit catch up with me now.*

Delph re-entered and pulled on his pants. Jessica tossed him the Prolert and turned toward the window. She could just make out the platform where the demonstration was taking place. All those Integrationist wackos in one place. It was almost as if they were asking to be picked off. That they chose to assemble across the street from the most important international summit since the FIO had voted to enforce a complete trade embargo against the United States just reinforced how bold they had become.

Jessica snorted. The Integrationists hid behind nonsensical rhetoric about restoring the Presidential vote, when all they wanted was to spring their terror-supporting leaders from Federal prison. *Fucking insurgents. We'll take 'em down a notch.*

Jessica's thoughts were interrupted by the subtle hum of Delph's heavily accessorized Wireman Wolf booting up behind her. To call the Wolf a console was actually an insult. It was more like having a suitcase-sized network nucleus to go. Delph had tweaked the system with every link loop, hack plank and troll switch she'd ever heard of—and a few she hadn't. He'd stolen his encryption code from the supposedly impenetrable Russian-built firewall the Federal International Organization had constructed to enforce their embargo across electronic tradeways—and upgraded it. One could say that Delph was now his own free trade zone. And those FIO dupes were none the wiser.

Delph handed her a pair of floaters, which she wrapped around her eyes with a quick twist of her wrist. The main platform in Central Assembly Square came into sharper focus and enlarged. Delph amazed her once again. He had taken a pair of high-end virtual reality goggles and transformed them into the most powerful online binoculars she had ever used. She tucked the ends of her hair behind her ears. Using a single-handed dedo controller, Jessica accessed the options displayed in her peripheral vision. She scanned the crowd and noted the number and placement of the OCD ARIels. One thought ahead of her, Delph said, "If you want to access the individual ARIel feeds, tap the numbers running up and down the left and right. She raised her hand and tapped the number 26. She was instantly transported to the point of view of an ARIel positioned on the top of the platform's overhang.

Jessica heard Delph moving around behind her. She knew his routine by heart. The pattern he used to flex his hands as they slid into his platinum-lined double dedos, the barely perceptible string of tones as he scanned his floaters for unauthorized overlays. The quiet grunt as he keyed himself into the Wolf and dropped into the Parlor of his heavily encrypted nucleus.

Jessica continued monitoring the Square while Delph's dedoed fingers flew through the air accessing the Office's nucleus and the other ARIels monitoring the flow of people through the City. "I'm reading approximately fifteen hundred people on site," Delph said. "Five hundred more are converging on the area, mostly via subway. There are seventy-five police marking the perimeter of the protest area."

"They were going to leave us an opening. Is there an opening?" Jessica interrupted.

"Looks like Channel Path is mostly clear between the gate and the pillar."

"Can I get a view of that?"

A succession of images blinked by like a slide show that had OD'd on Pollies. It threatened to make her dizzy. Finally, she picked up a view of the north side of the park. One lone officer had been placed to guard the rear exit gate and the fifty yards from it to the Pillars of Liberty monument. He looked to be about sixty-five or seventy years old. The furry caterpillars of his eyebrows worked up and down above the silver surface of his floaters as the officer tried to make himself comfortable in his new gear. *Nice work.*

The sensor belt he wore was a mid-range model typical of municipal forces. It had the basics: thermo graphic sensor, night vision and a perimeter alarm with targeting aid all hooked into the standard issue floaters that were troubling his eyebrows.

"That'll do. Mark my entry by the Pillar end. I think a Class II interference signal should be enough to confound his belt."

"I thought I'd do an overlay, if that's all right with you. You know these old-school cops. When the equipment gets screwy, they get suspicious right away."

"You can do that from here?" Jessica asked.

"Sure. I came over last week and set up a signal amplifier under the gate posts by the northeast Pillar."

Jessica smiled and shook her head. One more point for Delph. Entry would be easier than she had ever hoped. With the officer seeing nothing but the holographically projected image of the park sans intruder—her—she would be able to dispense with the thousands of potential excuses she had invented in case she was caught climbing over the wall protecting the staid monument from the ordinary rabble. She smiled and mentally completed her route to the main platform.

While Jessica was engaged in her own thoughts, Delph surveyed her through the smoky brown tint of his floaters. *I'm a step ahead again.* He liked impressing Jessica. She was a perceptive intelligence agent and feared nothing. She respected him, which made him feel free to suggest alternatives and new approaches. With Jessica, he was free to creatively push against the boundaries of his expertise instead of just punching buttons like the tech jockey most of the other agents expected him to be. Jessica had freed his mind and captured his fascination. It didn't matter to him that she didn't feel for him the way he felt for her. She needed him and kept him in closer proximity each time he pleasantly surprised her with another peacock's feather of technical artistry.

Jessica finished her visual walk-through of the mission, tossed the floaters onto the bed and shrugged into her vest. She conducted a quick inventory of her tools and decided she was good to go. She donned her mission floaters and grabbed the wireless earpiece that would keep her connected to Delph until the mission was complete. *If things go well enough,* she thought, *maybe I'll do him again before we pack up.* She smiled. That would be a nice way to cap off the day. She pushed the doughy plasticine of the earpiece into her ear canal and used the tip of an extended paper clip to turn on the transmitter.

Delph inserted his earpiece as she exited. "Check, one, two."

"Loud and clear." She said as she headed for the elevator.

"Be careful out there," he whispered.

Jessica smiled to herself. *Careful is for cowards,* she thought. The elevator door closed her in with a soft thud.

The roadways to Freedom Park were thronging with protesters, their foes and others who just wanted to try to get a glance of the dignitaries walled inside the British Embassy. The crowd had grown to nearly two thousand people by the time Jessica rounded the corner toward her access point. She brought up the visual of the regional leader of the Integrationist movement, Marcelo, reviewing his dark features.

Jessica passed a small cluster of media vans, their antennae clamoring for airspace. She turned her head as she passed the Total Wire News Service Van from which her young and impressionable colleague Carrie was broadcasting her first live feed. She looked fragile in her new silver Layer suit. It would be replaced in post-production with an appropriate persona selected from a focus group screened database. Jessica had to hand it to Carrie though, her voice carried more confidence than her demeanor displayed.

"The demonstration is being held in the Central Assembly Square region of Freedom Park. This is within view of the British Embassy, where President Fein is entering into talks with British Prime Minister Tyler Grey and select members of the FIO Security Council to negotiate for at least a partial lifting of the international economic embargo against the United States. The central disagreement during these talks is likely to be the FIO insistence that the United States submit to inspections of their cloning facilities—public and private—to disprove allegations by British Prime Minister Tyler Grey that the United States is involved in human rights violations surrounding the production of human clones. To date, the Prime Minister has been elusive in describing the exact nature of the alleged violations. President Fein is appealing to FIO leaders to insist that Prime Minister Grey produce evidence of human rights violations, or withdraw his claim."

A few minutes later, Jessica positioned herself at the northwest corner of Freedom Park where the massive wrought iron and electric razor wire fencing met the Pillars of Liberty. She stepped gingerly around the pile of empty syringes, discarded muddy underwear, and used condoms and crinkled her nose against the acrid stench of urine. Above the detritus flew a banner of graffiti—*Archive this, Homers!* Beside it, emblazoned in hunter orange spray paint was an enormous missile head in the shape of a penis penetrating the buttocks of a spongy-looking hog.

Homer was tired slang for her current position as an agent of the Office of Civilian Defense, a holdover from a time when the agency defined homeland security as more of an external than an internal threat. Jessica didn't take it personally. Most people simply didn't understand the stakes. They didn't understand that the Office of Civilian Defense was the only line of protection between average citizens and forces that sought nothing less than the complete destruction of the United States of America.

She smiled at the archaic name still ascribed to Office agents. Along with the 2039 name change had come a massive reorganization that resulted in the creation of three distinct nodes: the Local Forces Node, the Bio-medical Node, and the Military Node. Her division, the Media Node, was created in 2047 in response to criticism of the lack of transparency of OCD procedures. It was the most covert Node, largely unknown to the Local Forces Node and with limited ties to the Bio-medical Node. Total Wire News Service was the perfect partner in this venture, as its market share eclipsed that of any other media service in the country. In her five years with the Office, she discovered the inherent flexibility of her position. TWNS provided her with ample opportunities for cross-node projects and this suited her just fine.

Hunkered in the shadows of the desecrated monument, Jessica waited for Delph to tell her she was clear to go. She pictured whatever small clan of barely post-pubescent rebels who had come before her gripping their spray paint, emboldened by intoxication of the inhaler-based dilute hallucinogen XRG and the cover of darkness. Such energized sincerity could be an asset, if they only had a little education. Education like she had.

Jessica had been a Pollie-subdued college senior when a story she wrote for the campus newspaper caught the eye of TWNS Bureau-chief, Tripp Thompson. The story commemorated the fifteenth anniversary of the United States pulling out of the United Nations. She provided a comprehensive review of the politics of the United Nations at the time, including its subsequent re-formulation into the Free International Organization. She outlined the idealistic goals of international unity proposed by the FIO and capped the paper off with a compellingly self-righteous editorial arguing for re-integration of the United States into the community of nations.

The boldness of her argument veiled the ennui that accompanied her feelings toward her chosen course of study. Through her education in the foundations of discourse and rhetoric, she discovered that she could argue most any point from whatever perspective was convenient. The development of this skill, however, left her feeling ethically rudderless, truly believing in nothing in particular.

Tripp invited Jessica to dinner at Chez Jacque, where dinner for two could top four hundred credits. They debated for two hours about the relative importance of national self-determination. She made a game out of presenting opinions that were on the opposite pole of the political spectrum from his, providing consistent, rational arguments to support these views. Tripp appeared to respect that, continuing their verbal jousting with a smile in his voice. By the last bite of her crème brulee, she began to suspect that he knew that she was full of shit. Afterward, they went back to his condominium on the Upper East Side. He was okay.

In the early hours of the morning, as he was getting ready to drive her home, Tripp looked at his watch and asked Jessica if she'd like to see the truth. She wasn't sure what he meant by that, but it sounded intriguing. *What's the worst that could happen?* She thought. *I could end up with my next story.* So, she followed him to his car.

Tripp drove her to the TWNS Bureau office where he led her through a darkened maze of cubicles to the rear conference room. He closed the door. The moonlight cast shadows across rows of executive chairs that looked like shark teeth. Tripp rotated open the fancy Wireman Alpha console at the end of the table, donned some floaters and slipped his hands into a pair of dedos. Jessica had never seen this equipment up close before. She wrestled herself into the oversized guest floaters he handed her and watched in stunned silence as he used the dedos to masterfully manipulate a holographic image of the world that floated over the table.

He zoomed in to an apartment complex in the suburbs of Tijuana, blithely hacking through FIO satellite seals. He tuned in to thermal imagery of a small group of people around a table. A twitch of Tripp's tan wrist and Jessica could hear their voices in her head as they planned a terrorist attack on Texas' main irrigation channel. Suddenly, the door to the group's little hideaway burst open. Three figures, clad entirely in black, save for the iridescent glow of small American flags sewn on each left arm, lay into the planners with a spray of gunfire. It was over in 30 seconds with the conspirators dead and the room in flames. The three figures tossed a few microcell charges into the detritus behind them for good measure and disappeared as quickly as they had come. The holograph disappeared abruptly.

"Your tax dollars at work." Tripp said. "So, do you want to work for me, or not?"

Jessica sought Tripp's gaze through the glassy surface of his floaters, but only saw her own reflection. His hands were outstretched as if in anticipation of her answer. The gold and copper wiring of the dedos' connection to the console glinted in the recessed lighting. They ran along the tendons of his hands, around his wrists like rapier hilts and draped regally toward the floor. Her eyes flicked back and forth between the floaters and the dedos. Tripp walked up to her and lay one finger under her chin. The electrode was cool and smooth. "What do you say?"

He was no better the second time around, but she took the job any way.

"Okay, Jess. The overlay is up and running. All clear for go."

Jessica started out of her daydream and replied, "Copy that, Delph. I'm on my way in."

Jessica peered across the length of the fencing and saw the lone officer standing by the gate, smiling, leaning down, talking to what he thought was a five-year old girl with the cutest pig tails he'd ever seen, but which was really thin air. Delph's overlay had him completely fooled. Jessica started at a hissing sound from behind her, but it was only a Scrubbie doing its duty for the citizens of midtown by cleaning their garbage from the street. *Focus, Jessica, focus.*

She pulled some grounding clamps from her gig bag, clicked one end of each to the recessed metal contacts on the soles of her climbing shoes and wrapped the other ends around the base of the fence post. Rubber-handled shears between her teeth, she shimmied up the vertical fence railing. At the top, she balanced herself on top of the four-hundred volt electric wiring and clipped a hole through the razor wire above it.

She pushed off hard against the wire, propelling herself through the hole, flipping in a single somersault as she did so, twisting her ankles to release the grounding clips. She landed in a squat. The grounding wires swinging freely wrapped themselves once or twice around the fence post with a clang. The officer looked in her direction, but all he saw was a nonexistent dented metal trash can rolling against the fence after having been kicked by the ghost of a stray dog that was now running away. Nothing out of the ordinary there. He turned back to the little girl.

Jessica stuffed the shears back into her gig bag and slung it casually across her shoulder. She walked along the side of the monument to the front stairs. A cluster of people wearing slogan t-shirts and carrying foam core signs was shuffling toward the main platform. She blended in, nodding from side-to-side as the lefties greeted each other with hoots and hand gestures. *Yeah, power to the people...right on.*

Nearing the platform, she saw Marcelo. He was tall and lean. The early summer sun had already tanned him more than his file picture showed. He gave the impression of being a man who worked out—a lot. His face was hard and mistrustful. He had high cheekbones and the eyes of a predator. She would have to be careful. Her only job was to get close enough to him to dab some of the marking gel on his skin. The nano-probes in the gel could then penetrate his skin and send signals to the OCD nucleus, where he would be tracked back to his organization's headquarters. With that knowledge, the Office could easily neutralize the threat he presented in the least public manner possible.

Jessica positioned herself near the center of the main platform, pretending to read a program she found on the ground there. She looked at the rag tag group gathering around

Marcelo like filings to a magnet. They hung on his every word and would follow him anywhere. A precious few of the leaders would follow him back to his headquarters as well, where they would be dealt with. The truth is that people follow. Ultimately, people always follow.

Jessica worked her way around the platform, discreetly setting microcell charges at each corner. After marking her subject, she would detonate the small, harmless devices to create just enough of a pax that the leadership would retreat to their hole. A few lefties standing near the charges might take some shrapnel but they'd be all right in the end. It would be enough to land the blast on the evening Wirecast, where the Office could blame the insurgents themselves for the attack. *Brilliant.*

As Jessica rounded the corner again to the front of the platform, Marcelo looked directly at her, despite the persistent tugging at his arm by a co-ed sporting short shorts and a colorful butterfly tattoo underneath her left ear. Jessica bared her teeth into a forced smile and pumped her arm in the air. Marcelo scanned her once more before turning his attention to the clipboard being offered by the co-ed.

Jessica guessed she needed to work harder to fit in. Spinning abruptly, she bumped into a stumpy, sweaty fifty-something struggling to tie a sandwich board around his portly shoulders. She helped him finish the job, patted him on the back and watched him waddle away.

It was three thirty before Marcelo took the stage. He was preceded by a folk singer, whose guitar should have been confiscated for all the skill he had in playing it. The crowd hadn't seemed to notice, though. They swayed and sang and cheered throughout the dismal display. Jessica armed the microcells remotely and waited for her opportunity.

"Friends!" Marcelo announced to a resounding cheer. "It is a great honor for me to address you today. You have all come out, some at immense personal risk, to raise your voices against the tyranny of open-ended terms of office. We stand united today, to send a message loud and clear to President Fein that we demand our right to the Presidential vote be returned to us. We demand the dignity of choosing our leadership, to live without fear of reprisal for our beliefs, to enjoy our families and foster friendships in peace and privacy."

The crowd roared. The time for action drew near. Jessica scanned continuously for signs of trouble. As usual, she found some. A man dressed in gray, slid around the corner of the stage and casually dropped a puck-shaped object into a trash barrel. *Was that a Boulder-charge? Where would a civilian get a high-powered grenade like that?*

"Delph." Jessica whispered into her headset. "I'm seeing activity down here. Do you read any agents other than myself? Is there a second team here?"

"Negative. What are you seeing?"

"Zoom in on the trash barrel by the podium. Scan it." Jessica pushed through the crowd toward the stage.

Chanting rose up around her "The vote is mine, President Fein! The vote is mine, President Fein!"

Jessica watched the man in gray disappear behind a stall selling bio-engineered "organic" soy granola bars. She banked left to intercept him.

"Jessica, get out of there!" Delph cried out. "It's a boulder-charge. It's a boulder-charge! Get out!"

Jessica broke free of the bulk of the crowd. The man in gray looked back and saw her following him. He broke into a run. Jessica followed.

She was halfway to the west gate when the first explosion rocked the park with a force that knocked her to her knees. She scrambled up and looked back at the platform, from which a dark plume of smoke was rising. A large section of the stage and surrounding audience had collapsed. Marcelo was splayed out, one arm dangling off the jagged edge of the stage.

Jessica turned back to the gate, just in time to see the man in gray speed away in a porter without identity tags. "Shit!"

"I'll get the porter." Delph offered. "You get Marcelo. You can still make it, if you hurry."

Delph was right. All Jessica had to do was tag Marcelo. The nano probes would penetrate his skin before the ambulance arrived and no one would be the wiser. They'd just have to wait to track him until after he healed—if he healed. Jessica spun on her heels and ran full force toward the stage. Just then, another explosion rocked the ground. This time, Jessica took a hit of debris full-force to the abdomen. She crawled in small circles on the ground panting to get her breath back, then she took stock. No blood. No broken bones that she could tell. Pulling herself up, using a park bench, Jessica looked toward the stage. Sandwich-board man was lying in a charred mass underneath a fallen support beam. Smoke and survivors blew in every direction.

Jessica stumbled toward the stage. She pulled a folded particle mask out of her kit and covered her face. What remained of the platform appeared to her like castle ruins. She came to a shocked standstill. Marcelo was gone. She scanned the bodies and debris around her. Certainly a great deal of damage had been done, but not enough to incinerate an entire body. Where could he have gone?

"Delph, I can't find him. He's gone."

"Gone? I'll put a trace on his subdermal." Jessica heard the Wolf whirring and the whooshing sound of Delph's dedos as they cut the air. "Nothing. I'm not coming up with anything."

"Someone knew, Delph. Someone knew and they got here before us. We've been compromised."

"The OCD Local has been mobilized, Jessica. Get out of there, now!"

"Naw, I thought I'd stop for coffee," she quipped.

Jessica could hear the roar of the approaching OCD helicopters closing in on the park. She pulled her vest around her and turned her face to the ground. Hers had been a secret mission—as always—and she was certain that she'd have a difficult time explaining the remaining charges left in her vest, along with the remote detonator and various other toys. She fled for the temporary security of the trees along the wooded area of the park. Black paddy wagons with the royal blue stripe of the Office pulled up along the western wall of the park. Jessica turned south. Her lungs burned as she pushed ahead faster, finally outside the gate, behind the gathering crowd of on-lookers and around the western corner of the park.

Rather than crossing the lobby of the hotel, she used her room key to swipe herself into the stairwell. She climbed to the third floor before voyaging through the hall to the elevator.

Delph was already loading the Wolf into its bag when Jessica burst into the room.

"I'm calling Tripp." Jessica said, pulling out her Mate and tapping the Bureau's code. "Someone knew. I want to know how this happened."

"Don't freak out. It'll be okay. We'll just explain what happened."

Jessica gave him a morbid look. "No one's answering. This is bad. This is very bad." She shoved the Mate back into her vest pocket and ran her fingers through her hair.

"Let's just get out of here, okay? We'll figure it out later, right?" Delph hoisted the straps of his cases over his shoulders.

Jessica nodded and looked at Delph just before she turned back toward the door. She was so distracted that she didn't have time to register the look of dismayed surprise on his face. As she turned, her head hit something very hard. The world fell away with an echoing boom.

An Undisclosed Location: A Secure Communication Line

"What happened?" The Voice was angry.

The Observer tented his hands in front of his face and remained silent.

"Marcelo is missing. The public is in an uproar. You couldn't have fucked this up more if you had tried."

The Observer stared across the room at the intricate pattern in the molding of his mahogany walls. He breathed in and out slowly to the count of ten. "The situation is being controlled.

We fed the wire within the hour. There was no time for speculation."

"There is always speculation."

"Use it to your advantage."

The Voice was quiet.

"Spin it, sir. Look at how quickly the Local Office responded. Find some widows; give them checks. You'll be a big Integrationist hero."

"What about the girl?" the Voice interrupted.

"I don't think she was involved, if that's what you're thinking."

"All I know is we've lost our best chance of finding out where those bastards keep their stronghold and their leader has gone underground. What am I supposed to think about the girl? We need to cut our losses."

"She's the best operative I've ever had," the Observer warned. "We need to try to salvage her."

"Filtering leaves too many tracers. I can't take that risk."

"There are...other options." the Observer suggested.

The Voice was silent.

"I understand the new interface looks promising."

"And I understand the last trial was an unqualified disaster." The Voice replied.

The Observer rolled his eyes. *Politicians.* "I'm sure you understand that some collateral damage was inevitable when developing a weapon of this scope."

"It's too risky."

"Of course it is. That's why T-Col is so important. To eliminate that risk." The frustrated Observer started tapping his fingers on his desk. "One success is all we need. Then we can make so many of your other problems simply disappear. Then reappear of course. And no one will know. Somebody's just got to be first."

The Voice played with the moldable pile of magnetic pellets he kept on his desk, pulling the pieces into a thin tower. "I thought you liked this girl. What do you get out of having her converted?"

It was the Observer's turn to be quiet.

The Voice continued. "You need to understand. If the procedure goes wrong, we may still need to sacrifice her."

"I do understand," the Observer replied. "But it's worth a try, don't you think. If not her, who? If not now, when?"

"All right. Go ahead. Transfer her to the Chilling Zone." The Voice agreed

The Observer fist-pumped the air. "First thing tomorrow. I'll give them the head's up right away."

"By the way, Officer."

"Yes?"

"Screw up again and I may find I don't need you any more."

The line went dead.

Central Senate Leader David Marks' Home: Alexandria, Virginia

Senator Marks sat in his study, contemplative. His evening glass of Port sat untouched on a coaster in the middle of his leather-topped desk. The room was dark with the exception of a single Tiffany floor lamp behind him. His neuro-diode console perched inside a custom cherry cabinet near the door. Marks always kept his console in Screen mode. He felt reality was far too important to dissolve himself with the seduction of either the projected holograms or the immersive VR settings that the console was capable of. VR was a tool. Reality needed him. Even with the objective distance of 2-D to protect him, the evening Wirecast dismayed Marks. The perky anchorwoman standing by the Total Wire News Service van near the entrance of Freedom Park seemed unfazed.

"At least ten people were killed and thirty six were injured when two explosions rocked a gathering of protesters who were calling for a return of regular Presidential elections. Among the dead is the group's leader Evan Marcelo. Sources say that Marcelo was the target of the attack, which may have been perpetrated by members of his own movement.

"Marcelo has been connected to several terrorist organizations in Canada and Mexico. It is thought that Marcelo turned against his supporters as part of a plea bargain and provided the Office of Civilian Defense the names of two operatives who were planning a hi-jacking of Labor Department computer systems. The OCD arrived on the scene quickly, cordoning off the area and transporting the wounded to area hospitals. President Fein will address this latest terrorist attack in his scheduled post-summit speech this evening.

"News from the FIO summit meeting itself was not encouraging. Sources close to negotiators state that the Security Council continues to investigate the baseless charges by British Prime Minister Tyler Grey that the United States is engaging in human rights violations in its cloning facilities. President Fein argued that nothing less than the sovereignty of the United States is a stake in this debate and that the United States has demonstrated its commitment to the Human Dignity Clause in signing on to the International Accord on Human Cloning twenty-one years ago."

Senator Marks powered down the Newswire and covered his face with his hands. Ten dead. Thirty-six injured. *Was it worth it? It has to be worth it.* Marks stood and wandered over to the liquor cabinet by the neuro-diode console. He exchanged his Port for Scotch, downing it in a single gulp.

The Chilling Zone: Boston, Massachusetts

The Chilling Zone was nestled among the cluster of nondescript research laboratory buildings that were wedged between and around the large teaching hospitals of the Longwood Medical Area on the western boarder of Boston. Architects over the past century had gotten creative in terms of maximizing the potential for additional square footage, which resulted in a hodge-podge of heights, styles, and shapes of buildings. Even Longwood Avenue, the street for which the district had been named, was turned into a tunnel when the overhead space was claimed by Children's Hospital and a collection of small research firms who catered to it and other nearby facilities. The only thing distinguishing it from the favelas of Sao Paulo were the stark straight lines of the structures and the well-maintained shiny exteriors.

The employees of the various institutions feigned casual collegiality. They gathered at their journal clubs, chatting and laughing around tables full of cafeteria catered wraps, chips, and generic Polly-cola. Each had their own personal point of pontification that the others understood and tolerated. Department chiefs shook hands and touted the mutual benefits of inter-institutional collaboration. Underneath the formalities, however, everyone knew that patents were at stake, along with access to the ever-shrinking pot of federal research funding. Trust was only smile-deep.

This environment of cordial suspicion was the perfect location for a secret government facility. Cloaked in the cover of medical innovation, the Chilling Zone appeared no different to the denizens of the Longwood Area citizenry than any of the other paranoia-driven high-security labs that were its neighbors. From the south, the rhythmic flapping sound of a black and gold OCD Medical chopper grew louder as it approached the Chilling Zone's helipad.

Dr. Ames placed his briefcase lightly on his glass-topped desk. He glanced over his chair and out the window to the central courtyard where some of the night staff were enjoying a free breakfast before heading home. The mostly twenty-something lab techs scooted around the enclosure, the collars of their jumpsuits open, smiling. Every so often one of them sent a hash brown airborne into the back of the head of a friend. Dr. Ames' skin itched. There was something going on. Walking down the hallway, he had heard the Director's voice floating jovially through the air. Before ten a.m.? Never. Dr. Ames lowered himself into his high backed leather chair. His console was blinking. Red. Someone wanted his attention the minute he got in.

[Retrieve message]

A woman's voice spun a smooth web over the phone line, pulling him in. It was the Governess. "Dr. Ames. It's time. Our girl has a name. Meet me in Surgical Bay 2 at eight. Don't be late."

[Delete]

Dr. Ames turned in his chair and looked at the techs again. Two teams had now formed, each with one individual riding on the shoulders of another. They ran toward each other like jousters. The teams were laughing and cheering. They appeared to be in some sort of race to grab a bagel that was being held aloft on a stick. The diffuse light from the frosted glass above them gave them a matte finish. Their edges seemed to glow. They knew. They all knew and none of them were going home until the Transformation Protocol was completed.

He couldn't blame them for their enthusiasm. It was difficult enough for these kids to work nights in a lab without being able to tell anyone what you do. To work like that for years without results was discouraging. Besides, T-Col was abstract to them, science fiction come to life. None of them were forced to watch the horrible reality of the procedure as it was performed. They could afford to be festive.

Even prior to his current spiritual crisis, Ames had always been the sensitive one. His colleagues hassled him about it at lunch regularly. It's what prompted them to honor him with his mission name "Daddy." Nonetheless, he had maintained the professional composure he needed to get the job done, and he was good at what he did. So, he was tolerated.

Turning away from the window, Dr. Ames went to his closet and perfunctorily climbed into his clean room jumpsuit. He double-checked his reflection in the small mirror that hung on the inside of the door and replaced the worry lines with his practiced look of unsuspicious bland complicity.

When Daddy finished scrubbing, he entered the Surgical Bay. His hands felt cold and disconnected from his body. He hoped the Governess wouldn't smell his doubt. Two gurneys lay parallel to one another. His girl, neutral and placid lay awaiting the infusion of an identity. *If the interface holds...* He remembered again the screams of their previous experiment. He could smell the molten stainless steel fiber core as it burrowed through the cortex of the primary, mapping her relevant history. He flinched at the thought of so much blood. After the transfer, the recipient clone had lost its mind, tearing at its own flesh and beating its head against the headboard until it died. A prickly flush crept up Daddy's arms to his shoulders. His heart palpitated briefly and he had difficulty swallowing.

He needed to focus. Daddy turned abruptly to the second gurney. On it lay the Primary, a shortish woman, well-muscled. Her almond-shaped eyes stared blindly up at the ceiling. *At least the paralytic is working.* He was drawn in by their surprising shade of green. *What is she thinking right now? Can she think in this state?* Daddy found himself pulled deeper into her eyes, seeking some remnant of her humanity. *I can't do this any more.* He felt his airway constrict. He began to wheeze. *Look away!* He admonished himself and busied himself with his work breathing in slow, controlled waves.

At Daddy's command, a small flock of ARIel helper robots, descended on the Asian woman's gurney with frenzied glee, taking vital signs and inserting IV tubing up and down her limbs. These ARIels were designed for hospital work. They were almost human in their form with long finger-like probes that were surprisingly precise in their movements. Their attachments could change from needle to scalpel to suction catheter.

Daddy injected 10 mg of growth hormone activator into the clone. He flinched as the ARIels blandly penetrated the Primary's skull with three-dozen five-inch probes. The computer monitor above her head sprang to life vomiting a river of data as the Primary minutely twitched and jerked a tear rolled down her right cheek. *Okay, so not a complete paralysis. Breathe. Breathe.*

Once the neural mapping process had begun. He couldn't watch. He thanked whatever God would still have him for the Primary's silence. His gaze remained fixed on his girl and he tried to picture her transformation. One IV ran into her right arm. The bag up above contained the enzyme that would prime her cells for receiving the primary's DNA pattern. *All I would have to do is replace it with saline and this insanity would end...*

Daddy felt the air in the room condense and rarify, shifting the wrinkles in his bio-suit, as the Governess entered from the negative pressure chamber. He felt her black eyes settle on his back. He turned to look at her.

The Governess' pure white hair was pulled back starkly into a bun. Her smooth albino skin looked iridescent in the full spectrum lighting of the Surgical Bay. Daddy could never get used to the trails of pink that her blood vessels made under her skin when she was excited.

"You should go now," the Governess stated coolly.

He remained still for a moment longer, casting a glance at the rigid form of the woman simply known to him as F-03. Soon she would be someone with a name and a life all her own.

A mixture of guilt and dread spread hotly across his neck. *So what if I broke the rules?* So what if he stroked her head, freeing his hands for one minute from the sticky confines of his rubber gloves. Who could know he had whispered small comforts in her ears and sung her lullabies? There was nothing yet to receive. *Probably.* Nothing had been mapped yet. *So it was okay—I think.* Daddy trembled to think of what the Governess would do to him if she found out, but his face remained placid. He remembered the gentle pressure of his lips on her unmarked forehead as he'd kissed her good-bye last night, when he was finally alone. *No one needs to know.*

"Dr. Ames," the Governess said, slightly impatient this time.

Daddy looked at his colleague, meeting her ice-blue stare long enough to prove he was not compromised. He crossed the room in three fluid strides, pushing his way through the negative pressure chamber, barely stopping to peel off his bio-suit. He tossed it in the soiled laundry bin next to the door and picked up his pace as he walked down the hall.

His assistant tried to flag him down with a small stack of file folders when he passed his cubicle, but he ignored him. Daddy almost jogged past security in the main lobby, threw his shoulder into the tempered glass of the main entrance and gulped a fistful of unseasonable June humidity.

Traffic noise assaulted his ears. Somewhere to his left a sprinkler was helping the colorful annuals that surrounded the flagpole to beat the heat. Daddy's senses, sterilized in the lab awoke to the smell of mulch and hot asphalt. He broke into a run past the fountain, past the perfectly calibrated line of maple trees flanking one side of the road, through traffic and into the park on the other side. He didn't know where he was going, only that he would not return.

Delph Crane's Condominium - Sprie 2 West 75th Street: New York, New York

Delph woke up in his condo, face down in the carpet. His vision spun briefly when he lifted his head. Thankfully, the cloudy sky sheltered his eyes from the sun. The light angling through the sliding glass door turned his surroundings to a dull gray. The scrolling stock ticker on the high rise next to his building revealed he had missed four days. The Wolf was logged on and spun in stand by mode. He was surrounded by a debris field of Pollie-cans and XRG inhalers. A pair of women's underwear lay by his neuro-diode console. It was a perfect still-life of the aftermath of a party gone wild.

Delph pulled himself to his feet, using an end table for support and wiped a short string of drool from the corner of his mouth. Wandering through his kitchen, Delph listened to the many messages left for him by his mother, his programming contract agent and two friends asking to be hooked up with access codes to an exclusive Gentleman's Club nucleus. It was reasonable to find himself passed out on the floor on a Sunday morning. It was not reasonable to discover he had been lying there for days.

Furthermore, the XRG inhalers made no sense to him. He was a fan of the drug in the early days of its release because of the clean high with no hangover. Since then, however, street hustlers had corrupted the recipe to get more doses in a batch. One particular encounter with this tainted brew sent him to the hospital in respiratory arrest—and earned him thirty days in a daily counseling group for addicts. After this incident he swore off street XRG and had made his own ever since.

It was clear that someone wanted him to believe he had partied himself unconscious. He tried to remember the last thing he did before blacking out. He noted the wooziness he felt; the blank spaces in his memory. Suddenly it clicked. *Damn, I've been filtered!* He thought. *Some major shit must have finally gone down.*

Fortunately, Delph was a man of forethought and preparation. Over the course of his first six months as an agent, Delph collected all of the algorithms he could find in regard to the associative filtering process and built a reverse filtering tool. It required frequent backup neural mapping, which he performed on himself just prior to each mission. He surmised when he first joined the Office, that he might find himself in this situation some day and figured that his ability to retain information the Office wanted lost, might provide him with certain ammunition, should they decide to try and fuck him over. After tossing back a cup of coffee to clear his mind. He re-booted the Wolf into a phase-shifted configuration.

Delph hid his neural maps across three Hermit drives controlled by biosealed troll switches. His reverse filtering tool was designed to re-assemble the neural map and re-potentiate the synaptic connections for missing memory traces, leaving unfiltered memories intact. He could have won funding for his own research lab, if the OCD knew the extent of his programming capabilities. Unfortunately, he could also win a one-way ticket to T-Col, once he no longer served a purpose. He had other ideas about how to spend his free time.

It took the Wolf two hours to sift through Delph's map tracers and bring him up to date, three times longer than he estimated and still there were holes. That's when he used the back door in the filtering lab's nucleus to scour their records. Piece by piece memories of the Freedom Park bombing reassembled themselves. Jessica's panicked call over the wireless. The gloved hand winging a steel-reinforced billie club across Jessica's left temple. He remembered seeing blood seeping from Jessica's nose and ears. He remembered running like hell.

As the uplink took hold, the tens of thousands of synapses associated with that particular experiential sequence and the hundreds of thousands of linked subsequent connections reached the threshold for firing. His memory started sliding into place and his recollection crystalized.

Having lived and breathed technology, Delph maintained a certain sense of security in the amount of control he could wield over it. Some of the adventure though resided in those few brief times when technology could surprise him. This was one of those moments. Just before the uplink disconnected, a small chunk of code escaped the confines of it's security level and fell in line with the other data flowing into Delph's mind. Rows of beds. Pale skin. Missing limbs. A warehouse the size of an airline hangar. He briefly stopped breathing. This was information he definitely didn't want to know. Every justification he'd accepted for every ethically questionable action he'd taken in the past three years became transparent for the covert manipulation it really was. Until that moment, Delph had been completely confident in his ability to avoid being controlled in that way. *It's all true,* Delph thought. *The farms are real.* The problem now was to figure out what the Office would present him with next and what to do about it.

An Undisclosed Location: A Secure Communication Line

"Daddy left home," the Voice said to the Observer. He clocked out at fourteen hundred on Monday and hasn't been seen since. I'm concerned."

The Observer licked his lips. "We continue as planned."

"He knows everything. We need to take precautions."

"I'm on top of it, sir." The Voice heard squeaky crinkling as the Observer shifted his weight in his leather chair. "We'll find him."

A piercing hum filled the headset of the Voice as the Observer casually ran his dampened finger around the rim of his crystal rocks glass. The Voice adjusted his sleeve and twisted the hinge of his cufflink absentmindedly.

"This is a complication," the Voice warned, "I don't like complications."

The Observer smiled to himself. He had the Voice right where he wanted him. After this mission was successful, his apprehensive master would have no choice but to turn the executive director's chair over to him. He'd only managed to hold Congress off as long as he had by playing the "no-suitable-replacement" card. Well, he'd just been dealt a full house. "Trust me. This is what I do."

"We should lay low for a while."

The Observer rolled his eyes and turned his chair toward the window. This is what he hated about politicians. They always misplaced their balls at the critical moment. He scanned his gardens for inspiration, and breathed out audibly to the count of ten. "Why don't you just do your job, Sir. And let me do mine."

"I'm counting on you."

"Good. Until Friday, then." The Observer hung up before the Voice could change his mind and switched his console to "Reply only" mode. No more interruptions. No more second-guessing. As a sub-director of the Office of Civilian Defense who was in the trenches every day, there were things only he could do, decisions only he could make, a big picture only he could see. *The plan is good*, he thought. *Things are under control. We are ready.*

Mount-Sinai Hospital: Manhattan New York, New York

Jessica was aware of the cool, sterile, filtered air before she could open her eyes. It burned her nostrils. She tried to lift one hand to scratch the itch on her cheek, but found it difficult to move. It felt like someone had attached lead weights to the palms of her hands. She tried curling her fingers into a fist. The weakness of her muscles astonished her. It was almost as though her brain were calling to her limbs over a black-market hermit line. Sometimes the message got through, sometimes it didn't.

After what had to be ten minutes, Jessica managed to bend one knee, resting the sole of her foot against the crisp, bleached sheet. The fabric scraped roughly against her skin as she shifted. It was surprisingly painful. She moaned.

The AImee, an artificially intelligent monitoring program without a programmed personality, hummed above her head as it detected Jessica's increasing alertness and updated her status. A shot of warmth spread across her right arm, which was mildly concerning, but when her pain began to fade she was grateful. After that, Jessica drifted in and out of consciousness for an indeterminate period of time.

At last, she opened her eyes just as a pair of ARIels—one pink and one green—entered the room, carrying trays of supplies. They appeared to be glowing from within. Their edges were fuzzy and they left trails along her line of vision as they moved. Everything else in the room was blindingly white. Squinting, she was able to make out a few straight edges in space that vaguely resembled a rectangle. She guessed that was the door. Jessica blinked and coughed.

The ARIels approached her. The pink one appeared to be a newer model than the green one, Jessica decided. It was outfitted with jointed legs and virtually silent hydraulics. Her rubber-coated finger-like probes organized the small vials of fluid and tools that were laid out in her tray. Green-girl on the other hand sported only roller style propulsion that whirred as she moved about. Notwithstanding the different models, the two robots had their programming entrained to operate as one functional unit, initiating and completing tasks for each other with efficiency and silence.

Jessica tried to address the pair, but all she could manage was a muffled "Grrkk". It felt like her tongue was wrapped in an old gym sock. *Ugh!* "Maa...ungh." With that she gave up.

The AImee beeped and Green-girl plugged one probe into the console to receive a download. When it was finished, Pinkie tilted Jessica's head back and released two drops of liquid into each of her eyes. It stung—*Wow!*—but it helped. Her vision began to clear.

Green-girl folded Jessica sideways at the waist and injected something into the middle of her spine. The benefits of this administration were not immediately clear. Jessica began to twitch violently throughout her body, which made her cry out several times. Pain like steel blades sliding along the length of every nerve radiated from the point of injection in every direction, across her torso and to the ends of every limb. A disturbing pressure then swelled up her spine, through her neck and into the middle of her skull. Just when she thought her head was going to burst, the pressure released her from its chokehold.

The twitching subsided too and the AImee beeped again. Pinkie ambled over to the AI monitor's console and began pushing buttons. Suddenly, there were colors. The white room resolved into a soft pale green, her white sheets turned light gray. The unbroken, blinding field of white of the floor developed flecks of pink and aqua. Even the ARIels themselves morphed from pink and green into Maroon and Navy blue. Jessica was so mesmerized by the transformation of her surroundings that at first she failed to notice she could move again.

Instinctively, she reached up to touch her face. Then she spent a moment staring at her hands, manipulating her fingers and wrists, proving that they belonged to her. She found the sight of her own body to be disorienting, as if every part of her had been reorganized as she slept. *I must have been hit by a truck or something.* She thought.

Jessica sat up and the AImee started beeping loudly. Suddenly dizzy and nauseous, Jessica listed to the right. Immediately, both ARIels were beside her. With a click of one button, the bed transformed into a kind of hospital-issued Barka-lounger. She rested her head against the Intelligel pillow. The dizziness subsided, but the nausea did not. She wretched and vomited forcefully all over her hospital gown and sprayed a corner of the mechanical face of the now Navy blue ARIel.

"What. Happened. To me?" Jessica asked quietly.

The ARIels, of course, did not respond with anything useful. "You are in the hospital. Please relax and we will clean you up." The maroon ARIel's voice was pleasant, but neutral. It echoed like the sound was bouncing off the sides of a ravine.

Navy left the room, momentarily, and returned spic and span, carrying a new gown and clean sheets.

Jessica decided to try being more specific with the assistive robots. "Why am I in the hospital?"

"You are very sick." Blue. Less reverb. More mechanical.

"You need to rest." Maroon.

The ARIels were quick and efficient in changing both her and the bed with little input from her. They quickly lifted and pulled and draped and tied as though she were a loaf of bread being packaged for sale.

"How did I get sick? What exactly is wrong with me?"

"You were hurt,"

"In the horrible terrorist attack,"

"Thursday before last."

"You were hit on the head."

"You are very sick."

"You need to rest."

Jessica leaned her head back against the pillow again in frustration. Ordinarily, nursing ARIels were employed to familiarize patients with their surroundings and to aid in reality orientation by relaying the facts of a patient's injuries consistently and in detail. These ARIels were obviously programmed to give her as little information as was needed to facilitate her care. *But why?* Jessica closed her eyes. The machines whizzed around the room tapping on various monitors and machines. Before leaving, they downloaded instructions into the AImee above the head of her bed. Then she was alone again.

Surprisingly, Jessica noted that she no longer felt too badly. Yes, she was groggy. And her limbs tingled, like they were just waking up from being asleep. But otherwise, she felt pretty good. She lay quietly for a moment, trying to organize her thoughts.

The Observer noted Jessica's lethargy through a closed circuit connection embedded in the AImee's monitoring eye. Strange. He'd expected her to fight more, for information, for action. He had not expected her to be so complacent. The Observer hoped that, given time, her original enthusiasm would re-emerge or else she would be useless to the Office. All of the effort he had made to keep her in the game would be for nothing.

It was rare to find an agent with intelligence of her caliber who was also able to follow orders while maintaining a singular focus on mission goals. Even in the face of collateral damage, Jessica could keep her head together. She could improvise strategy when needed without going rogue. Having cultivated her for three years, he was furious when Jessica was compromised. He vowed to find and torment those responsible for the fiasco. His vengeance would only be more potent if she had to be sacrificed.

During Operations training, the neurologist in charge of teaching new officers the complex protocols surrounding candidate selection for Associative Filtering made the risks of taking short cuts quite clear. He told them about the incident in 2046 when Special Ops Unit Commander, Phil Weiss, underwent Associative Filtering subsequent to his return home from Mexico City. He appeared to have acquired a standard case of post-traumatic stress disorder, suffering night terrors and random flashbacks triggered by loud sounds and sudden interruptions. Released from the hospital with a clean bill of health, he became the top weapons trainer in the country and was subsequently stationed in Austin, Texas.

No one knows for sure when the tracers began or for how long he managed to suppress them before breaking. All they figured out was that Weiss re-gained gruesome memories of Mexican civilians torn apart by boulder charges and pin grenades. He remembered following the orders of the chain of command to neutralize a building near the main market. Its occupants fell to the poisoned fog of six Breath of God podules before Weiss and his few remaining men stormed in to find almost six dozen dead children huddling around their equally rigid caretakers.

The random selectivity of tracer-retrieved memories determined that he would not remember the civilian-led rocket attack that killed half his unit in under five minutes. He did not remember seeing his attackers flee into the building holding the day care center before receiving the order to fire. Weiss became secretly convinced that the American government had set him up to perpetrate human rights violations against the Mexican rebels fighting for US withdrawal from their territory, and quietly bent himself on revenge.

In his end game, Weiss corralled an entire class of Special Weapons recruits into an abandoned bunker in the desert, on the pretext of running an escape scenario. The Breath of Gods had not quite killed most of the recruits before Weiss' strategically-placed boulder charges blew, bringing the building down on their heads. The base's emergency response unit arrived just in time to see Weiss blow his own head off by biting down on a chunk of polarized-ion putty.

The Observer understood that Jessica's current predicament had the potential for propagating a fiasco of equal proportion to the Weiss parable. That T-Col had its own risks was assumed. He just wished he knew what those risks entailed. It was a wild card he preferred not to have in his deck at this time. Still, Jessica was his best agent. He needed her, at least for now. When her mission was complete, he could re-evaluate. Until then, all he had was statistics. Associative Filtering carried with it an eighty-five per cent success rate in erasing undesirable memories without tracers, while even the T-Col failures had documented a ninety-eight per cent success rate. *Good enough for government work.* He chuckled to himself.

There was movement in Jessica's hospital room. *What's this?* Jessica was now standing on her bed, holding her self-extracted IV needle. She was using the needle to attempt to break into the casing of the AImee. Her aim was a little off and she lost her balance a few times, but he could see her trying to focus.

Won't stop until you get an answer, will you? That's my girl.

Jessica almost had the front panel of the AImee free of the device when there was a knock at the door. She looked over just in time to see a squarish man wearing a suit enter, carrying what looked like a thick black suitcase. They each remained still for a moment locked in each other's gaze. Jessica thought to herself, *who the hell wears three-piece suits any more?*

The man introduced himself, "Jessica Butler, I'm Doctor Moore, a neuropsychologist here at Mount-Sinai."

"So that's where I am?" Jessica interrupted.

The doctor appeared nonplussed for a moment, then collected himself. "I'm going to be looking at your cognitive processes to make sure you haven't suffered any losses in your accident."

Jessica eyed him suspiciously, "and what accident was that, Dr. Moore?"

"Please, sit down, Miss Butler."

Jessica maneuvered herself into a sitting position without removing her eyes from the doctor. She decided she didn't trust him, although she didn't know why.

"So, you're having difficulty remembering where you are..." Doctor Moore began.

"I was unconscious and was never *told* where I am." Jessica rebutted.

"I see." Doctor Moore entered some notes into his clinical portfolio. The AImee, unperturbed by Jessica's assault beeped cheerfully.

"And you're feeling angry?"

Jessica was silent and glowered at him. It didn't help that she didn't know exactly how she felt. She inherently did not trust this hospital or its staff, but she didn't know why. Something seemed off, but she couldn't define it. Furthermore, she was having significant difficulty remembering large chunks of her life.

She had conducted an inventory right before she decided to mount her stealth attack on the AImee. Her childhood memories appeared to be intact—until somewhere in college, when things got fuzzy. She remembered that she worked as a reporter for TWNS, but she could not remember which Bureau office or what current stories she was responsible for. And she certainly was not going to tell Doctor Twenty-Questions here that she had no memory of what she had been doing when she was hurt, how she had been hurt, or that she was afraid to stay in this place any longer than she needed to.

Doctor Moore placed a deck of cards face down on the table in front of her. "I'd like you to sort these cards into two piles based on the clues that I give you. Each time you place a card, I'll tell you if you're on the right track or not."

Jessica tried to read his face. *He can't be serious.* "Okay." She decided to play along. She lay one card down. Seven of spades. Nothing. She picked up the next card—three of hearts—and put it in a second pile.

"No."

Jessica raised her eyebrow in mild annoyance, tossed the second card on top of the first and picked up the next card. Nine of clubs. She looked at the pile in front of her and placed the nine of clubs into the second pile.

"No."

Jessica took a long impatient breath in and breathed out through pursed lips in the Doctor's general direction. She watched his eyelids flutter as he tried to ignore her breath fluttering against his eyeballs. She placed the nine of clubs with the first two cards and picked up a fourth card. Six of diamonds. She considered the cards laying in pile one for a moment and decisively placed the new card in its own pile.

"Yes."

Finally, she understood the pattern to the Doctor's responses. Jessica had always been good at discerning patterns, visual and otherwise. She picked up the next card, two of spades—pile two.

"Yes."

Five of diamonds. First pile.

"Yes."

Ace of spades. First pile.

"Yes."

Four of hearts. Second pile.

"Yes."

Jack of clubs. *Hmm. Tricky.* First pile.

"Yes."

Three of diamonds. First pile.

"No."

Jessica locked on his bland expression. The left corner of his lip twitched under her gaze, but gave no other clue as to his intentions. *He's changed the pattern,* she thought. She looked at the next card for a long time. Ace of hearts. She watched his eyes follow her hand down to the table. His Adam's apple rose and fell as he swallowed nervously. First pile.

"Yes."

And so it went for four hours, by her estimation. Doctor Moore presented her with a series of seemingly inane tasks, each of which proved to be surprisingly esoteric, yet ultimately interpretable. By the end, Doctor Moore appeared to have satisfied himself that she was mentally acute. *As long as he doesn't ask me what I was doing two weeks ago Thursday.* He didn't.

Instead, he excused himself with a snap of his briefcase. "Good day, Miss Butler. Much luck in your recovery." And then he was gone.

Jessica stared at the closed door for a minute or two, half expecting some being—living or robotic—to enter, as if on cue, after the departure of the neuropsychologist. *What happened to all your fine orchestration?* She thought. *Things are getting pretty shabby around here.*

She scanned the room for anything to amuse herself. Briefly, she considered resuming her dissection of the now-battered AImee that kept pinging away at intervals, but decided against it figuring that whoever programmed the ARIels, probably programmed the AImee as well. Therefore, there was likely to be little information to be had there. She sighed and closed her eyes again. Man, she was tired.

With her eyes closed, the focus of her attention once again shifted to her limbs and that strange tingly feeling. It still felt like she had been electrocuted and every cell was leaping with excitement. She reached her hand up to her face, missed and re-targeted her forehead. Fear trickled over her like rain. It felt like her limbs had forgotten how to move. *It's natural to be disoriented after a traumatic event,* she tried to reassure herself. *Remember,* she thought. *What can I remember?*

Jessica visualized herself. She was wearing floaters and dedos and was interfaced into the TWNS network. She tapped herself into a file on the Intergrationist insurgency.

Cut to: A microphone in her hand, she makes a report:

"...is denying any affiliation with the Integrationist assertion that they are the legitimate government of the United Stated of America."

Cut to: A perky blonde woman with hair that curls up at the ends. She is in a café. She pops a Pollie into her iced mocha latte. Ah relaxation. *So...what was I just thinking about?*

Cut to: Graduation. A short, trim man. He smiles

Cut to: A burning nightclub east of Mexico City *¿Qué pasó aquí?*

Cut to: A closed fist extending toward a trash barrel. Something falling in.

Cut to: Sound. *Boom!*

Jessica emerged groggily from her sleep, twisting the sheets around her torso. One eye opened suspiciously. Someone had turned on the neuro-diode console at the foot of her bed. *I don't remember a panel being here before.* A woman in a perfectly pressed red suit and a blonde bob smiled into the camera.

"Today marks the twenty fifth anniversary of FDA approval of the popular neuro-relaxant beverage additive Polythanidone. Affectionately called "Pollie" by consumers, Polythanidone works it effect directly on the amygdala and other parts of the limbic system in the brain, producing a feeling of calm and confidence."

I know her...

"Detractors of Polythanidone argue that the drug has a similar effect as the long-banned club drug Blue Sabre and that the only purpose it serves is to sedate a stressed-out population without addressing the source of the problem."

Carrie...

"Bubbly Bistro Technologies, which remains the sole manufacturer of Polythanidone due to a special extended patent issued in October of last year, plans to celebrate the anniversary by distributing a VRoupon at their corporate nexus (one per household port) between July 1 and August 1."

"Carrie Ann. Yes! Carrie Ann. I know you." Jessica half laughed and half sighed with relief. *Carrie Ann. Of course.* "Now, who the hell is Carrie Ann?" She squeezed her eyes shut in frustration and cursed her ongoing confusion before drifting back to sleep.

The next time Jessica awoke, she saw herself—or some likeness thereof—had taken over the neuro-diode panel. *What the hell?* Her overlay was dressed in a conservative pastel power suit. A single silver chain adorned her neck. Her pin-straight, jaw length hair had been overlaid with helmet-shaped hair worthy of the best Home Trust party Senator's wife. A wide gold band flanked by a three-quarter caret diamond dressed the third finger on her left hand. She hardly would have recognized the image of herself, if she had not suddenly remembered creating the ring. *Yes!*

She had been sitting in Tripp's Thompson's office reviewing an overlay she created utilizing templates pulled from the best of successful news anchors over the past hundred years.

"There's something missing." Tripp said matter-of-factly.

Jessica looked at him questioningly.

"How are people going to know that you're a stable person who can be trusted? You look so young. It's going to be difficult for you to reach them." He continued. "I'll just marry you."

Jessica let out a surprised laugh, tinged with fear. Tripp could be somewhat unpredictable, but marriage? Before she had the opportunity to clarify his meaning, Tripp pushed a few buttons and up popped the ring. Originally twice the size, Jessica commented that it looked like the thing was holding her finger hostage. So, he reined it in a little. The overall effect was striking. And truth be told, she liked the idea of being a part of a giant conspiracy. Americans had no idea the people they turned to daily for information, or during crisis for inspiration were no more than overlaid concept pieces gleaned from their own collective cultural sub-consciousness.

Jessica became fascinated by her confident self, talking at her from the screen. "…in 2026 when seven Manhattan College students were arrested during a protest that turned violent. On November 27th, several hundred students gathered in the street in front of the school angry over a recent wire rumor claiming that the Fein administration was suppressing scientific reports about the safety of the recently approved hybrid wheat stock, which the students blamed for an increase in miscarriages among the farming communities in which it was grown. The Fein administration denied the claims, but could not keep the rumor from spreading to the international press.

CUT TO – Doug Rothstein – Secretary of Agriculture between 2027 - 2042: "Despite the lack of evidence, or perhaps because of it, the international community by and large banned the production and import of Genetically Modified Organisms in their food markets. The reduction in exporting opportunities was devastating to farmers across the country and family farms were lost at an alarming rate."

CUT TO – Jessica Butler: "The crisis continued to expand over the ensuing six months until Congress passed the landmark legislation the Standardized Safety in Food Act, which not only set certain specified standards for the testing of new GMO's but banned the distribution of food from non-licensed sources to increase the safety of the existing food chain."

Jessica tried to remember researching the report she was delivering. She could not. Just then, Tripp Thompson poked his head in the door and grinned widely, pulling her out of her thoughts. His fine sandy blonde hair fell carelessly this way and that over his eyebrows. His blue eyes shined warmly into her own. Jessica smiled back with relieved pleasure. "Heeeey, Tripp."

"Jessica, baby, you're awake!" Tripp strode into the room confidently, gestured for the neuro-diode console to go into sleep mode and kissed her on the cheek. Then he presented her with a large bouquet of early-summer flowers. "A little piece of the great weather you're missing." He pushed the call button. A moment later the Navy ARIel appeared. "Please get us a vase for her flowers. Thank you."

"Yes, sir." The robot replied and rolled away.

Jessica felt comforted to have her boss with her. After their initial sexual misadventures, they had formed a strong mentor-mentee bond that endured beyond her initial apprenticeship into her professional career. It was Tripp who introduced Jessica to the fine points of navigating the VR newswire, who taught her how to stream herself through the TWNS nucleus, collecting nuggets of information like some people used to pan for gold. He showed her how to circumvent the troll switches in the FIO firewalls that had been constructed to maintain the isolation of the United States from the greater world of nations. And it was Tripp who recruited her into the Office. *The Office?* Some memory wiggled around in the back of her mind.

"The Office..." Jessica blurted out, surprising herself.

Tripp looked briefly unnerved. The ARIel returned with a vase of water into which it placed and arranged the flowers. Tripp's wary expression broke, and he returned to his broadly smiling self. "We were very upset to hear how hurt you were. What happened out there anyway?"

Jessica eyed the ARIel as it left the room. "That's just it, Tripp. I don't remember what happened. Not where I was, not what I was doing. Nothing."

"Hmm. Tough break, Jess. That happens sometimes though. I wouldn't worry about it."

The pieces of her fractured thought slid into place with sudden clarity. "I was on 'official business', wasn't I? And I don't mean the newswire."

"As far as I can tell, yes." Tripp paused. "You remember the Office, then?"

It was Jessica's turn to hedge her answer. "Vaguely. Why don't you fill me in?"

Jessica waited impatiently while Tripp considered his options. He examined her demeanor and expression. Jessica Butler had one of the best poker faces he'd ever seen. He had no doubt that if she wanted to get something out of him, she would, one way or another—eventually. But she appeared to be genuinely struggling to understand who she was and how she came to this place. In order for her to be of continued use to him, the T-Col team had been required to leave her tactical training intact. He decided he needed to take the chance. If there were any undesirable tracers lying in wait, it was best they be triggered now and not later, when they thought they could trust her again. He pursed his lips formulating exactly which information he should include and what should be left unsaid.

Jessica sensed Tripp's hesitation. He was hiding something from her. Correction. He was figuring out how to hide something from her. Her warm relief cooled and she drew a thin veil of distance between them. Through it, she could see out, but he could not see in. And if she played her part right, he'd never even know it was there.

"You are a news anchor for the New York Metropolitan Bureau of the Total Wire News Service. I'm the Bureau chief and you are my top anchor of national and international politics." He paused to test her reaction to this piece of information. She remained placid. Tripp locked the door and activated the com scrambler on his Mate. He leaned in close to her ear. "You are also a secret agent with the Office of Civilian Defense. I am the division-director of the Media Node of the Office, which includes Intelligence. Your specialty is uncovering and identifying internal threats to the political stability of America and at times defusing them."

"And I do this how?"

"By collecting information and evidence and helping to bring people in for questioning."

"Hmm. And this has been going on since…"

"Five years. You've been an agent for five years."

"So, one could presume that I've accomplished many missions in this time." She proposed blandly.

"You're one of the best, Jess. You're top in the game."

Jessica shifted her eyes from Tripp to the neuro-diode panel, to the door, and back to Tripp. She leaned in close to him. "So." She began, intimately. He leaned in further. She could smell the cologne on his neck. On another man, this would have turned her thoughts to more prurient interests. "So…" She licked her lips before yelling, "why don't I remember any of this!"

Tripp recoiled from the volume of her shout, shocked, but ultimately not surprised. Her timing was impeccable. She hadn't changed. In some ways this made him trust her more. He knew this side of her. He understood it. He could work with it. He thought about the Voice's order before leaving to come here. *Explain it to her so she'll understand and ask no more questions. Shut her up and get her in the game again.* "You've been filtered, Jessica."

"Excuse me?"

"You've got it straight. You were on a mission. The mission went wrong. The Office had no way of knowing whether or not certain Top Secret information would be compromised, so they took you in for Associative Filtering to take out everything that could be…problematic." Tripp gave Jessica his best you-got-me shrug.

God, that explains everything. Jessica felt thoroughly violated. With all of the holes she felt in her mind, she must have had access to quite a bit of Top Secret information. At least she now understood why.

"I know you feel a little disoriented now. That's just the residual effects of the drugs they use to elucidate the pathways targeted for de-potentiation. More of the missing pieces will come together over the next day or two. The doctor says you'll be able to go home by Sunday."

"Speaking of doctors, when am I going to see one?"

"Just relax, Jess. How often do you have the opportunity to just sit around and do nothing?"

"I wouldn't know." She allowed a sardonic smile to slip around the corners of the veil.

Tripp raised his finger and shook it slowly at her. "You rest up!"

Asleep again, Jessica turned and twisted in her bed. Visions and voices played across her mind in surround sound and Technicolor.

You…you're going to be someone special. I can feel it. You're different.

Mom. Dad. Auto accident. Dead eyes staring at her upside down. Hiding under a bush until the fire fighters find her.

You'll be someone special one day.

Someone is stroking her hair.

French braids. Her first. She is in the girl's room at school, cutting them off with a pocket knife. She admires the jagged edges and smiles. Sister Mary is crying over all her hard work.

Bright circle of lights over her head. She must close her eyes. Cannot. Pain. Is her head exploding?

Puppies and kittens.

What?

His lips, so close to hers, she can smell the peppermint on his breath. *You're going to be someone special. I just know it. Don't be afraid.*

Paper cut from a manila envelope. She is running. Under the bridge, behind the package store no one ever goes into. Scaling the fencing on the other side. Twenty-foot jump.

A warm kitchen. She and Mom making brownies. The chocolate tastes so good. She licks it off her fingers. *Mmm. Mmm. Mmm.*

"Mmm. Mmm. Mmm!" Jessica's eyes rolled up to the back of her head.

The Observer, mildly concerned, folded his hands across his stomach.

Year: 2051 (eleven years earlier)
Ground Zero: Lower Manhattan New York, New York

The celebration at the re-built Nine-Eleven Memorial was reaching its giddy height. The top ten high school marching bands from across the country had formed a temporary union for the show. As almost three hundred horns, flutes, and drums projected the National Anthem across the Hudson River, a brilliant color guard spun their flags eliciting cheers from the gathered public. All that was missing were flaming batons.

Clowns on stilts wandered the crowd handing out bouquets of balloons. They wisely avoided a fifteen-foot radius around the 20-story spires that stood where the North and South Towers of the World Trade Center had once reigned. The winds ripping up their smooth sides were likely to drag the tottering Bozos into their chaotic vortices, if they weren't careful. Several dozen souvenir hats were already in the water en route to Liberty Island due to these same winds.

The dignitary platform had been erected underneath the soaring archway that framed the site's entrance from Liberty

Street. President Andrew Fein observed the scene with satisfaction from behind dark sunglasses. The appropriately proportioned smile beneath his sizeable mustache let the audience and media representatives see how proud he was to be among them. He casually ran a handkerchief across his bald head and behind his neck. He tapped the toes of his silver-tipped cowboy boots in time with the performance below.

Fein's gamble had paid off. The re-building of the Nine-Eleven Memorial, destroyed in 2037, had been just the right vehicle to remind the population of what it ought to fear. As a result, they sought safety in the familiar and the stable, which Fein worked hard to make sure was represented by his congenial presence.

The band was winding down and the emcee, a long-haired heartthrob of Wire drama fame slinked up to the microphone. Shrill screams from the assembled women converged into a single whoop. Somewhere from the back one woman called, "I want to have your baby!" The pretty boy star put on his modest face and demurred. The dimple on his left cheek pinked and deepened.

"Ladies and gentleman. It's an honor to be here today." Reprise. Screaming. He spread his fingers, palms down and pressed the crowd to quiet. "Today, I have the privilege of introducing the most influential man in the world. This man, with the help of the Home Trust party is almost single-handedly responsible for restoring dignity and integrity to Washington. Please raise your hands for the President of the United States, Andrew Fein!"

President Fein stood and smoothed his jacket over his slightly rounded stomach. *Show time!* He thrust the sunglasses into his jacket pocket, approached the boy toy and shook his hand sincerely. Cheers deferred to hushed whispers and finally silence in the face of Fein's bowed head and dramatic pause before beginning his address. He paused a full five seconds to increase the anticipation. When he lifted his face to meet the crowd, his eyes glistened with tears.

"Who among us will forget the sadness of loss fourteen years ago when our most precious memorial was desecrated by a terrorist attack? Who will forget the sight of the crumbled mass of granite bearing the crumbled names of the two thousand nine hundred seventy seven heroes who died on September 11, 2001? Who could imagine that thirty six years later, when I was a young New York state representative, I would stand in this same place mourning the loss of three hundred twenty eight more American lives to the ongoing tragedy that is terrorism?"

Fein paused to gauge the crowd. They were quiet. They remembered.

"The symbolic nature of that attack was not lost on me. Terrorists were hidden among us, thumbing their noses at our inability to protect even this most revered treasure. The purpose of that attack was not to test us. It was to mock us. The timing too collided unfortunately with a new low in the trust between Americans, their government and the world. We folded into ourselves and abandoned this place and left it shrouded in rubble.

"Addressing you today amidst the majestic reclamation of our national heritage, reignites my hope that one day we will all be free from fear, free from lies, free from the mistrust that has drenched and threatened to drown our public spirit.

"When I took office two years ago, I promised to completely uproot the treasonous infrastructure of the Kessler administration and eliminate the threat of terrorist reprisal from within your leadership. I promised to finish the job that the brave agents of the Office of Civilian Defense began when they stormed the White House on February 23, 2049 to reclaim your right to honest and true governance."

Fein was interrupted by a sudden swelling of cheers from the audience. Media drones buzzed over the heads of the crowd collecting images of face-painted children and teary-eyed ironworkers waving pocket-sized American flags.

"Earlier this week, I fulfilled that promise when one hundred and three former Representatives and Senators from across the country faced a Grand Jury and charges of aiding and abetting known terrorist organizations. With this final cleansing, we will stop over two hundred and fifty million credits from being transferred to foreign interests this year alone."

The crowd cheered again. Hand-painted banners and American flags waved vigorously. The squawk of several air horns reverberated off the walls of the surrounding buildings.

"Unfortunately, the sudden departure of so many law makers and the difficulty of screening those who would jump to take their place puts a heavy burden on our government. For this reason, I have authorized a streamlining of the United States legislature into one Central Senate, which will be comprised of those current legislators who have proven their fealty to your trust. This body will convene under the leadership of Senator and Atlanta Bombing investigation hero, David Marks."

Fein gestured grandly to the chair in which Marks was sitting. The crowd hollered. Senator Marks stood and bowed. Fein noted a small scuffle in his peripheral vision to the right, but it cleared quickly and he refocused on managing the expectations and responses of his current audience.

"My fellow Americans, I feel your frustration. You're frightened and you're fed up. You want answers. You ask, for how long must we endure these threats to our well-being? Rest assured, this administration prioritizes your safety above all else. Under my direction, the Office of Civilian Defense has collected its creative resources to generate solutions to the fear that has taken root in the American soul.

"To those who would criticize my decision to temporarily retain my position as Executive Director of OCD during my term of office as President, I urge you to look at the results I have accomplished to date. Domestic terrorism has declined over twenty-six per cent in two years."

The crowd burst into another stream of applause.

"We are taking back our streets, we are taking back our parks, we are taking back our public squares and freeing the

American people to move about and conduct commerce as they please. Mark my words. Better days are right around the corner. Thank you for your kind attention."

Fein turned from the lectern. The band played *Hail to the Chief* while the audience clapped along. The sun slipped in and out from behind a small cloud, reminding Fein to retrieve his sunglasses from his pocket. His Secret Service team formed a small circle around him and led him toward a waiting limousine.

Senator Marks approached him from behind. "Sir, aren't you going to stay for a while? There are quite a few babies' cheeks to be pinched out there. And some of the media may have questions about your announcement."

"I have to get to a meeting." Fein waved his pudgy hand dismissively. "Besides, you'd better get used to pinching a few babies' cheeks yourself, Senator." The Secret Service waved Marks back and helped President Fein duck himself into the waiting vehicle. Moments later, the motorcade powered up and was gone.

Rolls Royce Limousine Porter: Lower Manhattan New York, New York

Andrew Fein reclined in the adjustable cradle of the limousine and turned on the lower back massager. An aide whose name he couldn't remember leaned close to him holding a net-connected scratchpad called a Cloud Folio. "The initial response to your speech looks good, sir. Our chatter monitoring shows that listeners overwhelmingly support the ongoing rousting of those who support the old administration. On the fringes some rabble-rousers are floating questions around about the constitutionality of changing the structure of the US Legislature. I think it's manageable, though. The comments aren't really gaining any traction."

Damn right, it's manageable, thought Fein. *And it's about to become more so.* He tuned out the persistent yammering of the aide, allowing his eyes to fall shut behind his glasses. Alone in his own mind, he could see his path more clearly.

As far as he could figure, Fein faced one major obstacle to keeping his job indefinitely—the recession. Economic uncertainty was the most potent wrecking ball any administration could be faced with. The wealthy getting wealthier? That's easy to handle. All you have to do is keep people believing someday they could be a member of the one percent and they'll support any status quo. Isolationism? No one even notices. Take away people's stuff and their credits though and they get unruly and start rebelling against the rightful order of things. Unfortunately, the trade restrictions imposed on the United States by the FIO pretty much ensured that the recession would be long-standing and perhaps deepen. Strong leadership was needed to ensure that disruptions to the necessary streamlining of capital resources was minimized. Thank the stars for Pollie. Its broad use guaranteed that the public wasn't as generally excitable as it was in earlier decades and it was easy to tax.

"...and the Coahuila solar array is going online again at the beginning of the month," the assistant droned on. "We've installed the new management team and left a small contingent of OCD on site to prevent any further sabotage."

Fein tuned the assistant out again and thought about the Mexican energy auction of 2016. That one brilliant move ensured Mexico would become the power house of all central America, Columbia and Brazil. The continued corruption at all levels of their federal government ensured it was easy to take control of. Now that US troops had reached the border with Guatemala, it was only a matter of time before key members of the FIO, Brazil and Venezuela to be precise, would understand that the main source of power for their massive urban population centers was going to be taken under US control. President Fein felt these governments would be much more engaged in the negotiation process if he were all that stood between them and rotating blackouts. Somehow, he thought they would see the wisdom of lowering those trade barriers just a little.

Fein didn't expect that rationalizing an escalation in the region would be too difficult. Eighty per cent of the US population was already convinced that Mexico was the instigator of the sabotage of GMO seed stocks in the mid 20's. He could build on that with the proper supports. *Yes, this is going to work out just fine.* The President allowed his mind to wander further as the luxury porter swept through the city.

Waldorf-Astoria Hotel: Manhattan New York, New York

President Fein and his entourage swept into their suite on the secure floor en masse. Fein tossed his sunglasses onto the antique half round table by the door and proceeded into the sitting room.

The sun peeked diffusely through the curtain shim, illuminating the Swarovski candy dish delicately laid out on a lace doily in the center of a mahogany end table. Next to this a short young man with sandy blonde hair stood at attention when he entered. The man's earnest blue eyes reflected both respect and fear. Fein faced him directly before speaking. "Tripp Thompson, I presume."

"Yes, Mr. President. It's a pleasure to meet you." Tripp stepped forward and extended his hand. Fein shook it.

Firm grip. Not overconfident. This is good so far. The President gestured to the seat Tripp had abandoned and crossed to the wet bar by the window. The thickly padded navy carpeting gently gave way beneath his Bruno Magli's. "Can I get you something?"

Tripp sat. "Scotch, please."

The boy has taste.

Fein's security team spread themselves strategically throughout the suite, maintaining two agents within easy reach of Fein's invited guest. Fein pleasured in the weight of the solid hardwood doors of the suite's bar cabinet. Fully opened, one pressed into the heavy maroon drapery framing his view onto Park Avenue. Traffic was at a standstill. *Rush hour.* He retrieved two glasses from the shelf above.

Fein turned back to Tripp and found him following his every movement with his eyes. *Observant.* He handed Tripp his drink and settled into the firm cushions of the settee. "I love New York."

Tripp smiled and snorted at the cliché.

"I do. The energy here is different. Washington? Everyone's got an agenda and it's usually contrary to your own. You spend your life maneuvering around each other and never get anything accomplished." He swirled his glass and observed the flow of the fluid. "New York? Everyone has an agenda, but they're too busy going after it to even notice if it's contrary to your own. And if it is? Eh, you'll figure it out." Fein took a sip and swallowed. "Why did you go into media, Mr. Thompson?"

Tripp raised his eyebrows and inhaled. "I like knowing things."

"Things, Mr. Thompson? Like what color handbag is going to be 'in' this year? Things like that?"

Tripp stifled a grin and tilted his head side to side. "No. Things like, why would the President of the United States request a personal meeting with a mid-level news segment producer he's never met before?"

Touché. Fein took another sip of his drink. "I was very impressed with your piece on the history of the FIO trade embargo. It was very balanced."

Tripp nodded once. "Thank you, Sir."

Fein sighed dramatically and placed his drink on the coffee table in front of him. "I need help, Mr. Thompson. I need an outlet that I can rely on to not…turn the public against its own best interests."

"You want a shill." Tripp stated simply.

"I want someone who understands." Fein countered. "Mr. Thompson, I would like to make you an offer. You will be promoted to Division Director of Total Wire New Service's New York Bureau. You will simultaneously obtain access to certain privileged information within the database of the Office of Civilian Defense, in order to increase the accuracy and timeliness of your reporting."

"And?"

"From time to time we may call on you for some investigative work."

Tripp locked eyes with the President.

"You will of course be allowed to choose your own team."

Tripp took a sip of his drink.

"You will also find that there will be a variety of opportunities for advancement in the Office. Your position would be crucial to maintaining an appropriate flow of information to the public."

"When do I begin?"

Fein smiled. "You just did. Welcome aboard."

Year: 2062
Park Avenue South and 96th Street: Manhattan New York, New York

Tripp waited in his porter at the traffic light and mused about how the balance of power had shifted since his first meeting with Fein in his Waldorf-Astoria suite. He hooked a secure line off of the OCD nucleus and pinged Fein's private line. The Voice answered deliberate and neutral. "What's the status?"

"Better than we imagined. Her confusion is clearing. She remembers her training and her role, but so far there's no sign of anything that could be considered problematic." Tripp declined to mention the new information he had constructed and overlaid with the memory transfer. It would only upset the man without benefit.

"This is encouraging."

"The success of this operation leaves you with a lot more options. I have some ideas that may enhance the usefulness of this new tool."

"We'll discuss it at our next briefing."

"All right." The line was dead before Tripp even replied.

Tripp's porter weaved slowly through the rush hour traffic. Laser tags mounted at the corners of each intersection flashed silently as they read the identity badges on each car traveling in the Central zone. The tax had done little to stop the lawyers and shoppers on the Upper East Side from driving to and from their destinations. Now if you really wanted to get somewhere in a hurry, 116th street was usually wide open. Tripp sighed, reclined his cradle and took inventory.

Jessica seemed okay. For that he was truly glad. Yes, he would have sacrificed her if he'd needed to, but he would have felt badly about it. She didn't appear to have any recollection of her experience in Freedom Park, or the events immediately prior to and after it. She had accepted that she was filtered and appeared to be okay with that.

Delph on the other hand was still something of a question mark. He had been hurriedly packing before the real shit went down. So, Tripp wasn't worried there. Just in case, they'd brought him in and filtered some small segments in the timeframe of the event itself. He thinks Marcelo is dead, which is okay, Tripp supposed.

Less certain was Delph's relationship with Jessica. In their last meeting together, Delph had hammered Tripp with questions about where she was and if she made it. Tripp had been vague at the time, because he didn't know Jessica's long-term prospects yet. Tripp thought Delph left the meeting assuming that Jessica was dead.

The boy's clear affection for Jessica could be seen as a liability, or it could be an asset. If he loves her, he's going to want to protect her, no matter what the cost. He won't let her out of his sight. Delph had been briefed, very loosely, on the existence and purpose of T-Col. His unparalleled programming and hacking skills demanded that he become a part of the project eventually. Tripp knew that Delph's biggest test was yet to come.

That was Tripp's wild card. *What will Mr. Crane do when he finds out his partner has become quite literally a new woman? Will he reject her? Even kill her perhaps?* Tripp didn't think so. His initial response to the idea of the project was one of general intrigue. Would he reconnect with her? Protect her? Tripp didn't know, but he was due to find out soon.

Mount-Sinai Hospital: Manhattan New York, New York

The slant of the sun cast wiry shadows across the mess of sheets that lay piled at the end of the bed in which Jessica had been confined for three weeks. *At least I was asleep for two of the three. Otherwise, ah!!!!* The room smelled stale to her, despite the efforts of the squad of Scrubbies that descended on it daily. The probe ends of the AImee dangled toward the floor like tentacles. Jessica rubbed her forearms where until only two hours ago the surgical glue had held them fast to her skin. The reams of discharge paperwork lay carelessly clipped together on a rolling table.

Jessica sat on the edge of her bed, leaning over to lace up her Doc Martins when Boo arrived. Her presence was announced by the entrance of two petite combat boots topped by thigh-high lace stockings. Boo's real name was Betty Anne. At some point in high school, Jessica remembered, Betty had become Boo, there was a funny story behind that, but for some reason Jessica couldn't remember it. The left boot turned sideways impatiently, tapping its toe three times. Jessica looked up.

"Come on, let's go before I kick ya' in the face."

That was Boo. Straight to the point. Today she was wearing a plaid mini, cinched at the top with a wide plastic belt and silver buckle. Her athletic shape was emphasized by the thin silk fabric of her red cami.

"Cool it sister, I'm just making sure I don't fall on my ass on my way out of here. They might have to keep me then."

"Traffic sucks." Boo flipped her head and her short, perky platinum curls bobbed cheerfully back and forth. She paced back and forth, gnawing on the side of one fingernail.

"Big surprise." Jessica sat up too quickly and the world made a pirouette around her. She splayed her arms out on the bed to stabilize herself.

"Whoa, chica, you okay?" Boo reached out and grabbed Jessica by the shoulders.

"Just a little light-headed. Haven't been out of bed for a while."

"No shit! I'da turned into spaghetti by now—overcooked."

Jessica smiled and stood, feeling better now. "Toss me against the wall. Let's see if I stick."

Boo laughed as Jessica crossed to the guest chair to grab her jacket. "Still, three weeks. And no visitors allowed. You'd think you were the fucking President or something. How did you keep from going insane?"

Jessica crossed to the pile of paperwork and flipped through it looking for signature lines. "Mahjong. You wouldn't believe the tournaments they have over in the brain injury unit. They're out for blood, man."

"You suck!" Boo laughed and pulled a dented pack of sugarless Pollie gum out of her bag, stuffed a piece in her mouth and offered the pack to Jessica. "You were out like a light for what two weeks? Looked like shit too."

Jessica popped a piece of the Pollie gum in her mouth and dropped the pen on top of her paperwork. She grabbed her black bag, hoisted it to her shoulder, then adjusted her collar around it. "I thought you said they didn't allow visitors."

Boo paused almost imperceptibly, then wrinkled her nose. "Pah!" She waved her hand through the air dismissively and followed Jessica to the door. "That's what the nurses told me on my way in here any way."

Jessica started to form a question in her head, but as she did, the Pollie-laced gum released its calming tonic into her bloodstream. As she walked with Boo to the elevator and into the garage, small fragments of half-formed thoughts fluttered away like butterflies on a mountaintop. She slid into the passenger side of Boo's red Parsec 8000 luxury porter and felt the seat shift when it recognized her, retrieving the guest settings for her optimal comfort. The car smelled like a blend of Jasmine and Lavender.

Boo keyed in her security code. "Jessica Butler. Residence." The porter sprang to life. Boo played with the stereo settings as they merged with the traffic toward Roosevelt Drive. Finally, Blu Jackson crooned through the speakers in quiet tones. Jessica's head gently pressed into the back of the cradle as the porter accelerated to cruising speed.

On the other side of the window, the world spun by. The two dozen people huddled around the hospital's free clinic check-in kiosk turned to a blur as another wave of dizziness engulfed Jessica and flitted away again. Her eyes couldn't keep up with the pace of the road as they merged onto the highway. Billboards smudged themselves through her line of sight without resolution. All of the trees appeared to have grown cotton blobs on the ends of their branches. The lines in the road pulsed past, threatening to give her a migraine.

Jessica squeezed her eyes shut and rubbed them with her left thumb and index finger. When she looked up again, Boo had pulled out a lipstick and was amply applying it to her already screaming red lips. With her curly hair and her neo-trash cutie-pie outfit, she looked like a down and out Betty Boop. *Boo—Boop. Was that it?*

"Honestly, I thought I'd be carrying you out in a wheelchair, Jess. You look pretty good for it all."

"Thanks."

"So, do you like remember getting hit by that truck?"

"Truck? Oh. No." Jessica reminded herself that the average person had no idea Associative Filtering even existed and that the secret agent thing was between her and her God. It was for the best. "I don't even remember getting up that morning."

"Wow, that's weird!" Boo's eyes widened beyond usual. "Once, when I was in fifth grade, I got hit in the head by an ice ball. That was Shiri Tyrell's idea of a Valentine's Day card. I forgot what I had for breakfast that morning." Boo nodded soberly.

The porter banked right to exit at the old UN Plaza. Jessica remembered viewing the plaque commemorating the workers who had died in the destruction of the UN building soon after the United States' withdrawal from the agency. The diplomats were gone. So, the only casualties were of low-level staffers who had been left behind to pack up the offices of everyone who was anyone. Given the how key the event was to subsequent actions of the agency under its new title of the Federal International Organization, she was surprised that there hadn't been a big old memorial built there. Instead, the site had been repopulated by a gated community of expensive condominiums, with its own dedicated shops and service facilities. Jessica lost sight of the complex as they turned right on First Avenue, toward East 57th Street.

"So, what's happened since I was put out on the curb?"

"Same old, same old." Boo replied casually. "Remember that guy I went out with a couple of times back in March?"

Jessica didn't. "Yeah."

"Well, he called me up out of the blue last Wednesday. And he's all, like, 'Hey, how's it going' and I'm telling him, 'Hey, you haven't called me in three months'. So, it turns out he went to England or something—had to get, like, a fake passport and everything—to protest the international trade embargo. He gets caught. He's thrown in prison. I didn't even ask how he got back. Can you believe that?"

"I can't believe someone's stupid enough to try to get around the travel ban. All FIO passports have DNA-tagged identity planks in them now. Very tough to forge" *For an amateur,* she thought. "How do people think they're going to get away with shit like that?"

"He almost did."

"Hmm." Jessica turned her eyes back to the buildings rolling by. "So, you gonna see him again?"

"Already did."

The Parsec flanked Freedom Park on the South side. Jessica watched a family of four clustered around a pretzel vendor each using their new EASy chips to make their purchases.

Jessica recognized the wide-eyed thrill of the novelty that would wear off eventually along with the surgiderm that sealed off their incision sites. *Bleep! It's so EASy!* The youngest girl, who had to be about seven or eight giggled as the vendor swept the scanner over her arm. Then she held out her snack for some mustard.

Boo continued her monologue. "I also hopped down to Miami last week for a two-nighter. Shirls won this special deal at Caesar's Park. All we had to do was spend at least a hundred credits on drinks and, well—come on! That's easy. I wish you could've come with."

The signal at Columbus circle changed and Boo and Jessica swept through Broadway, underneath the hulking forms of the Unibank complex and bore left on West 62nd Street. Unibank's monolithic chrome boxes at Columbus Circle stood in stark contrast to the decorous open spaces and brick and glass structures of Fordham University. Passing through their campus was always restful and Jessica came here to walk whenever she could.

"…so we just bought both. Do you like it?" Boo smiled and turned her face side to side. Jessica realized she hadn't been listening to Boo's latest shopping monologue. *Is this the first time she's breathed since we left Mount-Sinai?* "Sure, it's great." *The lipstick? The mascara? Oh, hell!*

The car turned into the security buffer at Jessica's condo complex. It wasn't upscale like the towering filaments on West 75th Street, but it was clean and secure. Flowers bloomed along the inner driveway throughout the spring and summer and there was a jogging ring outside of level 4. Jessica was comfortable here.

The first gate opened, granting the porter access to the inspection alley next to the guard post. Boo commanded the windows to glide down. Jessica held her wrist out the window so the uniformed officer who approached could verify her identity. He ran portable scanner over it, while his colleague completed the thermo graphic scan of the porter.

"Glad to see you're well Miss Butler. Will you and your friend please step out of the car for scanning?" As they did, two women approached from the guard post carrying wands. When the ladies were finished running their wands over Jessica and Boo, the second gate opened. Boo and Jessica drove up the hill toward Bay 8.

"Your people are pretty efficient here." Boo commented.

Jessica shrugged. "Next time we'll take my car." Suddenly, she was very tired.

Jessica lumbered toward her door and touched the thumb reader. Boo dropped Jessica's bag in the kitchen, near the door and headed straight for the sofa and the projection console in the living room. She slipped on the single-dedo control as Jessica wandered into the bathroom to splash water on her face. Boo disappeared into the sofa cushions as she keyed in to Jessica's console and dropped into her personal Parlor.

On her way back to the kitchen, Jessica vaguely noted the clipped sounds of pieces of news stories, soap operas and commercial jingles in the background as Boo scanned her entertainment options. She looked at the photographs lining the hallway and paused to review her image in these little snippets of time. Jessica backstage at Madison Square Garden with rock star Nate Winchester. Jessica with Tripp in the Palm Room with Pulitzer Prize winning news anchor Petra Jackson. Jessica in Vermont with Tripp on a ski slope. Jessica on an airplane with Iraqi Prime Minister Al-Faedra. She was vaguely surprised not to see a picture of Boo in the mix. After all, they'd spent so much time together. *What was the last movie you went to?* Jessica reached out her hand to touch a blank space on the wall.

"Jessica. Thank you. I will get you and friend something to drink?"

Jessica jumped, startled at Mabel's sudden intrusion. "Yes, Mabel. Clear water. Thank you."

"Clear water. Yes."

Jessica watched Mabel's smooth movements as she pulled open the cabinets to retrieve two glasses. She remembered one time sitting on a plane next to a man whose job it was to sketch the neural pathway templates for the Janitor Scrubbies at the Cifex Building. Even single-purpose machines like that were so complex, that a PhD and a two-year internship were the only ways to break into the field. She vaguely understood that the technology was based on a combination between traditional computers and the plasticity of rat stem cells, but that was about where it ended. Mabel collected two ice cubes and filled Jessica's glass with water from the filter. *You know, I think I kind of like the purple after all.*

Mabel cut into Jessica's thoughts as she passed into the living room. "And Friend? To drink?"

Boo replied. "Name. Friend. Boo. Diet soda."

"Diet soda. Yes. Boo. Yes."

The Scrubbie glided toward the kitchen to finish pouring the drinks. Her pacing seemed different tonight. Jessica listened to Mabel bustling about the kitchen. Clearly, she was preparing a lot more than simple Clear Water and Diet Soda. Why?

As promised, it seemed Mabel was moving beyond her original programming, learning the likes and dislikes of her owner and accommodating them. Responding to the…*oh*… Jessica remembered a night she came home cranky as a hornet. It was only a few days before she was hospitalized. She'd been working for eighteen hours straight on…*what?* She didn't remember.

Jessica spun around and ran her fingers through her hair. *I was working on*…something. Anyway. Mabel asked if Jessica wanted a drink. Jessica ordered a clear water and, when Mabel brought it, flew off the handle because she hadn't brought a scone too and didn't she think that 'after a long day I might be hungry.' It only happened once, but Mabel adapted quickly.

Jessica focused her mind by squinting at her reflection in the glass covering the picture of her and Tripp. She pursed her lips over it, checking to make sure no lipstick had smeared outside of the lines. She arranged a few limp tendrils of hair and headed into the living room.

When Jessica arrived, Boo was watching a Spanish soap opera while searching the local nucleus for a place to go out. Jessica stifled a yawn.

"Boo, I'm not sure I'm up to..."

"Oh, hush. You are just in serious need of some lushin' and lovin'."

Jessica chuckled lightly and sighed.

Mabel entered carrying, as predicted, a tall glass of clear water and a diet soda along with a light dinner of finger sandwiches and green salad—well almost green. Jessica thought the lettuce had retained a bluish tinge ever since the Iowa flood of '25.

"Thank you," Mabel blurted. "Will you have a snack as well?"

Did Jessica note a slight tone of fear in Mabel's voice? *Do Scrubbies feel fear? Do Scrubbies feel?*

"I'll have some of these. Thanks, Mabel."

"Yes. Jessica. Boo. I will be at my station." Mabel bent stiffly at what resembled a waist and retreated to the back of the condominium.

"Okay." Boo started. "There's this place. It's in the Old East Village. Oldies. Professional crowd. Low key. Come on. Let's go."

"Boo..."

"Come on..." She smiled her most winning toothy smile for emphasis.

"At least let me shower."

"Yes!" Boo stuffed half of one sandwich in her mouth.

Jessica picked one up and tasted it. It was good. Impressive. She looked up at the console "Enjoying your show?"

"Riveting."

"You don't speak Spanish."

"Ah, but we all speak the language of love." Boo said, in a mock fluid French accent.

Jessica looked at her sideways with a half smile. "Tell me what happens." She turned and headed back down the hallway to the master bedroom suite. *Shower,* she thought. *And you'll be a whole new person.*

Iris, St. Mark's Place: Old East Village New York, New York

The shower did the trick. Well, that and the Pollie-laced raspberry double espresso—times two. Jessica and Boo sat in a corner booth at Iris with Jim and Steven, two guys Boo met at a cousin's wedding a few weekends before. It was quite convenient, really. Not two minutes after Boo and Jessica had bleeped themselves into the club's Cash and Security system, Steve and Jim were on the opposite side of the violet-lit bar, waving and hollering. It didn't take Jessica long to figure out that Boo had arranged the whole thing. It was a nice gesture and Jessica tried to relax into the atmosphere. The four of them ate, drank and flirted for hours.

The music was Low Rhythm Pulse, Trance Jessica thought they used to call it. There were lots of low frequencies floating on a rhythm the speed of your heartbeat. The DJ, tucked away behind a double pane of bulletproof glass, mixed in ambient sounds, high, tense strings and voice samples. The overall effect was to provide just the right balance of hot and cold to let the Pollie-drunk wallflowers nod and to egg on the pairing of strangers on the dance floor, enticing them into the forty credit per hour love suites sprinkled discretely around the room. The DJ was good.

Steve led Jessica to the dance floor. The suspended floor vibrated with the pulsing bass. There was a subtle crack as strategically placed containers of dry ice opened around the club. The edges of every surface blurred and faded. Steve pulled Jessica against him, moving lithely with the music.

At some point between the fog rolling in and a quick huff of XRG, Boo and Jim melted into the shadows. Jessica made some smart remark about Boo always getting her man.

"And you?" Steve asked, drawing one finger along her jaw line.

Jessica didn't look away, sizing him up. His onyx eyes revealed brooding intensity. He was the kind of man who cared about how he looked. The waistline of his pressed trousers lay smoothly across the crests of his hips, revealing a triangle of smooth skin where his silk shirt parted at the bottom button. It was the color of caramel and just as enticing.

"Taught her everything she knows." She met his eyes.

Steve smiled. He ran his hand up her leg to where her thigh-highs ended in a delicate lace band. He tucked his finger beneath and ran it in a circle around her leg. This was a man who wasted no time. *Seize the day.* Jessica cupped his face in her hands and covered his lips with hers. His lips parted and began kneading hers. Jessica let out a low sigh. She hadn't realized how tense she was. *Thank you, Boo!* Steve escorted Jessica to the farthest room to the back, near the DJ's booth—it was always the cleanest.

An Undisclosed Location: Harlem New York, New York

Delph was blindfolded and being escorted down the street by a large muscled man who smelled like sweat and dirt. His right hand firmly gripped Delph's bicep and his left cupped Delph's left elbow. His guidance was firm but cordial as Delph was maneuvered up a small flight of stairs and into a cool interior. Delph wiggled his eyes against the blindfold, but it shifted only slightly. He could see nothing.

A door shut behind them and a hardwood floor groaned petulantly under Delph's sneakers as he and the stranger passed deeper into the building. Somewhere someone was cooking. Chicken and cilantro mixed with basil and perhaps mint, he couldn't quite tell.

Delph's guide stopped abruptly. A door squeaked open and Delph felt a distinct temperature drop as he was led forward, down a flight of stairs. The smell of the chicken cross-faded with must and dampness. His guide seated him in what felt like a folding chair. Across the room, someone cleared their throat. Muscle man removed the blindfold.

They were in a basement, which was dimly lit by two compact fluorescent bulbs on each end of the long space. His chair had been placed in the middle, between two metal support poles. Across from him, looking cocky with his arms crossed and his legs splayed open, was the man he had come to see—Evan Marcelo.

"You look good for a dead man."

Muscle man got stirred up by the comment. "Watch it Homer, or I'll…"

"Ace! Cut it." Marcelo interrupted. Ace and his biceps withdrew to their previous position behind Delph. "My unfortunate demise was necessary to avoid capture by your office." Marcelo stressed *your* as if Delph had any input into its activities. "Now, I have an associate who tells me you have information about certain OCD projects that you're suddenly willing to share. Why?"

Why now is more like it, Delph ruminated. His understanding of the depth of power the Office was seeking had come into sharp focus for him six months ago when he reviewed the specs for the insurgent neutralization program they dubbed T-Col. That's when he began to harbor doubts. With T-Col, the Office had moved beyond simple intelligence-gathering and spy operations into a realm of moveable ethical boundaries. It was a place he wasn't sure he wanted to go. That's when he was first contacted by the Integrationists.

At the time, he hadn't been ready to commit to flipping on the Office. Besides, he understood the basic need for the program when Tripp explained the urgent security dangers it addressed. He naively thought he could maintain the integrity of the Office through his efforts on the inside of the organization. So, he declined the Integrationists' offer of partnership.

The turning point had been his experience reconstructing himself after having been filtered. Subsequent efforts to establish Jessica's whereabouts, even to the extent of not knowing whether she was even alive further alerted him to his precarious position in the Office. He finally internalized the fact that no one was ever so integral to the Office's operations that they weren't dispensable, not Jessica and not even Delph Crane. The terrible unwanted images from the top secret file he accidentally received haunted him. Now T-Col was imminent and he had to stop it.

Marcelo shifted, awaiting Delph's reply.

Delph remained casual on the outside. "I decided it's time for some new blood in the White House and this is as good a place as any to start."

"Three weeks ago you were setting me up to be killed. Now you expect me to trust that you and I have common interests?"

Trust. Delph didn't think he could trust anyone now. He remained vague. "It's not safe for me any more at the Office. I'm seeking new shelter."

Marcelo popped his lips. "So, if you were cozy and safe under OCD protection, you'd support their operations, but given the uncertainty of your future you're trying to team with me."

"I've learned some things." Delph stated honestly. "Things I'm not sure I can live with."

Marcelo sauntered over to Delph's chair and hovered over him. "What do you know about a certain project that aims to replace dissidents with facsimiles of themselves?"

Delph paused for a moment, locking onto Marcelo's eyes. *Is this it? Is this when I turn traitor? Is this the right man to follow?* Marcelo bent down and faced Delph nose-to-nose. His hand reached out and grabbed Delph firmly by the throat. Ace stirred in his position, ready to be called to action. Delph swallowed hard. In truth, he knew his decision was made before he'd turned himself over to thugs to be blindfolded and taken to wherever this god-forsaken place was. All that was left was to speak.

"The project is called the Transformation Protocol. T-Col for short. Their goal is to perfect the art of neural pattern transfer through combination electronic interface and clone technologies. The Primary is dumped. The Dupe picks up where they left off, perhaps with a slightly different agenda though."

"And you feel they are close to being able to achieve this."

"I used to think not, but now I'm not so sure. I don't think they would have showed me the protocols if they didn't expect the next trials to succeed."

"And when will these next trials be, Mr. Crane?"

"Don't know. I'm sure they'll keep me in the loop though. I am after all their top programmer. Reliable. Trustworthy." Delph grinned with a confidence he no longer felt.

Marcelo laughed short and stood. "And you're willing to provide us with information."

"Hot off the press."

Marcelo stepped back slowly and crossed his arms over his chest. "I sense you're still not really sure who the good guys are, are you Mr. Crane?"

Delph regarded Marcelo suspiciously.

"Allow us to provide you with a little intelligence of our own. Then you decide." Marcelo slipped a small cello tab into Delph's shirt pocked and patted it. The paper thin storage device crinkled softly under the pressure. Delph felt a sudden stinging in his arm. "Call me." Marcelo whispered as Delph lost consciousness.

Jessica Butler's Condominium – Amsterdam and 61st Street: New York, New York

In the morning, the first thing Jessica was aware of was blinding pain. That and the need to vomit. And what was that noise?

"Jessica. Yes? You are oversleeping? Yes?"

"Yes." She mumbled into her pillow.

"Yes?" repeated the Scrubbie.

"Yes." Jessica said more emphatically, but still muffled.

"Yes?"

"Yes!" Jessica shouted and sat up. She held her shattered head in her hands and wondered where was the last place she left her Accelliprofin.

Mabel stood quietly. Stunned, you might say, if you were referring to a human. "Breakfast is ready. Yes?"

"Yes." Jessica said quietly.

Mabel turned to leave.

"Mabel," The Scrubbie turned toward her. "I'm sorry."

Mabel stared at Jessica enigmatically and exited more quickly than usual. *What the hell?*

Jessica paced a few steps and ran her hand through her hair. She stumbled into the bathroom where she found the bottle of pain killers. *The elixir of the gods.* She thought as she swallowed down three. She looked at herself in the mirror. *Damn, girlfriend, didn't you get beaten with the ugly stick.*

The previous night's make up—having never been removed—had tried to make a run for the border but instead bivouacked in a glorious blotchy lavender and blue theme in the hollows beneath her eyes. Her short hair, usually cooperatively smooth, had gone solo and danced toward the ceiling in spiraling exuberance. The one testimony to her little one-on-one with the advertising executive who had a penchant for folk singing was a large red bite mark at the right hand corner of her neck where it met her shoulder. She briefly considered which scarf to wear, but decided that brushing her teeth was of greater urgency at the moment.

A few minutes later, Jessica wandered into the kitchen. Mabel had set up a pretty display of light fare. A small dish of plain yogurt with a scattering of granola sprinkled on top. A peach, scrubbed and sliced in sixths. Two slices of plain toast. Off to the upper left was a large mug of strong coffee. To the right hand side was a bud vase with a silk daffodil in it. The stem end was partially obscured by tiny clear beads, playing the role of water, that sparkled in the morning sun like ice crystals. Jessica had to admit Mabel had style.

"Thank you. May I get you something else? Yes?"

"No. Thank you, Mabel."

"Thank you. I will get your clothing." She said and slipped quietly away.

Jessica tapped into her Mate, which was next to her plate and swiped through a few of the morning's news stories. Uninterested, she decided on the newswire instead.

"Command. Projector. On."

Across from the breakfast bar, the receiver pad blinked on and small figures appeared in the standard anchor/story array. The images resolved just in time for Jessica to see rescuers in hazmat suits carrying stretchers of injured landfill mining employees away from the site of the latest industrial calamity. The Service Workers Union had long criticized the mining companies for denying the clone workers access to the personal protective equipment that is required under the SWU contract for non-clone employees. Today another company executive was defending their policies by promoting their proprietary genetic pre-programming technology, which allows the company to "naturally inoculate our workforce against the parasites and pathogens that took such a heavy toll on non-clone workers in the early days of the industry." He hailed the technology as both safe and cost-effective. *Liar.*

Jessica scraped the last of the yogurt from the dish and started in on the toast. Bored with the newswire, she turned her eyes toward her folio again. The screen had refreshed with a picture of British Prime Minister, Tyler Grey, looking worked up about something. *What did we do now?* The corners of his mouth were turned down in a hideous caricature of self-righteousness, his left index finger jousted the air in silent accusation. The headline read: *Grey Flouts Re-Alliance with US.* The story beneath the headline rehashed the British Prime Minister's accusations of human rights violations in the United States and the breakdown of talks between the United States and the FIO to end the embargo. *Nothing new there.* The article went on to imply that the British Prime Minister was said to be secretly funding the activities of the Integrationists, who were planning on mounting a counter-coup and that he was under suspicion of funding terrorist attacks to bolster his case for opening the United States up to investigation by the international community. *Hmm. Now that's interesting.*

Jessica quietly sipped her coffee and considered the meeting she had scheduled with Tripp at ten thirty. Instinctively she knew she would be assigned to this story. After all, Tripp assured her she was the only reporter in the bureau who was also an OCD agent. In fact, she was the only one who even knew about Tripp's connection to the Office. Jessica liked a challenge. She drained the rest of her coffee in one gulp.

Total Wire News Service – Manhattan Bureau: New York, New York

Jessica's first trip back to the Bureau was somewhat overwhelming. For some unexplainable reason, she decided to walk and take the subway. Her time in the hospital had deprived her of fresh air and she thought the summer sun would help clear her head. Instead, the jostling and grinding with her fellow passengers had violated her personal space and reactivated her hangover. Alone in the elevator, she managed to compose herself for her reunion with her colleagues.

"Jessica!" Carrie Ann squealed as Jessica stepped off of the elevator and into the cube farm. In an instant, Carrie had wrapped herself around Jessica's shoulders, plastering her arms to the sides of her body. Jessica struggled to free herself.

"Hey, Carrie. Down, girl. Wow. I didn't expect this kind of reception."

Carrie reluctantly withdrew.

Bill Snow sauntered over from the other side of the reporters' Corral. "Man Jessica, we thought you were dead. I was vying for your wire station, but Tripp wouldn't have it."

"Some other time, Bill. You never know, some truck could come along tomorrow and finish me off. Keep hoping."

Bill smiled mischievously, "I'll keep my eyes open."

Jessica laughed.

"Good to have you back." Bill stuck out his hand; Jessica shook it.

"It's good to be here."

"But that's what brings us all to reporting, isn't it?" Bill said.

"What?"

"The adventure."

Carrie Ann giggled.

"We all have our reasons, Bill." Jessica turned and headed for Tripp's office.

"He's on a conference call." Carrie called after her. Jessica waved the air dismissively. She knocked as she opened the door.

Tripp's office was a study in minimalism. The centerpiece was a large mahogany desk he claimed was once owned by Ted Turner. Matching large mahogany shelves with elaborately trimmed paneling spanned the walls. His predecessor had covered the shelves with piles of half-finished research and published biographies on every imaginable public figure. Tripp had only a few sparse objects d'art casually arranged around the room. His in-box contained two neat sheaves of paper wrapped snuggly in elastic bands. Jessica didn't understand how he could command a newsroom of seventy-five with so little external chaos.

Tripp was angled on one elbow staring vacantly at his console. He was wearing his privacy earpiece. "I understand your concern, but I assure you we will provide you with all of our questions ahead of time." He paused. "Ah-huh. Yup."

Jessica flopped herself unselfconsciously into one of the springy leather chairs opposite Tripp, tapped her watch and shrugged expectantly.

Tripp shrugged back and repositioned his sheet of nanopaper. As he reached for his stylus, the edge of the paper pulled his shirt cuff back, exposing the thin white scar encircling his wrist. Jessica noted it was almost invisible now. She'd never thought to ask about it before. Tripp wrote, *Can't break free. Lunch?* Jessica nodded, stood up and stretched, exposing her gold navel ring at Tripp's eye-level. He shook his head, smiling and brought his hand to his forehead to shield his view. Jessica blew him a kiss and left, closing the office door quietly behind her.

Half a dozen pointless conversations about her speedy recovery stood between Jessica and the solace of her wire station. The passageways between cubes were so narrow there was no escaping the sequential looks of surprise and jubilation. *Yeah, yeah. Hugs and kisses. Gotta go.* Jessica smiled and bantered repeatedly about doctors and needles as she wormed her way toward the smoked glass at the far wall.

Finally, Jessica settled gratefully into her cradle and felt it subtly readjust to her form, filling the curves of her spine and lengthening to fit her limbs with ergonomic precision. She slipped into her dedos and floaters and dropped in to the TWNS nucleus, first for the Public Newswire—

Noc Owt, NYC has released its fall line of active wear for women, featuring form-fitting synthetics and stretch-leather. Essential to the lineless look is the implementation of zipperless closures created by the ability of the fabric to adhere to itself and separate again. Actress Linette Baldwin was recently seen wearing Noc Owt fashions at M-Zone in Los Angeles.

Streaming pop ups of Ms. Baldwin sipping a martini at the Medieval-themed Hollywood hot spot spiraled into Jessica's central vision while links to M-Zone's menu and reservation service and the Noc Owt fall catalog materialized on the periphery. Jessica used a flat hand command to wipe these away.

Drilling down through the list of developing stories, she found a nugget referring to the controversy with the British Prime Minister where he accused the US government of "the biggest abuse of humanity since the signing of the International Accord on Human Cloning." Jessica thought it was suspicious that Grey would not reveal evidence as to these abuses until some unspecified time in the "near future." A complete biography of Tyler Grey appeared collated and tabbed down the right side of her view. She saved this for future reference and wiped the rest back into the wirestream.

An interesting detail caught her eye; she tapped it. Underground polls distributed by leftist blogs asserted that President Fein's approval ratings had plummeted since rumors began circulating that the President had knowledge about the disappearances of several high-profile Integrationist leaders. Jessica couldn't remember the last time she had seen a Presidential rating poll. She tried drilling down into the source files, but there were no active links. *Someone's protecting their informants well,* she thought. She tried picturing Carrie Ann surreptitiously burning the backtracks to the source files without leaving a residue for her to follow. *Nah! Had to be Bill.*

Jessica wiped her space clean again and sighed. She needed something light and fun for her first day back. Things would get hectic again soon enough, she was sure. She lay into the scroll down control until a little summary blurb caught her attention:

"Two Philadelphia women were arrested yesterday for breaking the Standardized Safety in Foods Act. Over two dozen unstandardized plants were confiscated including tomatoes, peas, and green beans. Protesters marched outside the doors of the Philadelphia District Court this morning where Amelia Wynter and Susan Felt were being arraigned."

Hmm. Sounds easy.

A green light flashed in the lower right-hand corner of the screen indicating that the story was still available for Expansion and Elucidation prior to the Wide Band Channel Wirecast at noon. Jessica checked the time. It was 11:45 am. *No problem.* She lifted one dedoed finger and tapped in her Reporter Code.

The screen froze and the active story elements segmented themselves to the four corners of Jessica's field of vision: video clips upper left, photographs lower left, current text upper right, links to the public domain lower right. In the center, a message blinked awaiting confirmation. *Reporter Jessica Butler, E&E?* Jessica swept her fingertips across the confirm button.

Confirmed. Downloading sources. Assign persona?

While the computer accessed and downloaded all of the information currently available about the story she had selected, Jessica entered the Persona Salon. Arranged somewhat like a boutique displaying a selection of mannequins, Jessica scanned the images available to find the right persona for this story.

Her eyes gazed past a cheery red-headed twenty-something with pouting red lips and multiple decorative facial piercings. She remembered creating that persona when she covered *Revelations,* the hard core Christian rock band whose songs promoted capital punishment. Next in line was her political commentary persona: anorexic thin, with long painted nails, one pair of classic pearl earrings and matching single string necklace; conservative lavender and cream skirted suit. A blonde bouffant framed her face like the perfect Stepford Wife. Jessica laughed out loud.

The right look was essential to the success of a story in news. As Tripp always said, "Content without concept is content without comment." She learned that lesson the hard way her first year in the field. She worked for over a month on a hard-hitting investigative piece about price fixing between certain New York coffee-shop owners and the largest Pollie Manufacturer, Blue Sabre Technologies. She was particularly proud of the way in which she had been able to organize the quotes to make it sound like the two sides agreed with each other in the end. She uploaded the story to the Wire using a persona that looked like herself. At the time, young as she was, she still felt the need to put a personalized stamp on everything she did. So, she spouted garbage about not wanting to deceive Wire users by presenting the façade of a persona who didn't exist.

The story fizzled quickly with hardly a note that it ever existed. Tripp told her she could have had a Pulitzer for the content, if the execution hadn't been lacking. Now she was very careful—even for a story as banal as this one. Her reputation was at stake, even if her fans didn't have the slightest idea who she was.

Jessica settled on a middle of the road brunette standard "Anchor" persona—mid 30's—with sincere eyes. Sincerity was a must for emphasizing the potential public danger that these women posed to the community at large. This persona had to be a mother, someone she could use to swizzle viewer-moms into a whirlpool of concern for their little chickadees. She selected a casual silk suit in off-white and a pair of summer-friendly strappy sandals with two-inch heels for accent.

The system informed Jessica that all files were ready for access and editing. Jessica checked in on the time. Eleven-fifty. *Plenty of time.* If she hurried. She kicked back in her cradle and dug in, video clips first.

There were two-dozen clips to choose from. Jessica's Anchor persona sized and composited into view. She grabbed the arrest footage and forwarded to the money shots of Wynter and Felt taking the long walk from their front door to the waiting squad car. Then she dragged in the view of the basement — full spectrum lights, rows of bootleg vegetables. She tapped a dedo to the Command Frame and instructed the view to zoom in slowly, while panning across the rows. Green leaves and stems resolved into the frame and blurred again as they passed the field of vision. *Nice touch,* she thought.

Cut to: protesters outside of the District Court Building.

Close up: Signs – *Real food, no real danger; GMOs have got to go.*

Clip twelve was a historical montage depicting the history of the Standardized Safety in Foods Act. *Boring.* She sent the footage to the archive and moved on.

Security camera shot, a dark street in the Centertown. Wynter and Felt appear to be purchasing their seeds from a man in a long navy trench coat. Command frame – zoom in. It looked like there was something hidden in Wynter's palm during the transfer. *Enhance.* Not quite visible. Can't tell what it is. *Damn! Unusable.* Jessica poked the command frame. *Clip five archive.*

Clip six showed a fifteen-year old Felt in the middle of a field of corn on what looked like a rather good-sized farm. A thresher rolled by in the background.

"ID clip—time, place, relationship."

A status bar scrolled quickly across Jessica's vision. A gray square appeared, covered with text. *Susan Felt 2048. At home on her parents' farm near Tulsa.*

So, Ms. Felt was a farm girl. Interesting. "Insert Clip. Front end. Nine seconds. Play" The video sequence she created flashed to life around her. Halfway through, Jessica paused. "Revise. Clip Six. Duration eight seconds and twelve frames. Play." Once again, Jessica was surrounded by the life and times of Wynter and Felt. "Lock video." She commanded.

Jessica tapped the Sensory command. She scanned the list of available sense memories for farms. "Insert aroma. Clip Six. Freshly Cut Hay Four." Jessica's nose was filled with the scent of the farm on a rainy day. "Replace aroma. Clip Six. Freshly Cut Hay Three." The farm. Summer Day. Cut grass and hay. *Good, but it's missing something.* "Add accent aroma. Clip six. Honeysuckle." *To match my suit,* she thought. A strong scent of flowers mixed with the hay and grass. *Whew!* "Honeysuckle aroma. Fifty percent." *Better.*

Jessica selected appropriate scents and environmental sounds for each video segment she sequenced. She went to the still file and grabbed photos of each woman and intercut them with the footage of them being led to the squad car, adding slow zoom ins for effect.

A yellow light began blinking in Jessica's field of vision to the lower left. Three minutes to Wire Upload. Jessica felt the pace of her breathing increase. Her heart rate picked up a beat. *Plenty of time.*

"Dialog editor." A keyboard construct appeared in front of her. A selection of previously generated text items floated in space around a gray field. Jessica grabbed pieces of the text, arranging and re-arranging them. She typed in new dialog to inspire viewers into righteous indignation.

The yellow light turned red.

Jessica swapped one line for another in the opening. She pushed the text further back into Clip Six. *Let's keep it a quiet establishing shot. How about some quiet guitar music in the distance.* Jessica accessed the audio files.

A message appeared in the top center of her field of vision, in capital letters: *AUTOMATIC UPLOAD TO BEGIN IN THIRTY SECONDS.* Jessica smirked beneath her floaters.

She grabbed the audio file she wanted and placed it. She waved her dedo across the audio mixer to set the levels. She pulled up the persona she had selected and assigned cut to points throughout the piece. Her fingers worked frantically over the holographic controls. Finally she was satisfied. "Apply." Jessica commanded. The status bar rolled quickly across her field of vision.

AUTOMATIC UPLOAD BEGINNING. NO FURTHER ALTERATIONS WILL BE ACCEPTED.

"Oh. Yeah." Jessica said to herself and smiled. She pulled off her dedos and tossed them on the table in front of her. Then she flipped open the visor on her floaters and watched the feed go live on the Newswire nexus. *I still got it. Damn, I'm hungry!*

TWNS Newswire: 06 | 06 | 2062 | 12:00:00

CUT TO: Attractive woman with brunette hair in a fashionable off-white suit. Slight honeysuckle scent emerges subtly in the background.

"Two Philadelphia women were arrested yesterday for jeopardizing the safety of the food supply along the East Coast."

CUT TO: Farm scene. The scent of freshly cut hay blends with the honeysuckle.

"Amelia Wynter and Susan Felt, childhood friends from their days growing up together on Felt's family farm just south of Tulsa, Oklahoma were taken to Philadelphia City Jail for breaking the Standardized Safety in Foods Act by growing bootleg vegetables in their Center City basement."

CUT TO: Scene of Felt and Wynter being led to squad car in handcuffs. Quiet sound of city traffic.

"It is unknown for how long the two women have been harboring the potentially disease-ridden plants or how many have been distributed on the black market."

CUT TO: Plants in basement. Zoom in and pan across the rows of plants. A barely perceptible scent of garbage and urine lurks in the background.

"Over six dozen plants, primarily peas, tomatoes and green beans were confiscated in the afternoon raid."

CUT TO: Protesters outside of Philadelphia District Courthouse.

"Protesters gathered outside of the Philadelphia District Court this morning where Wynter and Felt are being arraigned on charges of endangering the public food supply and attempted assault at-large."

CUT TO: Close up of protester yelling uncontrollably into a microphone.

"The SSFA is an abject attempt by corporate farms to maintain sole control over the food supply in the United States. To push their agenda of selling exclusively GMO food products and producing a monopoly in the food we consume. The SSFA has got to go!"

AUDIO FADE IN: Subliminal "booing" mixed with traffic noise.

CUT TO: Anchor. Honeysuckle scent re-emerges.

"The US Department of Agriculture recommends that anyone who has bought vegetables that do not contain the seal of compliance with the SSFA discard them, in light of the potential danger of eating the black market vegetables. This is Jessica Butler for Total Wire News Service."

Generous Café – West 27th Street overlooking Chelsea Park: New York, New York

Jessica donned her sunglasses, even though she had settled underneath one of the comfortably umbrella-shaded tables in the courtyard of the Generous Café for lunch. She'd heard stories of a time when renowned reporters had to shade their eyes to keep from being recognized by their fans as they went about their daily lives, rather than to save their eyes from floater-induced light sensitivity. For her, the discomfort lasted no more than a couple of hours after she finished each report. There were some, however, who never made it out of journalism school because their eyes became so sensitive they couldn't look at their dinner in candlelight. She guessed she was blessed with a hearty biology—"sexy genes" as Boo would put it and that was just fine with her. Somehow, it was a little worse today. She guessed that a month away from the cradle would do that to a person.

The food service ARIel had just presented Jessica with her double Pollie-caramel cappuccino with cinnamon when Tripp arrived. "Sorry I'm late."

"It's fine." Jessica unwrapped a sweet stick and stirred it through the foam on her drink.

"I am Brian. Would you like something to drink?" asked the ARIel.

"Scotch on the rocks, please," Tripp responded.

"State law obligates me to tell you, sir, that it is twenty past noon. Should you feel the need to drink frequently at this time of day, you can call..."

"Interrupt script. Acknowledge."

"Thank you, sir. I will return in a moment." Brian rolled away with a quiet electric whirr.

"So, how are things going your first day back? Don't push yourself too hard."

"You know me, Tripp."

"Exactly. That's why I'm saying, don't overstretch yourself."

"Thanks, Mom." Jessica took a noisy slurp from her cappuccino. "Ah, now that's what I really needed." She took another sip, put her cup down and stirred it quietly as she felt the endorphins flutter through her bloodstream. *No worries.* She closed her eyes as she leaned her head back and breathed in deeply.

Brian returned with Tripp's scotch and Tripp awarded him four Service Points for speed and courtesy of programming. Jessica listened to Brian glide away. With her eyes still closed, she focused her attention on Tripp. "So, what's the scoop, Boss? Does this have to do with the British Prime Minister?"

Tripp shifted in his seat uncomfortably. She registered the sound, but chose not to comment. Tripp cleared his throat. He leaned in toward her and whispered, "What do you know about Grey?"

Jessica opened her eyes and drilled them into Tripp. "Only that he's making some pretty heavy accusations against the administration and I figured the OCD was going to want to keep an eye on him. That is why we're here, I presume."

"Can't get anything by you." Tripp sipped his drink stiffly.

Jessica took another sip of her cappuccino. Something was still bothering her about this conversation. Tripp was on tenterhooks. She wanted to know why.

"I need you to interview him. Tell him it's an in-depth feature. Get into his life. Find out...what kind of toothpaste he likes."

"And?"

"Find out who his connections are in the Integrationist hierarchy."

"I just don't get it," Jessica interrupted. "How do they benefit if the embargo stays? It's only going to hurt them too."

"They think the ongoing talks and the economic imperative focuses international attention on their issues."

"Are they right?"

Tripp swirled the liquor in his rocks glass and watched the glistening coating run down the side in amorphic patterns. He looked up at Jessica. "History tells us people get all foamed up about so-called government abuses with little evidence or provocation. It doesn't matter if their accusations are true. Only that they are well publicized. In the meantime, the stability of our entire government sits in the balance." Tripp swirled his glass again and took a sip of the spinning liquid. Jessica watched his neck move as he swallowed it down. A drop of scotch clung to the left corner of his lip for a moment, until he unconsciously licked it away and swallowed again.

To Jessica, it looked like he was trying to decide something. She was just about to ask him, when he continued. "There's something else." Jessica waited. "Grey has been implicated in a terrorist attack in Florida last year. Remember the truck bomb that exploded outside of the Miami Hyatt?"

"Of course."

"We have reason to believe that Grey was directly involved in planning that attack. There is...DNA evidence \ we collected from an Integrationist cell raid outside of Jacksonville, but since Grey is a diplomat, we don't have a pattern match template for him." Tripp paused.

"You need a DNA sample."

"Yes."

Well, geez, Tripp. Why didn't you just say so? That's a cinch."

Tripp relaxed a little around the eyes. "I didn't want to make you do too much your first week back. I want to make sure it's not too soon."

"God, Tripp. I've been aching to get going again. I can't tell you. Weeks in the hospital. It's enough to drive you nuts. Don't worry about me. I'll be fine."

"You're sure?"

"Yes."

"You don't have any...reservations?"

Jessica looked at him curiously. *What's up with that?* "Should I?"

"I'm sorry, Jessica. I just want to be careful I don't push you too hard. You're the best I've got."

"And right now, I'm all you've got. I'm fine. Really."

"Okay then." Tripp finished his scotch, put the glass on the table and stood.

Jessica nodded. Tripp left the restaurant.

Wirespace: An Independent Nucleus in the Non-Aligned Territory

David Marks was always amused at Grey's literal interaction with his wirespace Parlor. Today, he fussed with an elaborate tea set that was presented to him by a trim, well-pressed secretary. Marks had to admit the aroma was very inviting, but it was ultimately air and he couldn't get past that.

Grey pointed to an extra cup on his tray. "Are you sure you won't have some."

Marks shook his head. "No. Thank you."

"I mean, just because we've changed our perception of our bodies in space, doesn't mean we have to lose our basic civility." Grey lifted the delicate tea cup to his lips and took a sip.

Civility? He seems to have forgotten what we're here to discuss.

After a moment of tense silence, Grey set his cup down on the intricately engraved tray and sighed. "All right. Down to business."

Marks began. "All of the data from the T-Col procedure is stored in-house in a private nucleus that's not connected to the wirespace. My login is good for all level security clearance, but even I would have to be physically in the building to obtain the files."

"How will you justify accessing that level of documentation, except to claim morbid curiosity? Even then, someone's bound to pin it on you when I take the information to the FIO."

"I know. That's why I'm not going to do it."

Grey cocked his head. "Senator, I have risked everything…"

"I've found someone else. Someone better."

"I see." Grey eyed Marks dubiously.

"A high-level OCD wire monkey has joined the team. He will extract the data and transfer it to you."

"How?"

"It's not my job to know."

"Are you sure we can trust him?" Grey took a sip of his tea.

"He got screwed over by the department in his last mission and now his partner is missing."

"Wait. You're talking about Delph Crane and Liberty Park, aren't you?" Grey put his cup down. "His 'partner' is responsible for the disappearance of three of my staff members."

"You don't know that." Marks argued.

"I know enough. They've been on the same team for years. He's playing you."

"Crane's soft on her. She was gone. He started digging. The truth hits hard once you find it."

Grey opened the porcelain sugar bowl and added three heaping spoonfuls to his cup in progress. "We only have one chance at this."

"I know."

"Do you think the girl is really dead?"

"Not likely." Marks conceded.

"So, they finally succeeded?" Grey shook his head.

"They were very close last time. I invited some of the lower level chemists in the program over to the Capital for lunch and a private tour. None of them even know what they're working on. Not really." Marks smirked sardonically. They believe they're building an artificial intelligence system."

"Will they put her back in the game again?"

"My guess is that they already have."

Grey shook his head. "So, we could end up fighting the clone for access to the primary's records?"

"Pretty much."

"What a world." Grey smiled tensely, lifted his cup and toasted the air.

Total Wire News Service – Tripp Thompson's Office: New York, New York

Tripp Thompson paced his office restlessly listening to what the voice on the other end of the line was telling him. He passed a green glass paperweight back and forth between his hands. A small ring of dust revealed the place on the shelf where it had been sitting. The spot was highlighted by a ray of pink light from the setting sun, as it angled through Tripp's smoked glass window. Tripp was not pleased. "I see. When was this?" He listened intently. "No. Let me call him. He needs to know. Besides, now that the procedure is working, there's no reason not to do a little house cleaning."

There was a brief argument from the other speaker and a few words of warning. Tripp heard without listening and continued. "Just be ready. Your people are gonna start earning back your research funding now. Got it?" He cut the signal without waiting for a reply.

Tripp exuded nervous energy. Things were starting to come together. When Jessica delivered the British Prime Minister's DNA packet, the Office would be able to use the template to ensure his signature was found on every terrorist incident from New York to Juno. And now, if what his wirespace informant was telling him was true, there was a mole in the OCD hierarchy. He would be able to gain significant brownie points by exposing the traitor and bringing him to justice.

Tripp smiled to himself. Never in his childhood had he dreamed that a skinny kid from Bloomington, Indiana could become the leader of one of the most powerful OCD Node in the United States. Outside of the BioMedical Node, the Media Node had the most influence and the largest staff. If he continued playing his cards right, he was a shoe in for Executive Director, when Fein decided it was no long politically feasible to retain the position for himself.

The suite reserved for the Executive Director of the Office of Civilian Defense was at least three times the size of Tripp's Bureau office with twenty times the staff. He discarded the paperweight in a facsimile of its original position and toyed with the silk flower arrangement next to it. He considered who he would take with him when the day finally arrived.

A month ago, he would not have hesitated. Jessica was his workhorse; the one he could always rely on. With Jessica, there were never any excuses and never any uncomfortable questions. She executed her duty with finesse and dedication. Jessica's accident made Tripp nervous though—very nervous. It wasn't like Jessica to blow a rig early. And the order of the explosions had been so haphazard. Jessica was orderly, precise. That was how he knew that the incident at the park was too sloppy to have been her work.

Tripp wondered if Jessica would ever remember the events of that day. He hoped not. The Chilling Zone team had been very careful to only extract and transfer what was necessary for her to have continuity of consciousness and to continue functioning in her role with the Office. Still, with her being the first successful trial, doubts remained. Of course he wouldn't verbalize these doubts to anyone but himself. He simply took precautions. Unfortunately, she was going to have to prove herself before he would be completely convinced he could trust her again. If only he knew how much Jessica had seen before she went unconscious, any dangerous tracers lurking the in the shadows waiting to express themselves.

Tripp locked down his station for the night and tried to excite himself for another evening in front of the projection console with a freezer pack of dehydrated pork loin. His hunger passed away with the thought. He locked the door to his office and headed down the hall. At the end, in the reporters Corral, he could see the pink glow telling him someone was dropped in. Tripp knew who it was before he was halfway down the hall.

"Jessica. What are you doing here?"

Jessica jumped and lifted the visor on her floaters. "Tripp, you scared the shit out of me."

"Don't want to be surprised, shut your door." He patted the sound proofed barrier they'd constructed to keep Jessica's operations strictly confidential. "I thought you were going home early to get some rest."

"I am."

Tripp made a show of checking his watch. "Now."

Jessica parried. "Did you know that Grey was going to major in Criminal Justice, prior to transferring to the Poli-Sci department in his Junior year of college?"

"Yes, now log off."

"Liar." Jessica looked at him out of the corner of her eye and logged off with mock indignity. "There. Happy?"

Tripp smirked. "You know I'm not leaving until I see you outside of the building."

"Right." Jessica powered down and grabbed her bag. "Ready to go."

Tripp motioned Jessica ahead and pulled the door shut behind him. Sensing the lack of warm bodies, the lights turned off as Tripp and Jessica rounded the corner away from the Corral. Tripp watched the sway of Jessica's hips as she sauntered ahead of him into the elevator.

"As long as you're still here. Why don't you join me for dinner?"

"Tripp, we've been there and done that before. I don't think…"

"It's just dinner. Come on. I've been doing nothing but frozen since Cindy left me and there's never anything on the Wirecast."

Jessica kept walking. They reached the garage entrance.

"What do you say?"

"I say, that I am a little tired and I'm going to go home." She bowed slightly and walked off into the dim lanes of cars. Then she stopped briefly and turned. "Thanks anyway, Tripp." Surprisingly, she smiled. "Maybe another time." Then she was gone.

Delph Crane's Condominium – Spire 2 West 75th Street: New York, New York

Delph lifted the lid on his five-quart slow cooker and sniffed the steam that was released. Its scent was robust without being overwhelming. He poked around the stew with a fork. The onions were soft and the lamb had tenderized well.

He tasted a spoonful. *Oh, yes!* The twenty credits he spent on those two stems of bootleg rosemary was definitely worth it.

He closed the lid and crossed the rough-hewn slate floor to the utility cabinet. There was only one bag that was both large and strong enough to hold the weight of the filled cooker. Somehow it had migrated to the farthest reaches of the closet without leaving a forwarding address. Delph found the handle and gave it a yank, swearing once again to get around to putting those shelves up some time this year. The bag sprung free.

A high-pitched beep called to him from his waistline. Delph punched "Answer" on his Belt Mate. "I'm leaving now, I'll be there in five minutes. So stop calling me."

"Mr. Crane?" A smooth female voice oozed into his privacy headset.

Delph punched his forehead with the heel of his hand and began to pace the room. "I'm sorry, I thought you were my mother."

The Governess laughed in a throaty, deep voice. It was spooky. "Congratulations! We have a Convert. You're on."

Delph's heart rate nearly doubled. "So, there's been a successful trial?"

"I'm wiring you the locator data packet as we speak. We need to get the monitoring fishhook up and running."

Delph was charged with energy. Excitement, fear and doubt played ring-around-the-rosey in his intestines. He knew it would come to this eventually. Once he had something solid to report to Marcelo, he could earn some trust. He had to be careful not to give himself away. "Great. Where's the Convert?"

"Close to you, in Manhattan."

"How soon do you need it?"

"Immediately, Mr. Crane."

Shit! Delph thought. He was already an hour and a half late for his mother's little gathering. Not that he was all that excited to go. He knew she was just going to try to fix him up with some little blue-pumps, skirt-to-the-knees prim-rod, anyway.

Still, the lamb stew was a knock out and he never liked to disappoint his mother. "I can get to it tomorrow."

"Tonight, Mr. Crane."

Delph raked his long hair behind his ear and clicked his tongue barbell against his teeth absent-mindedly. *Can I make this quick?* He paced to the stainless steel sink and leaned on the edges with both hands. "Is it a clean link?"

"Clean as it gets."

"So its fresh, then?"

"Generally, speaking."

Delph could tell the Governess was hiding something from him. "We talked about running the fishhooks within thirty-six hours of the procedure, when there wouldn't be any risk of creating suspicious cognitive events."

"We had to be sure before we brought her live," she replied.

Delph sighed. So much for the lamb stew. "I don't know, M'am. It's going to be tricky."

"Mr. Crane, we have complete faith in your abilities. Ping us when you're finished." She terminated the transmission abruptly.

After Delph called his mother with a lame excuse about a burst water pipe, he sat down at the Wolf to start working. He downloaded the Governess' data pack and dropped it into the decryption program while he suited up. He could feel the pulse in his neck as he added himself to the datastream. He dropped into his personal Parlor on the public nucleus and fingered the blinking message icon to remove it from his peripheral vision.

To enter his secure area, Delph locked his sight on the image of Escher's stairways that hung innocently between the access panel to the public domain and a digital recreation of his favorite super hero, Spiderman. He blinked twice, rapidly. The photograph fell away, revealing Delph's private hallway to the OCD nucleus. He entered his forty-two character recognition string three times and saw the public sphere close behind him.

Reaching his arm forward in a shallow arc, Delph linked himself through the main OCD City nucleus, passing through to the Village links of the T-Col project. He was always amused by the anachronistic names developers had used to label the various sizes of and links between nuclei in wirespace. Designations like City and Village seemed to bear little resemblance to the flow of digital information he manipulated. Nonetheless, it did seem to make the less technologically savvy feel more at home in this universe.

Delph tapped the data packet to decompress it and threw the access code into the Troll switch that guarded the new Convert's files. Various data sets arranged themselves into Delph's field of vision and the figure of a woman resolved into focus in front of him, but not completely.

The outline was crisp, but all potentially identifying features had been pixelated so that he couldn't clearly see the target. Delph thought this was suspicious. Yes, he could still plant the fishhook, but the obvious attempt to hide the target's identity nagged at him, particularly since he had the highest security level for this project. Getting around this childish obstacle was not a problem for him. Considering his plans for his future alliances, the Office's obvious lack of trust could be.

The blocky smudge cleared. A body and then a face appeared - Jessica. Delph yelped like a hurt puppy and pulled the floaters off of his head. *This can't be happening.* He stood up and began pacing. He mindlessly bumped into a floor lamp almost toppling it. He grappled it back to place and stabilized himself on the wall. *She was dead. They let me believe she was dead!* Delph slid down the wall and closed his eyes. He searched his retrieved memories of the Freedom Park disaster, but nothing he recalled led him to expect that they would turn her into their first Convert.

Delph shook himself back to the present moment and looked across the room at the floaters that lay on the floor where he had dropped them. They glowed pink from the display that was still activated inside of them. He considered the fact that Tripp let him believe Jessica was dead. Now, the Office asked him to insert the fishhook, casually like it was no big deal. *They knew all along.* Delph felt his body chill in fear. *They've been planning this. They knew I would hack the ID.*

Delph lifted himself from the floor and sat back in his cradle. He placed the floaters back over his eyes. *Yes, it's her.* It was Jessica. *But why?* He thought. *Why make me believe she's dead and then ask me to put in the fishhook? It doesn't make sense. They know we were partners. They know, we...* Suddenly, it made sense to him. *I'm being tested,* he decided. *They're testing my loyalty, and if I don't pass, I'll be the next Convert hooked and reeled in.* Delph pictured his own clone template, which he was sure now existed, life on hold, lying in wait for the time when he became irrelevant to the Office's interests. He dreamed of performing the perfect hack, intercepting his own consciousness as it slipped from his body into the replacement form, saving himself from oblivion.

He looked at the compiled image of Jessica's face. It hurt to seem so close to her, but not be able to touch her, to smell her hair, to run his tongue up the side of her neck. Delph flushed with grief and fear. *Stop that!* He knew whatever feelings he had for Jessica, she didn't share them. Oh, she thought he was a decent partner and she trusted him. That he knew. He knew that he pleased her in bed. Still, when it came right down to it. Jessica didn't love him.

After the first time they had sex, Delph briefly clung to the naive belief that they could have a relationship. He invited her to his condo for dinner. She was suddenly sent on a fact-finding mission in Louisiana and forgot to tell him before she left. The lamb got cold and he'd gone through half a fifth of gin before he realized she wasn't coming. He decided soon after that she wasn't capable of loving. People were useful to her— practical tools. But if one or another person disappeared, Jessica wasn't going to lose any sleep over it. This was the quality that made her such an excellent agent, but it made Delph sad and intensified his longing for her. Looking into her future, he couldn't bear to see her old, broken and alone. Everyone needs someone to love. Why couldn't it be him? It bothered him that he hadn't seen this coming and been better prepared for it.

I need to concentrate. Think. What can I do? Suddenly, it came to him. He smiled. He looked at his clock. *It could be done. But can it be done in time?* In the point-of-view data stream, he walked up to the image of Jessica floating in front of him and air-kissed her on the lips. *Love makes a man do crazy things.*

Office of the British Prime Minister: Downing Street, London, England

Grey had been waiting for over six hours for the data package that included the contact information of the Marks' mole in the Office of Civilian Defense. Even accounting for the decreased speed of the black market hermit lines, the need for non sequential segmenting of the information and re-transmission from his staffer who was dropped into his personal nucleus at an internet café on Baker Street, it still shouldn't have taken this long.

He stared at the brass "OM" symbol inlaid in the handle of his letter opener and thought. He couldn't risk pinging the staffer. Maybe he could come up with some excuse for an official call to the Senator's office. Yes. He could do that.

Grey straightened his tie and ran a comb through his hair. Then he opened an official channel to the US Capitol and greeted the cheery red-headed secretary politely. "Good morning, love. May I speak with Senator David Marks, please?"

"I'm sorry he's not available. May I have him call you back?" Grey relaxed a little bit.

"It is rather urgent. I don't suppose you could have him interrupted?"

"Truth be told, sir, no one's seen him for a couple of days now." The skin on the back of Grey's neck prickled. "Word has it he's been ill. Some are saying they heard it was encephalitis. We don't know when he'll be coming back. Is there someone else who can help you? Senator Wilson will be picking up most of Senator Marks' committee activities."

"No. That's fine. I'll manage. Thank you for your time." After disconnecting the line, Grey put his head in his hands. *God, no!*

Delph Crane's Condominium – Spire 2 West 75th Street: New York, New York

Delph's dedoed hands flew through the air with the precision of a fencer. He checked and rechecked the encryption loops that hid his private array from the main network. He chuckled to himself. *I'm just a little minion, peeking into the party through the servant's entrance. Just a programmer; the ones who think too linearly to make up our minds for ourselves. Well friends, you're in for a surprise.*

Delph saw the Hermit line access on the Wolf blink, indicating that a link had been established from the main OCD nucleus. The fishhook was ready to go live. This would be the delicate part.

The instant the fishhook went live, he tapped a simple switch. Somewhere in Wirespace the hook code was enabled in the OCD nucleus, loading the fishook's corresponding data to a concealed site in the Executive Director's nucleus. Once the Director's nucleus confirmed the link, Delph rerouted the data stream using the Wolf as a conduit, which syphoned off a copy of Jessica's current neural map to his self-contained Hermit network, where it could remain unaltered. Afterward, he deleted the data hallways to his hidden nuclei and reset the passwords. It was the best safe haven he could devise on short notice.

Now that Jessica's consciousness was safe, and he knew where she was, it would be safe to contact her. He wondered what she would say. Had they filtered him out of her memory along with the mission? *Will she remember me?*

Jessica Butler's Condominium – Amsterdam and 61st Street: New York, New York

Jessica bent over the toilet as another wave of nausea enveloped her. Boo knocked on the door softly. "Are you okay? Can I get you anything?"

Jessica vomited forcefully a third time and spit. "Not right now. I just need to wait for it to pass." She was surprised by how swiftly her stomach had turned on her. She was just sitting with Boo in the living room eating popcorn and grousing about the poll results on their favorite reality game show when it hit. Pow! Thankfully, it seemed to be passing as quickly as it started. The ringing was subsiding from her ears and she could move her head without the room spinning.

"I'll just go back to the living room. Holler if you need anything." Boo padded softly away as Jessica reached for a towel. She dragged herself up from the floor, wiping the sweat off her face and rinsed out her mouth with water. *Must've had some bad clams,* she thought.

Delph Crane's Condominium – Spire 2 West 75th Street: New York, New York

Later that night, Delph sat on his deck nursing a tall glass of lemonade and a bag of Crunchips. One benefit of living on the twenty-second floor was the serenity. He was far enough above the street that the sound of the cars was drowned out by the wind as it wound furiously around the corner of the building into the side of his face. The feeling reminded him of a trip he took once to first deck of the Eifel Tower. It was like standing in front of an industrial-sized vent fan, but in his current state he found the feel of the air sliding across his skin soothing.

In over three hours of consideration and four vodkas on the rocks, Delph still couldn't conceive of how events at Freedom Park could have gone so wrong. It was a simple mission in the scheme of things. Make a distraction, tag Marcelo and follow him back to his headquarters. Jessica was never careless. He realized that small, but disturbing holes remained scattered through the sequence. Even after all of his effort, the neural repotentiation was flawed. Delph closed his eyes and inhaled deeply.

Take stock. He remembered seeing the explosions and thinking to himself it was odd she had let them go early. He remembered boulder charges, but he didn't remember packing them. After her call, he'd packed up the monitoring equipment more quickly than he had ever done. She looked like she'd been through a maelstrom when she ran into the room. Her hair was sticking out at odd angles and she wore an expression he'd never seen before on Jessica's face—terror.

Delph remembered seeing the man in the sunglasses before Jessica did, but he was unable to speak until it was too late and she was unconscious on the floor in front of him. The man in the sunglasses looked at him. Delph had a fraction of a second to decide what to do. *What would Jessica do if she were me?*

His mind turned to the data on his system. He didn't know who the man in the sunglasses worked for. If his system were dissected by the wrong people, it could be—misunderstood. Delph grabbed the Wolf. Instead of resisting Delph's escape, however, the man leaned over Jessica and injected her in the arm with something pink. Delph dropped everything but the case carrying the main processor. He reminded himself that Jessica didn't love him, but that he was still an agent. He flung this remaining bag over his shoulder and ran for the fire escape.

The man in the sunglasses looked up at Delph, but Jessica moaned and stirred. As he climbed through the window, Delph could see the man looking between Jessica and himself in a moment of indecision. Jessica moaned again and began to pull herself up. The man turned to face Jessica squarely as Delph mounted the stairs and ducked out of sight. He heard a gunshot when he was halfway to the ground. He never looked up to see if he was being followed. He didn't want to know.

At the bottom of the fire escape, Delph flattened himself against the wall and quickly side-stepped to the front of the building. He could see his van waiting across the street. He could also see two more men in sunglasses hovering around the front of the hotel talking to each other—or so it appeared. As they chattered, they looked around, clearly looking for him. *Mega shit!* Delph thought and tucked his head safely around the corner again. *Dead end!* He looked back the way he came and could see the first man climbing out of the window and onto the fire escape. He was trapped.

Just then, a door in the building on the opposite side of the alley opened up, and someone's sous chef trundled out with a bag of garbage. Delph leaped past the man, who turned in astonishment, and ran into the kitchen. The door shut securely behind him and he heard the muffled ranting of the sous chef on the other side.

He stumbled over a crate of tomatos and caught himself by grabbing the vertical bar of a steel shelving unit. The shelves teetered precariously as Delph pulled himself upright, spilling several clean stew pots on the floor. As one of the kitchen assistants tried to grab Delph, he accidentally kicked one of the stew pots, sending it bouncing off of the nearby wall and back into his own shin. The assistant doubled over, holding his leg. Delph turned to run and slammed into a steel prep table. A large knife spun quickly off of a cutting board, just missing Delph's abdomen. He hopped back and ran to the right toward the front to the restaurant.

Delph's breath was coming hard as he burst through the swinging doors into the dining area. He ducked quickly under a tray being carried by a stoic watier in a tuxedo without breaking his stride. He weaved through the five tables that were celebrating "Jack and Francie Forever" - according to their rainbow bedecked banner - and gave the happy couple a thumbs up as he made a b-line for the entrance connecting this restaurant with the Silver Screen Mall.

As he streaked down the open lane of stores and turned the corner, his ribs gave him a stab of admonition for the lack of warning—or training—for this little jaunt. He doubled over to catch his breath and scanned the mall for a place to hide.

In short order, Delph selected a clothing store. He figured a change of clothing might offer enough protection for him to make it beyond the perimeter of the OCD search. Fifteen minutes later, Delph emerged, a shining bastion of MBA sensibility. He was dressed in an almost perfectly fitting Italian suit with loafers and was carrying a briefcase, into which he had quickly stuffed the processor and storage unit. His hair had been gelled and combed. He slipped into a pair of fashionable mirrored sunglasses on his way out the door, confident that he was now perfectly unrecognizable. He got home safely. Whether or not they found the van, he didn't care.

Delph's eyes snapped open again when a particularly feisty gust of wind whipped the swizzle stick out of his glass and sent it sailing over the rail of the balcony toward the street. Delph watched it float lazily out of his sight. The numbers of the stock ticker across from his balcony marched endlessly along the wide ribbon of LEDs. So many of the numbers were in the negatives.

Delph's experience waking up filtered several days after the Freedom Park incident was his only proof that those who were after Jessica eventually found him. He considered what he knew and what *they* knew that he knew. *Clearly, Jessica had information I didn't know about. Otherwise, why T-Col?* Her conversion in the T-Col process and his close call convinced him that what Marcelo had shown him on his cello tab was probably true. He was going to be doing one hell of a balancing act for a while. One thing was certain. He had to find out what Jessica no longer knew.

"Heads!" he called as he tossed his glass over the edge of the balcony.

TWNS Newswire: 07 | 28 | 2062 | 10:15:03

Local Home Trust Party leaders are hailing the citywide implementation of head counts in public spaces to ensure that the same number of people exit as enter. Proponents of the new system cite the improved security of knowing how many people are gathered in public spaces and whether or not they are all accounted for at the end of the day. For the time being, the head count is being conducted by low-end thermo-graphic scanners designed to calculate the number of entries and exits across multiple access points.

City officials are currently negotiating with service providers of the popular Express Access Subdermal chips—called EASy chips by their users—to hook the people counters into their systems thereby gaining access to important demographic and criminal records information about those who are utilizing public spaces. Mayor Richard Fevor fervently supports the system against its detractors. "This is the most powerful tool to date that will allow us to facilitate the tracking and capture of criminals and terrorists in our city. We welcome the participation of the EASy service providers in law enforcement and look forward forging close ties with them in fighting crime. The new system will even allow us to better allocate our transportation and tourism resources by providing us with information about the direction of travel and destinations of our park users."

Integrationist Candidate for the Central Senate, Mark Brimmer, spoke out against the head counts at a press conference this morning. "There is no excuse for the further erosion of personal privacy in the name of crime control. History has proven time and again that a prosperous society discourages criminal activity. We should be pouring public resources into economic development, not putting government eyes on every street corner."

The debate is likely to intensify as more individuals choose the convenience of EASy chips over carrying wallets and purses.

Freedom Park: Manhattan, New York

The Pedestal was never empty for long. Prominently situated near the 48th street entrance to Freedom Park, it stood as a memorial to free speech and freedom of assembly. It was no more than a foot square, but was open to anyone who had good enough balance and the ability to climb the foot-and-a-half rise. Jessica saw a decent crowd of people had gathered around the Pedestal's current occupant. Many had situated themselves in small clusters with blankets and picnic baskets spread around them. For some, a trip to the Pedestal was a weekly outing for the whole family.

Intermittent herds of Integrationist children chased each other among the narrow isles formed by their parents playing "Protester and Civilian Defense Officer". They were well-dressed in hemp blouses and sweaters with animal-friendly Synthete sneakers. Jessica thought the adults should be watching them more closely. The City is a dangerous place.

The speaker was tall, at least six foot five in Jessica's estimate. He was more attractive than most of the Integrationist kooks she had encountered. He had jet black skin and thick dark dreadlocks highlighted with copper streaks around his face. His long fingers traced images in the air reinforcing his spoken messages. *Yeah, I'd do him.* She thought and chuckled to herself at the thought of having an affair with an insurgent. His words washed over her as she approached the area.

"...the very concept of humanity. It is not our bodies that are being challenged. No. Our government wants you to think that we must defend our physical form, because it distracts us from the real issue. It is not our bodies being challenged, but our souls. The relevance of the human soul is being challenged on every front. To what end is it that we dedicate ourselves to greater investigation of ways to replace our humanity with mechanized impostors of ourselves? To increase efficiency in business? To improve the economy? Not at all, our business leaders have already proven the uselessness of clone and AI technologies to increase the wealth of this nation. All savings that are realized go right back into the pockets of the corporate leaders who implemented these programs. The real reason humanity is being marginalized in favor of cheap imitations of ourselves is control. Humanity is an uncontrolled variable with which business interests have decided they no longer want to deal."

The speaker's words became louder as Jessica wound her way through the enraptured audience and faded away as she continued toward the pond in the center of the park. To her left, a young but tired looking woman adjusted the top of her sleeping toddler's stroller to shade him from the sun. Ahead, an older couple sat facing each other in meditation.

"You may ask yourselves how this is relevant to me? Why should it matter if humanity helps itself evolve into a more placid version of itself? We're already here. We're irreplaceable. Right? Don't be so sure. The tricks and technologies around you are only the ones they want you to see. As we sit here contemplating, there are government laboratories that..."

Jessica usually let the psychobabble flow through her. Today though, it made her agitated. She'd heard it all before. Conspiracy theories about armies of cyber-clones marching in to destroy the last of the human race. *If they only knew the truth.*

Jessica continued down the cement pathway slowly, breathing deeply. She was struck by the aroma of a tall purple flower that lined this portion of the path. She stopped to look at them more closely. She didn't remember ever having seen this flower before. She picked one and carried it to the side of the pond where she sat down in the grass.

Jessica continued smelling the flower, trying to remember if she knew its name. She looked up to the sky and saw a turtle in the clouds. It looked like it was racing a fish to a football goal and it was losing. She shook her head. *What's that? Stupid.*

A couple of boys several yards down the shore on her right were "fishing" in the water. Every few minutes they pulled up another wriggling, blinking fish. They swiped the bar code over the reader on their poles and tossed it back. In between, they splashed in and out of the water flicking drops at each other.

An older couple in their sixties or seventies were walking around the opposite side of the pond. Their quick strides moved in time with each other. It looked as though they had been walking this way for a very long time. Sadness crept up on Jessica as she watched the couple ambulate behind some trees. The feeling was unfamiliar and disturbing. She was lonely—that was it, lonely. She didn't remember ever feeling lonely before, not like this. Not with a knot squeezing tightly in her belly. Her eyes welled up with tears she couldn't explain. The couple laughed at some private joke. Clearly they enjoyed each other's company. She wondered how long they had been together.

Jessica thought about her grandparents. She tried to recall their faces and the things they used to do together, but realized that she couldn't. She narrowed her eyes and thought harder. She remembered a house with a yellow kitchen. The ancient appliances hummed loudly. Jessica used to pretend she was an astronaut. She would sit with her legs up against the chilly metal of the refrigerator and count down. *Three, two, one...blast off!* The refrigerator roared to life, rumbling her body. She pushed buttons on the array of pots and pans she had scattered around herself to be the controls. Her grandmother would come in...laughing? Scolding?

Feet. She remembered feet. Her grandmother, always having a forward fashion sense wore what were then the brand-new Synthete leather sandals. No stockings. Jessica closed her eyes and tried to recall her face. Nothing. Strange since she had spent a great deal of her childhood living with her grandparents. *How many years?* When her parents died...*left?* She and her brother went...*I don't have a brother.*

The piercing alert tone of her Mate startled Jessica. She shook her head rapidly and blinked her eyes open again. Her heartbeat chattered violently inside her chest. *Woh, I must have dozed off.* Second tone. Jessica picked up. "Hello?"

"Hey, Jess, it's Boo. Some people are getting together at The Rack tonight. There's a guy I want you to meet. You coming?"

"No. I've got a new assignment I need to get a jump on. I'll be working late tonight."

"Oh, come on. Play the I'm-still-recovering-give-me-a-break card and get outta there."

"I really can't, Boo." Jessica checked her watch. "Look, I gotta go. I'll call you later."

"Sure you will." Jessica could picture Boo rolling her eyes in that way that she does. "If you change your mind, you know where I am." Boo clicked off.

Jessica stood up and looked around. The couple had long since moved out of sight and been replaced by a thirty-something walking a dog. Jessica felt off balance. Everything around her was a little too bright; the lines were a little too crisp. Her sub sandwich was crumpled at the bottom of her bag. In her distraction, she forgot to eat it. *So much for my picnic dinner.* She walked back toward the edge of the park feeling heavy on her feet. She wished she were safely back inside her VR wire station at work.

The Pedestal was empty when she passed it again. A team of park Scrubbies were sweeping up and emptying the trash barrels. A homeless man, who reminded Jessica of the janitor from junior high school lay on a bench a few yards away, several Pollie-cans lying around underneath his limp, dangling hand. The Scrubbie team whizzed by the bench, scooping up the Pollie-cans in their path. Jessica wondered how many people, perhaps just like this man, had been put out of work when park maintenance workers were replaced by the Scrubbie drones ten years ago. How many of them had any place but here to go?

Jessica! She argued with herself. *What's up with that? It's nobody else's fault that this guy didn't pay attention in school. If no one needs the skills you've got, get new ones. It's that simple.* Another, smaller voice expressed doubt from the fringes of her consciousness. *Unless you can't...*

Jessica passed through the gate that separated the city from the park. A dull clicking pattern resembling an angry squirrel acknowledged she had exited the area.

Jessica walked back to her condominium via Warhol Street. The setting sun showed orange and red in the chic displays, turning the mannequins into devilish alter egos of themselves. Jessica walked more quickly. She was unnerved. It felt like a piece of her mind was missing, but she couldn't pick out anything in particular that didn't make sense.

Not remembering her grandmother's face wasn't such a big deal. Plenty of people forget the faces of their dead family. Given enough time and distance, one's own face would begin to lose its resolution. That's what family photos are for. Jessica knew she could open up her photo file and find any one of dozens of pictures of her grandmother. There was something larger missing, something only her unconscious fight-or-flight system knew, and it was scared. She felt violated, like she was robbed but not sure of everything that was taken.

A display came to life on Jessica's right as she passed the Beauty Spot. "Sorry we're closed, but please…" The bloodshot sun peered around the side of a fifty-story condo complex three blocks away, making Jessica squint just before it retreated below the horizon for the night. She kept walking. Her breath came faster. She strode up to the manual access gate, and waved her EASy chip over the reader. She was admitted to a small vestibule designed to look like a cozy adobe home living room. Safety flame candles hung in sconces on the wall. The figure of the lead doorman appeared on the projection platform to the right of the inner entrance.

"Welcome home, Ms. Butler. Would you like an escort to your unit?"

"No thank you."

"Please provide fingerprint confirmation."

Jessica pressed her left thumb, then her pinky and finally her index finger, twice to the combination pad. The resident door swung open.

Jessica smiled at the man's friendly image. "Have a good night, Jerry."

The usually placid doorman looked briefly surprised, raising his left eyebrow a few millimeters. *A greeting from Jessica Butler?* He composed himself quickly. "You too, Ms. Butler. Let us know if you need anything." He disappeared.

Inside her complex, Jessica laughed at her previous panic. *Jess, hon'. You've got to get a grip.* She was glad she had work to distract her.

Wirespace: The TWNS Nucleus in the FIO Neutral Zone

Jessica and her informant, Rene Stone, walked in silence for a few moments down the simulated cobblestone street of the British nucleus of the world newswire. The Brits had upgraded since she'd been here last. She could hear the clacking of the heels of her shoes and feel the ocean breeze exhaling over her skin from the wharf. The designers had chosen a pre-industrial theme this time with ships littering the harbor and gas-lit pubs lining the frontage road. Her informant shrugged. "I honestly don't know what goods Grey has got on Fein and his clan."

"You've got friends high up in the organization, Mr. Stone, unless he's leading from a distance..."

Rene Stone interrupted Jessica. "I told you. He's not their leader."

"So, who *is* their leader?"

Stone paused and stared at Jessica straight on. "Why would I tell you that?" His lips thinned into a closed line. After a moment he continued meandering along the walkway.

"We've worked a lot of cases together, Rene. You've always done well for yourself. We'll take care of you. Trust me on that."

"This isn't just some *case*, Butler. This is people's lives. And trust you? Only when I'm looking you in the eye."

Jessica took measured breaths in and out, trying to contain her frustration. She had gotten no new information out of Stone and she couldn't stay much longer, lest the System Master check their IDs and start decoding their aliases. She tried to figure out an angle through which she could at least get some small piece of information.

"Word has it the Integrationists have a hit out on Grey because of his globalist policies."

"What?" Stone choked on his own saliva and looked at her skeptically. "First he's their leader and now they want him dead? You must be desperate, Butler. You're grasping at air. That's careless work for you." Stone stopped himself, breathed deeply, and looked carefully around to see if there were any other avatars in sight. "The Integrationists might be naïve, but they're not stupid. Ever since our brilliant politicians took it upon themselves to withdraw from the UN, this country has been fighting a rising tide of resentment. Globalist or not, Grey is the closest thing to an ally that the U.S. has got."

Jessica snorted. "Some ally, he's advocating for the maintenance of the international embargo against all US products and services. Even some nodes of the Newswire had to go underground."

"I don't know what to tell you. If Grey is being targeted, it's not by them." Stone shrugged.

"What information does Tyler Grey have against the United States regarding human rights violations?"

"You don't give up, do you?"

"Not easily."

"If I find out, I'll give you a heads up. I might not tell you everything, but I'll at least let you know something's going down."

"Fine." Jessica said, frustrated.

"I'll exit through the Adam's Apple Pub," Stone told her. "I'll give you a five-minute lead. You might want to try the boarding house on the other side of the bridge. Word has it they haven't been monitoring that portal very closely.

Jessica nodded and walked away without saying good-bye.

Jessica Butler's Condominium – Amsterdam and 61st Street: New York, New York

Disjointed images flashed through Jessica's mind as she slept. She dreamed about giving blood, which she'd never actually done. There were drains flowing out of her arms and legs. Was she supposed to fill the whole blood bank? *So cold.*

That smell. *So familiar.* A man's cologne. *Can't open eyes.* He's brushing her hair and singing? Something. He's kissing her on the forehead. He says he'll be back. *Wait, don't go.* "Come back!"

Jessica sat up straight in her bed. It was obvious she had been tossing and turning. Her heart was beating double time. She looked at the clock beside her bed. It was four thirty; almost time to get up anyway.

She slid her legs over the side of the bed and stood with a weak shudder. *Three hours of sleep. This is going to be a great day.* She wandered into the bathroom and washed up. The doctors wanted her to go three months without the Prolert. They were concerned about the brain bruises – as they called them. *If this is what it feels like to keep myself 'Lert free, I don't think I'm gonna make it.* She crossed the living room and went into the kitchen. No sooner had she pulled out a pan and a couple of eggs, when Mabel came bursting through the door to her cubby. Jessica started at the sudden movement and noise.

"Thank you. Very sorry. Enter new schedule?"

"No new schedule. One time event. Confirm."

"One time event. Confirm. Thank you. So sorry, Ms. Butler. How would you like your eggs cooked."

"Thank you, Mabel. I will do it myself."

An error registered at the periphery of Mabel's system software. *Do it myself?*

"Thank you. How would you like your eggs cooked?"

"Thank you." Jessica repeated. "I will do it myself."

The command wound its way through the maze of settings and preferences honed over two years of operation with the same human host. *I will do it myself?* File not found. New folder. Personality subtype. Change preference? One-time event? Unknown. Store for future analysis.

"Thank you. I will set out your clothing."

"Mabel." The command stopped the Scrubbie in her path. "I'm already dressed."

"Thank you. I will set out your clothing." Mabel's small, purple "Service" light came on and began blinking. Jessica sighed.

"Mabel. To cubby. Maintenance Protocol Three."

"Thank you. Maintenance Three. Confirmed." Mabel retreated back to her cubby where Jessica's unpredictable responses could be integrated with past behaviors.

Jessica wondered if Mabel were still under warrantee.

As Jessica scrambled up her eggs with a little cheese and mustard, she thought about the process of creating Scrubbies. First, a brain mapping was created from a human subject with the requisite skills for the Scrubbie class under development. *I wonder how much they got paid? Hm.*

The map was saved to computer then etched onto a silicone board impregnated with rat stem-cell serum. From there, the neural network grows on its own and is replicable through the entire class. Jessica wondered who was such a perfect servant that their brain was worth preserving ad infinitum. She wondered how much of the neural network was coupled to the programming devices, and how much was created on its own. And if a Scrubbie could form associations to guess her likes and dislikes and to anticipate her wants before she knew she had them, did that mean that the Scrubbie could think?

Jessica turned on the neuro-diode console. The morning news is so much easier than philosophy.

Total Wire New Service – Manhattan Bureau: New York, New York

When Jessica tapped into her Wire station at the beginning of her shift at TWNS, there was already a message waiting for her. It was from Tripp asking her to see him as soon as she got in. *So much for getting in early...*She wasn't sure she was ready for an earful of Tripp at this hour. She carefully opened the top of her coffee and reached into her desk drawer. She popped a second Pollie packet into the mix for good measure, swished it around with her finger and closed the cover again.

On her way to Tripp's office, Jessica passed Carrie Ann's station. Carrie Ann looked up eagerly. "Oh, Jessica! I just adored your piece on the Polythanizone election conspiracy yesterday. I'd love to sit in on one of your edits some time to see you work. I could learn so much. Would that be okay?"

Jessica side-stepped Carrie Ann's eager pose and nodded distractedly. "Sure. Whenever's good for you."

"Oh, thank you so much. I…" the rest of Carrie Ann's reply was lost in the din of the newsroom as Jessica walked away.

Jessica knocked firmly on the door to Tripp's office. Strange that he had closed it so early. She opened the door. Tripp was on the phone. He looked up and waved her in.

"Good as done." Tripp paused, listening. "Yes, I'm serious." Pause. "By the end of the day, I promise. Right. Good bye." Tripp hung up and looked at Jessica intently.

"What is it?" She took a sip of her thankfully loaded drink.

"There's going to be a little meeting tonight. On a ship two hundred and *one* miles off the coast of Washington, D.C.. Guess who's going to be there?"

"Chairman Mao." Jessica said with droll sarcasm.

"Tyler Grey." Tripp replied. "Along with a bunch of his insurgent friends. Sources say they'll be talking a little strategy. Could give you the opportunity you need to get an inside scoop on this story. And if you happen to get the 'package' while you're at it, well that'd be just an added bonus."

"Two hundred and one miles, huh?" Jessica took another sip of her coffee. "Better get me a really good wetsuit."

"There will be a skimmer waiting for you at two o'clock on Pier 5. Ask for Kyle." Tripp handed her a business card with the logo of a ship and cargo crane. "Door-to-Door Imports. Europe. Africa. Asia. Four hundred offices worldwide". *Not any more,* she thought joylessly.

"Well then, I'd better get ready.

TWNS Newswire: 07 | 31 | 2062 | 18:43:10

"In late breaking news tonight, the Total Wire New Service has just received word that Central Senate Majority Leader, David Marks was killed in an attack at his Washington, D.C. condominium early this afternoon. Marks' staffer, Jeremy Anderson noticed that Senator Marks missed several scheduled appointments in the morning. When Senator Marks did not appear for a luncheon with the Ways and Means Committee Mr. Anderson became concerned and contacted Capitol Hill Police.

Upon arrival at Senator Marks' residence, the Senator was discovered on the floor of his bedroom, where he had apparently been dressing for the day. Initial reports indicate that the Senator may have received a gunshot wound to the head, but details at this time are sketchy. Throughout his career, Senator Marks has been a staunch defender of Americans in need.

David Marks was a US Marine from 2022 to 2042. He first made a name for himself leading the investigative team that uncovered the individuals responsible for the destruction of the 911 Memorial in New York City in 2037. Upon his retirement from the armed forces, Marks ran for state legislature in his home state of Maine, winning by a landslide margin of seventy percent. In 2049, when former United States Senator Jerry Ottowind disappeared during a constituency tour, Marks was urged by his supporters to run for the vacant seat.

Marks joined the United States Senate after a special election in 2050. After an initially troubling three months, he became a champion for the chronically ill by advocating stem cell cloning for the selective growth of transplantable organs. The first recipient of such a transplant was five-year old Brendan Little, who received a farmed lung transplant to cure him of Cystic Fibrosis. Through his efforts, Senator Marks was able to quell the irrational fears of the American Public about human cloning.

Always a patriotic citizen of the country he loved, Senator Marks' latest efforts had been focused on negotiating with the international community to lift the international trade embargo against American goods and services. Particularly important to the Senator, was reversing the information lock-down that prevents United States scientists from gaining access to potentially life-saving research in the worldwide bio-medical industry. Ironically, Senator Marks himself had recently recovered from a severe encephalitis shortly before his death.

David Marks leaves behind his wife, Elsa, and two children, Isaac and Hannah. We gather in prayer to support them in their time of grief."

International Waters Off the Coast of Washington D.C – HMS *Firebrand*

Delph walked casually toward the stern of the HMS *Firebrand*, scanning the waters for signs of Jessica's skimmer. Calming piano music diffused through the doorway of the main casino room as he passed by. Jeweled women with intricate up do's and their men with shiny shoes and manicured nails lounged in the softly upholstered chairs that encircled the gaming tables. Small clusters of acquaintances eyed strangers in the room surreptitiously over the tops of the cards in their hand or over the rims of their martini glasses. The conversation was muted for such a large crowd.

Turning toward the railing, Delph pretended to be enjoying the glow of the moonlit ocean while he rechecked the fishhook locator beacon on his floaters. *Almost here.* The meeting of dignitaries inside the small unlisted private dining room near the stairway to the ship's bridge had been in session for almost two hours already. Initially Delph was concerned about how long it took for Jessica to follow the boat from the harbor, but timing had always been one of Jessica's strengths. If she wasn't here yet, then it had been part of her plan to wait.

Delph continued his stroll, blending in with the secretive, wealthy gamblers gliding from game to game as if this entertainment were perfectly legal. A perky cocktail waitress with a short blonde curly ponytail offered to take his order without asking for his passenger manifest card. No one on this particular excursion was eager to reveal themselves to the OCD database, which was convenient for him. Drinks were on the house. Delph waved the girl away and made sure he was alone before ducking into a small alcove near the stern.

Energetic pop music from the top deck trailed unselfconsciously over the end of the yacht. There was not a more perfect place for a meeting of international conspirators. The boat, a 122 meter Barklay Winger, was registered in Bermuda and never left international waters. The gamers wouldn't jeopardize their winnings or furtive business deals by tattling on the Commodore running it. The gamblers kept their eyes and ears to themselves. What happened on the *Firebrand* stayed on the *Firebrand*.

His hands in his pockets, Delph shifted restlessly in anticipation of seeing Jessica again. He had just turned toward the starboard railing, when he caught a glimpse of a silver trail about fifty yards behind the ship. Forty yards. Thirty yards. Twenty yards. A trim figure rose on the sliver of a boat and dived noiselessly into the water. *She's here.*

Delph could barely hear the whistle of the mini-TAIL grapple over the ship's engines. This was followed by a sharp snick as it attached itself to the baseplate of the deck's rail. He removed himself to an out-of-the-way corner under the stairs to the upper deck as Jessica hoisted herself onto the boat, landing on her swim fins with a gentle *flap*.

Just then a half drunk woman in a red dress and heels stumbled around the corner talking loudly into her Mate comm interface. "Can't you just transfer another ten thousand? Pleeeeeeeaaase! I came all the way out here and I'm broke before the big stake games have even started." The woman listened for a moment and scrunched up her face angrily. "Well, what good are you then?" She turned to storm away and almost ran squarely into Jessica. "Who the hell are you?"

Jessica heard the woman's caller mumble something over the comm. Before the woman could reply, Jessica pulled the Mate off the side of the woman's handbag and threw it off the back of the ship, into the water.

The woman looked after it. "Hey!" She yelled, "that was my..." She was silenced by Jessica's fist as she turned to face her again. Jessica pulled off her flippers and dragged the unconscious woman to a nearby storage locker. After heaping the woman into the back, she tossed her drysuit and other gear in on top of her. She quickly slid a waiter's uniform over the bathing suit she'd had hidden underneath—a perfect match to what the staff was wearing inside. Jessica straightened her nametag and strode officiously toward the dining room.

Delph watched her walk away remembering how the sensuous the curve of her waist felt under the palm of his hand. He was burning for her again. Delph forced his eyes away from Jessica's retreating form and back to his work. He triggered his Belt Mate, which he had hidden in his pocket. "The Princess has arrived."

"Watch her closely." The Observer replied.

Delph tapped out without replying and headed back toward the ship's function rooms. On the way, he nodded politely to some happy newlyweds. Then he quickly traced Jessica's steps to the Commodore's dining room. The spotless varnished cherry wood door swung open as he arrived. He casually turned toward the electronic wall display, pretending to review the list of upcoming games. In his peripheral vision, Delph saw Jessica serving a slice of cheesecake to a man with shaggy dark hair. She didn't appear to recognize the man, but the man recognized Delph just before the door swung shut again. Delph removed himself to the hallway behind the kitchen.

Jessica was surprised by the British Prime Minister's casual attire. Instead of his usual well-tailored sage suit and brown loafers, he sported a cream colored silk shirt and linen trousers complemented by gray Synthete sandals.

She placed the cheesecake, point forward, in front of each guest starting with a man with scraggly hair. She thought he looked familiar, but she couldn't place his face. Soon after she passed, he quickly excused himself from the room. Jessica refocused on her primary objective. She observed from a corner of the room as the group finished their desert and waited. *It's ironic,* she thought. *The same barons who hire robotic teams to serve their customers always insist on human servers for themselves.*

Delph didn't have to wait long for Marcelo to descend upon him and grab him by the collar. "What's she doing here?" Marcelo hissed in Delph's ear.

"Top secret," Delph mouthed silently.

Marcelo scanned each end of the hallway. "Secret my ass. She's gonna blow my cover."

"Don't worry, she's been wiped. She's clean." Delph assured him.

"You're thinking with your dick, Crane. You know she could throw tracers any minute."

"And you need to trust me on this, Marcelo. We need her on our side."

"What makes you think she'll decide to help us?"

"I have information she wants. She just doesn't know it yet."

Marcelo snorted. "If you screw this up…" He curled his fist under Delph's chin and walked away. Delph chuckled to himself.

The meeting was concluding as Marcelo re-entered the Commodore's Dining Room and re-seated himself. The delegate from Ohio was speaking his mind about the final agreement. "If you can give me a point list of how we're going to extricate ourselves from this once we effect a regime change, then I'm all for it. But unless you can give me solid conditions under which we can re-enter the international community, I'm not sending my people anywhere to do shit."

Grey was patient, but firm. "Regime change and a dropping of the outrageous importation taxes that your group insists on protecting. That and you're in, as simple as that."

"So, we help you only to get economically walked on when we open the borders again to a flood of cheap European and African goods. How do you expect us to pull our economy up out of the toilet if we can't make a profit?"

"You'll make a profit, Wellman. I promise you."

Wellman did not look convinced.

The group began pushing themselves back from the table. Jessica quickly descended upon the British Prime Minister's plate almost snatching it from the hand of another member of the wait staff. Carrying only that dish, Jessica worked her way around the delegates to the kitchen door. She passed the chef's staff as they cleaned up and prepared for the next event and found the narrow stairway down to the storeroom.

Seeing the first of the meeting participants exiting the dining room, Delph activated the Hermit line in his camouflaged floaters. The eye scan controls spread themselves over the inside of his glasses. Using his trace program, Delph watched Jessica wind her way back to the stern of the ship. He pulled up a schematic of the ship and devised the easiest route to intercept her.

The storage room smelled like garlic and chrome cleaner. Jessica shoved the dessert plate behind some jars of olives and carefully sealed Tyler Grey's fork into a waterproof pack. She tucked the pack into a Velcro pocket on the inside of her blouse and discarded the wait staff vest on a hook on the wall. She opened the door and looked both ways before turning right toward the staff lockers and the stern of the ship.

Jessica hurried to minimize the chance of anyone asking her why she'd left the service area. Luckily, there was no one around. The night was young and there were over five hundred people left to feed, two thousand drinks to be made, and a hundred and fifty six dinghies to be greeted, loaded with guests and sent home. There wasn't another staff member in sight.

Jessica pushed on the exit door at the end of the hallway. A sign directly in front of her said *Engine Room* pointing down and to the left. Jessica turned right. Rounding the corner she reoriented herself to the stern and bumped smack into a small man in portable floaters designed to look like sunglasses. *Didn't I have a pair of those once?*

"Jessica." Delph's heart rate increased hopefully.

She froze into a half-crouch. "Who are you? How do you know my name?"

Delph removed his glasses and reached out to touch Jessica's face. She pulled away. She had had just about enough of déjà vu for one day. Delph's hand remained suspended in the air for a moment before she grabbed it and twisted his arm behind his back, pinning him to the wall. She put her face close to his. "I said, who are you and how do you know my name?" Jessica noticed a trace of sadness cross his face.

He grimaced as he tried to turn to face her, but she tightened her grip. "I am your only friend."

"Phffff."

"Trust no one."

"Does that include you?" She mocked.

"I'm the only one you *can* trust." He replied. "Tripp won't tell you the truth, Jessica. Not about Freedom Park."

Surprised, Jessica's grip faltered just enough for Delph to spin and connect his elbow with her jaw, sending her stumbling into the opposite wall. He stepped uncomfortably close to her and whispered into her ear. "That's right, Jessica. Freedom Park. It will come back to you. It will all come back and I'll help you find it." Before he pulled away, he ran his lips down the side of her neck, leaving a trail of fire in its wake, and kissed the upper curve of her collarbone.

Jessica shivered and head-butted him violently and bolted toward the rear of the ship. She found the lowest deck balcony and dove kitty corner toward the following skimmer.

Delph patted a swelling bump on his skull and watched her swim away. He tapped into the com link again. "The package is sealed and delivered. She's clean." He didn't wait for a reply.

He disconnected and casually retreated to the upper deck for a game of black jack and some scotch.

Total Wire New Service – Manhattan Bureau: New York, New York

Jessica shifted in the Wire station cradle and rolled her shoulders in tight circles. She spun Tyler Grey's holographic image around in front of her using minute flicks of her wrist. The floaters shifted on her face as she raised her eyebrows and relaxed them again. Sixty-three years old. Leftie. In fine shape for his age—a triathlete. Former Royal Air Force Captain. Jessica took a sip of coffee. She had imported the cup's image into her VR-space so she wouldn't lose track of it. She continued rocking restlessly back and forth in her chair. The British Prime Minister had to be the cleanest politician she had ever investigated. No DUI's; no whores; no drugs. Unmarried—interesting, but not incriminating.

Jessica wiped the image in front of her and took another gulp of coffee. *If Grey was such an integral part of the bombing in Freedom Park, why have there been no previous accusations of supporting terrorist activities? A guy like this doesn't just flip out and start killing people.* From 2043 to 2055, when he became Prime Minister, he served as lead negotiator for the British FIO delegation. Per his file, he was known for his steady diplomacy and inability to be rifled. He was good at what he did because of his even-temperedness and ability to find solutions to benefit the most people in any discussion.

Nonetheless, Grey was vocal in his support of maintaining the FIO ban on all Genetically Modified Organisms in the food chain, a policy that when implemented in 2047 had devastated US farmers due to the drastic sudden demise of the international trade exemption. Grey was also one of the most forceful voices in the drive to investigate President Fein for human rights violations and the first signer of the formal FIO demand document requesting inspections to investigate alleged violations of the International Accord on Human Cloning.

That Grey has an anti-American bias seemed clear, but terrorism? It just didn't add up. Grey seemed to get what he wanted without the use of deadly force. What could a bombing accomplish for him that his diplomatic skills could not?

Jessica closed Grey's biographical file and re-entered the virtual hallway of the OCD nucleus. She paced back and forth a few steps, then tapped in her Tier Four security code. The hallway around her turned deep teal, signaling entrance into the high security portion of the system. She flung her virtual form into the air and flew down the wide corridors of sub-nuclei making swimming actions with her arms. She waved down next to a portal titled GMO Treaty and dropped into the Research space it contained.

From the look of the research space that had been designed for the GMO treaty work, it seemed that many people had spent a great deal of time here. The space was outfitted with gleaming white walls and large Paladian windows that looked out onto a grassy, tree-lined mall with a central fountain. A door toward the back of the room revealed virtual sleeping quarters. This was not the kind of environment set up for casual browsers. A great deal of time and money had gone into efforts to derail the FIO's plan to enforce GMO-free food. The presence of VR sleeping quarters told her that a team had been assigned to the task at a level of secrecy that demanded they be sequestered in wirespace for the duration of the assignment. So, while machines and medics minded the researchers bodies in the OCD Interface Laboratory in Seattle, the researchers occupied themselves with daily living in a virtual research library. Jessica wondered how long they had been confined here.

She scanned the rows of built-in file cabinets: NewsWire Clips, Public Opinion Polls, Economic Impact Projections, Jessica selected the Personalities drawer and was presented with dozens of options of prominent individuals involved in the conflict. Grey was not involved in the implementation of the FIO ban, but his contemporary of the time was equally as forthright in his opinions about GMO-free food. Jessica was just about to close the file when she saw a link to a Reference Document entitled "Report from the British Medical Association: the Safety of GMO's." She tapped the link. Nothing happened. She tried again. Same result. *That's strange.*

She swiped the file closed and requested an internal search engine. She entered the name of the report and the engine responded with a Primary Location Marker. Jessica tapped the marker. The icon blinked, but did not open. "Fine!" she huffed. She noted the Primary Location "Medical Reports" and swiped the search engine away. Looking around the room, Jessica finally locating the Medical Reports drawer between Marketing Efforts and Operations. She tapped the Primary Location drawer and was presented with a selection of documents, all of which appeared to comment on the safety of GMO's in the food chain. The report from the British Medical Association was near the top. Jessica attempted to access the document directly by tapping the direct access icon floating in front of her. This time, she was greeted by a gray box stating "Access Failure – Restricted to Tier Five Authorization Only". Jessica frowned.

For comparison, Jessica tapped the icon for the report from the American Medical Association. Instantaneously, the document lay on a table in front of her. She scanned the abstract.

> *American Medical Association Summary Report on the Safety of Genetically Modified Organisms*
>
> *Despite the widespread use of genetically modified organisms (GMOs) in the food chain since before the turn of the last century, controversy remains within the public about the appropriate use of pre-release research required to authorize GMOs for public consumption. Furthermore, international efforts to ban GMOs at a global level, increase the urgency of definitively settling the debate. The current authors performed a meta-analysis of over two hundred previous research*

studies, one hundred and fifty six of which were randomly controlled trials in an attempt to parse out fact from mythology regarding the potential negative effects of GMOs. This study concluded that, despite the large number of reports claiming adverse effects, rates of allergic response, and protein incompatibility were only marginally higher for GMOs food sources and did not reach statistical significance. These authors concluded that the benefits of a heartier and more reliable food chain outweigh the inconvenience of marginally higher rates of allergic response, particularly in the current environment of easy allergy control.

What could be so special about the report from the British Medical Association that it had to be hidden behind such a high security wall? Jessica was considering a variety of options for temporarily obtaining Tier Five access when her private com channel started blinking in the lower right quadrant of her field of vision. The red blur told her it was important. She shook her head in exasperation and tapped it.

The familiar Persona of her informant, Rene Stone, materialized in front of her, but vaguely transparent, clearly he was shielding his transmission. Jessica would appear hazy to him as well. In this high security zone, Stone would only perceive a neutral sandy gray box for her surroundings.

"Stone. What can I do for you?"

"We need to meet."

"We're talking now."

"In person. As soon as possible."

Jessica was surprised by his request. Stone was always adamant about maintaining his distance in the real world. "I could move to a hermit line." Jessica offered.

"I need to see you now." Stone looked over his shoulder, then crouched in a little and whispered. "I'll be at the base of the re-built Nine-Eleven Memorial at eleven o'clock. I'll wait for ten minutes." Stone signed off abruptly.

Stone was really edgy. The background noise and the poor quality of the transmission told her he was using public facilities, probably a cyber-café somewhere in mid-town. *This might be a sell-out,* Jessica thought. *Or he might have important information for me.* She quickly signed out of the nucleus and lifted herself from her station. She tipped her head to the left and right, relishing the sharp popping sound. *No better way to find out,* she thought, and hurried into the night.

Re-Built 9/11 Memorial: New York, New York

Jessica parked three blocks from her destination in order to mix with the foot traffic from a busy nightclub. A discreet sign at the height of the bouncer's elbow mentioned the availability of unadulterated XRG in the establishment. The "secret" code they used to avoid prosecution was amusing to Jessica. It read: *Pure Xcitement Really Great. No Fuss!* Jessica chuckled. Scanning the line of patrons waiting to get in, she though it was too bad she wasn't up to their dress code tonight. The music sounded good. Boo would know if it was worth checking out. She made a mental note to ask her.

Walking away from the inviting cluster of lights and laughter, Jessica zipped up her leather jacket and flipped the collar up around her neck. She had forgotten how cold it got around this part of the city. During the day, throngs of middle school children and their chaperones clogged the streets gawking at the souvenir displays and interactive educational kiosks that lined the streets. At lunchtime businessmen threaded their way through the giggling mass as they took pictures of themselves and the 20-story spires that stood where the North and South Towers of the World Trade Center had once reigned. Not now. It was late. The vendors had rolled up their wares and the school busses had rolled back to their comfortable suburbs hours ago.

This spot was the most isolated place in the city at night. Even the gangs and drug dealers were superstitiously spooked by the spiritual implications of its history. When the city darkened and the pavement cooled, the wind became voracious. Unfettered by buildings it spiraled up and around the stark spires of the memorial like ghosts haunting a murderer's consciousness emanating a shrill whine as it passed over the scaled surfaces of the structures. The site was shrouded in near darkness at night, receiving only a faint glow from the interior lights of the buildings surrounding it. Most of their shades were drawn.

As she crossed under the sweeping arches marking the entry to the site, Jessica remembered how much more she liked the original memorial than this one. She had seen it the summer before it was destroyed on a rare trip downtown with her grandmother. There had been a giant courtyard surrounding two modest modern office buildings. Throughout the courtyard were the bronze likenesses of two hundred victims of the Nine-Eleven attack—faceless, so as to represent the entire community of people lost on that day. Figures of firefighters and police officers mingled with business people and janitors and the entire tableau was ringed by flowers and a bench-height wall engraved with the names of all of the victims. The original memorial had been lovingly constructed in 2026 after initial design attempts had fallen victim to political posturing.

In the Winter of 2037, terror struck again at the sorely battered site. Fewer people died, thanks to the reduced size of the newer buildings and the advanced construction techniques that had been used to build them. But the creative spirit of the city had been broken. The people could find no adequate means of expressing the sorrow of losing more innocent people to terrorist bombs. Superstition grew about the site, businesses refused to re-locate there again. All that remained now of the nation's attempt to heal were the two stark wind-churning spires.

Jessica ducked around the corner to the side least visible to the road and waited. Her neck was tucked into the collar of her jacket like a turtle. Her arms were crossed over her chest for extra warmth. She dared not shiver or jump in place, lest she draw unwanted attention. She waited. *This had better be good.*

Not long after Jessica arrived, Rene Stone appeared to her right, as if out of nowhere. "Thank you for coming."

Stone's virtual Persona was somewhat more—chiseled— than the real thing, but he was taller than he appeared in the wire and maintained his air of presence.

"So, what's the big deal?" she asked.

"Senator Marks is dead."

"That's been all over the NewsWire. You should tune in once in a while," Jessica stated blandly. She was beginning to regret leaving the cozy security of her cradle. She turned to walk away.

"I know what happened to him."

Jessica stopped.

"And you're confessing this to a NewsWire correspondent because...why?"

"Something very strange has happened, Ms. Butler, I thought you'd want to know about it."

"Scoop of the year?" She asked skeptically.

"Cut the crap, Butler. I have my informants too. I know about your extracurricular activities with the Office of Civilian Defense."

Jessica looked around her quickly, expecting an ambush.

"I've come alone."

Jessica met Stone's eyes. She sensed a tension there she had never felt before.

"What do you want?"

"They found a data plank. When the cleaners were scrubbing the evidence, they found a plank on the floor next to Marks' body. It was bloody, like it had been attached to him in some way."

"And who are they, Stone?"

He blinked at her slowly and ignored the question. "Their team looked at the tissue remnants on it and determined it was neural matter. Marks'."

"So the guy had a neural implant. Probably just some kind of high security ident."

"They checked that out. It was not standard issue. And that's not all." Stone stopped speaking and paced back and forth.

"You're wasting my time, Stone."

Stone stopped, mid-stride, and looked Jessica straight in the eyes. "It was degraded. The DNA was degraded. There were strange nucleic acids at the edges too. Butler! Do you know what this means? Someone manipulated Senator Marks' mind, right down to the expression of his DNA!"

Jessica felt the world swirl around her. She swooned and grabbed the side of the spire to stabilize herself. The pointy edges of the scales pierced the palms of her hands. Images flashed in her mind. A hand touched her shoulder.

Cut to: A white room. Metal table.

Cut to: A hand reaching up toward her.

Cut to: Sound. Moaning.

"Butler, are you all right?"

Cut to: Mirror. Her face reflected.

Jessica straightened up, re-gaining control of her vision. "I'm fine."

"I know tracers when I see them. This plank means something to you. You've been filtered."

Jessica shook her head. "I'm fine."

"If you've been filtered, you don't know anything. Not even your name, unless they let you." Stone leaned closer. "But this plank. You know something about it. And how the OCD can control government officials."

"That's paranoid rhetoric and you know it!"

"Really? Don't you wonder why they killed Marks?"

"He's the Leader of the Central Senate. He represents..."

"He was on their side, Butler." Stone cut in. "He was working from within to procure evidence for the FIO tribunal. He disappears for a week. No one can find him. That's how I got involved. It was like the man dropped off the face of the Earth." Stone paced a small circle and continued. "The media spun some story about encephalitis and he suddenly reappears, but then what does he do? He pulls a complete one-eighty. He tells them they're a bunch of paranoid conspiracy theorists. He threatens to put everyone on the OCD watch list. That's when things got ugly."

Jessica shrugged. "So he smartened up? They're going to be in some deep shit killing Marks. "

"Late effects of encephalitis. That's all anyone knows." Stone looked at Jessica, desperate. "How did an ally in the fight against human rights abuses suddenly switch sides? It's this plank. I know it!"

"Oh that's rich, Stone. I can't believe I trudged all the way out here in the middle of the night to catch an earful of this nonsense. You want a voice in Washington? Pay for it, like everyone else."

Jessica turned and walked toward the open pavement. Stone grabbed her shoulder to stop her. He pulled her arm to turn her. When she lifted her hand to hit him away, he stuffed a small biohazard bag into her fist.

"Take it, then. You have better resources than I do. See for yourself." Stone let her go.

Jessica looked at the inert square enveloped in the crinkly plastic.

"Where you go from there is up to you." Stone turned abruptly and disappeared into the darkness.

The steady, low hum of the porter's hydrogen converter lulled Jessica into a semi trance as she slid her way back uptown. She blinked hard to keep herself awake, briefly considering transferring to Auto Control. She pictured herself at the guard station, snoring away while the guards called an alert on the bulletproof porter that refused to identify itself for entry, and decided to stay in Manual.

She glanced toward the glove compartment where she kept some Prolert. The doctors wanted her to wait, but she was wasting so much time sleeping she felt like she couldn't get anything done. She turned on the radio to wring the last drops of adrenaline from her soggy brain. Her head drooped forward.

A horn sounded from behind. "Shit!" Jessica popped her head up and slammed on the brake. "Fuck 'em! I can't live like this." She dug around the glove compartment as she sped through the next five blocks of green lights.

"Ah!" Jessica pulled out the bottle of fuschia-colored pills and flicked the dispenser open with her thumb. She dumped two in her mouth and swallowed hard. "I feel better already."

Jessica slammed on the accelerator, but missed the next traffic light. She stopped abruptly, an inch from the radar line. A teenage boy in a supped-up classic Parsec 2051 looked at her admiringly from her right. He revved his engine twice. The roar of the old combustion system, such an ostentatious presentation, made her laugh. She deliberately leaned back sensually in her chair and looked the other way.

To her left was an enormous billboard advertising the benefits of the EASy chip credit authorization system—*Cash in a flash!* Hard to steal, hard to forge, easy to track. A terrorist's nightmare. The photograph showed a smiling couple entering an exclusive nightclub. Enormous italicized script announced, "BLEEP YOURSELF IN—IT'S SO EASy". Jessica laughed to herself again. Millions of Americans had fallen for the prestige advertising blitz and the initial promotion when the EASy chips were introduced. The things people will do for vanity. For Jessica, it was a purely practical matter. In quick, out quick, mission accomplished.

The light turned green, and the too-hot-to-handle boy tossed out another burst of engine revs before speeding off. Jessica pulled ahead slowly and turned left at the next block to the entrance of her condominium complex. She rolled down the window and waved her EASy chip over the ident scanner. The guards cross checked that with her car and waved her on ahead.

It's so EASy.

The Chilling Zone: Boston, Massachusetts

Dressed in the characteristic tan khakis and blue button-down shirt of a low-level OCD technician, Delph stepped out of the elevator on the executive level of the Chilling Zone. He was impressed by the comfortable office environment he walked into. It was as if the people who worked here needed to convince themselves that what they did was nothing unusual and so they surrounded themselves with the trappings of a typical executive suite. The walls were covered with fabric wallpaper of attractive psychometrically analyzed blues and greens to encourage calm and productivity. Plump sofas and easy chairs were stationed in sporadic conversational clusters with potted plants and snack vendors scattered throughout the facility.

Of course the Chilling Zone itself was different. That was a clean room, only accessible with Tier Four security clearance and a sonic shower. Even Delph wasn't allowed to enter the negative pressure chamber that separated the administrative and office suites from the scientists' work area. It wouldn't do to have just anybody walk in during a T-Col procedure, especially those brainiac rookies who still believed they were working for an AI-obsessed gaming company.

Delph's shoes sunk into the plush carpet as he casually walked down the hallway, keeping his head bent to the particular angle that would obscure his face to the security cameras with his hat brim. It wasn't that he wasn't authorized in this area. He just didn't want his presence to be immediately associated with a major network hacking incident. He entered on the premise that he had been called in off hours to search and destroy a particularly virulent worm that had taken up residence in the Biomedical Node sub-director's stationary console.

It hadn't been as difficult as he thought it would be to set up the remote virus scan alert that would log itself in and place an automatic call to his pager. He was, in fact, disappointed to learn there were no secondary security systems in place to

143

prevent such an intrusion. He had been looking forward to the challenge.

Delph bleeped his EASy patch over the staff access on the sub-director's office door and heard the automatic locking system click open. He shut the door behind him and surveyed the sub-director's office. He was known to be an organized man, but his office did not represent an obsession with orderliness. He had his share of personal trinkets and knick-knacks on his desk and shelves. A crayon drawing labeled "Daddy" was prominently displayed on the corkboard beneath a paper printout of a Project Manager timeline for renovations and expansions to the facility. *Okay, so he's a little retro.* A large American flag was mounted on the wall opposite the director's seat almost filling it.

Delph sat at the sub-director's station and opened his bag of tools. He plugged a ferret clip into the maintenance port on the sub-director's system and connected it in a daisy chain to a 3CM storage plank. He slipped on this floaters and the air in front of him filled with the sub-director's default parlor. Delph logged in as an administrator and began a standard virus scan of the director's system. He set the preferences for "vacuum scan with bit verification" to give himself more time.

When the scan was in progress, Delph pulled on his dedos and floaters and accessed the ferret clip. He ran a scan operation for anything related to Jessica or the botched mission at Freedom Park. Surprisingly, he found nothing.

After attending to several verification requests from the virus software, he turned his attention back to the sub-director's files. He opened a duplicate desktop and began scanning all files for keywords: Butler, Jessica, Freedom Park, and mission compromise. He keyed in every known alias for Jessica, himself and the mission. The search resulted in one reference to Freedom Park, but the file appeared to have been removed to a remote site.

"What the hell?" Delph drummed his fingers on the sub-director's console platform and looked around the room.

The virus software announced that it had finished the scan and discovered a rather common Trojan horse of the kind that high school students play around with when the teacher leaves them alone in the computer lab. Delph looked back at the childish drawing on the wall. *Smart kid.* He destroyed the virus and requested a re-scan. He was running out of time. His every move was being logged in central system. If he spent more time than was necessary to debug the sub-director's station, a cadre of security guards would descend on him in short order. He was sure the sub-director had files relating to the event in question. He just needed to find him.

If I were the Subdirector of the Biomedical Node of the Office of Civilian Defense, where would I keep my remote storage?

Delph stared across the room at the enormous flag and had an idea. He displayed the search field again and typed in "flag".

Nothing.

"Stars and stripes"

Nothing.

The virus scan showed eighty percent complete. Delph closed his eyes tightly, trying to remember every common phrase the director had ever used. He had one more thought "Old Glory".

Bingo. A Hermit link appeared on the desktop and requested a password. Delph immediately implemented his decryption sequence.

Virus scan ninety-five percent complete.

Password located: Log In Complete.

Virus scan complete. This station does not carry any known viruses. You have thirty seconds to log out.

Delph visually scanned the files available to him on the Old Glory drive. There were hundreds of them. There was no way he was going to be able to sift through them all in the amount of time he had.

Command: Dump Duplicate: Drive: Old Glory:\ To Drive: X:\ Enter.

Delph listened for voices in the hall. He heard nothing.

Dump Duplication Complete.

You have exceeded your log out time. Automatic log out sequence commencing.

Delph quickly unplugged the ferret clip and processor and stuffed them back into his bag. He closed up the sub-director's station and hurried to the door. As he opened it, two uniformed OCD police officers arrived in full body armor.

"Woh, can't a guy even do his job here?" he said nonchalantly.

The officers scanned his bleep chip. "Well, Mr. Crane, what took you so long?"

"Just cleaning up my gear, you know?"

"It is necessary to log off in the appropriate amount of time."

"Yes, sir. I'll be more careful next time."

The officers looked at each other. The second officer passed his thermo-graphic scanner over Delph's bag. They seemed satisfied. "Move along."

"Yes, sirs. Thank you, Officers." Delph swung the bag over his shoulder and strolled out of the building, thankful for the thin lead padded pouch he'd added to the bottom.

He smiled at the front desk guard as he left. "Good night, Gary. See you soon."

"You take care, Mr. Crane."

Delph waved as the door shut behind him.

FIO Headquarters: Warsaw, Poland

After the United Nations' split with the United States, the soon-to-be-renamed organization moved their headquarters from New York City to Warsaw. The move did wonders for the local economy and the city afforded the Free International Organization with ample facilities to carry out their work. The main chamber featured comfortable Intelligel chairs with personal nucleus docks for each delegate and their assistants. Each station looked like a mini-corporate box seat at Yankee stadium.

Tyler Grey spoke to a house that was three-quarters full. "Without a thorough search of America's cloning facilities, we cannot ascertain the extent of their violations of the Human Dignity Treaty." He paused and slowly scanned the faces of the FIO assembly. His frustration surged as he watched the members leaning and whispering to their assistants, answering messages and making dinner arrangements during his speaking time.

"The Fein administration has had over a year to respond to the allegations that they are cloning human beings for spare parts." He paused again for emphasis. "Spare parts! Can you imagine the torture of the lives of hundreds of clones of wealthy, powerful individuals as they are slowly whittled away piece by piece on an as-needed basis? Human beings, living without arms and hearts and eyes. Never knowing when the primary donor will make its next harvest."

The FIO Chairman interrupted. "You too have had over a year to present to this council with evidence for your accusations against the United States. Yet, you continuously refuse to present it. We cannot make a considered decision without access to such evidence."

"I am certain the FIO understands the delicacy of the current situation and that we must take a measured approach to our revelations." Grey countered.

"Measured and yet eventual."

"Three of my top agents on this assignment have already gone missing."

"And one has turned against you, Minister Grey, saying that you are on a vendetta against the United States for not forewarning you of their intention to neutralize a cell of terrorists in the Mexico City Hilton, which resulted in the death of over two dozen undercover British operatives. Why would one of your closest allies contradict you in such a manner?"

Grey looked down at the podium and then back at the Chairman. "I cannot say, Counselor."

"You have until the end of the month to present your evidence, Minister Grey, or the FIO will not consider the matter further in this session. Do you understand?"

"Yes, Mr. Chairman, I do. I thank you for the FIO's time and patience."

"Let us adjourn for lunch." The Chairman struck his gavel on the desk in front of him with a resonant bang.

Kiki King Sushi & Grill: New York, New York

The press corps descended upon the Asian-fusion restaurant like a swarm of bees, buzzing, strutting and posturing. Jessica mingled toward the rear of the group, listening. She tucked her press pass into her shirt pocket to stop it from being continually tugged by passing members of the crowd. The wirelink to the FIO working session had given her a lot to think about. The British Prime Minister seemed too impassioned to have been putting on a show for the FIO and international news agencies. Then there was that data plank from Senator Marks' head. Now seated at the long sushi bar, Jessica ordered a sashimi special for one and a ginger ale.

"Did you see his face when the Chairman smacked him down for hiding all of this 'evidence'?" a young reporter from the Washington Post said laughing. "I thought he was gonna spring a leak right in front of us."

"I cannot say, Mr. Chairman," mocked another.

The Post's boy continued, "We'll give 'em holy hell one of these days. Isn't he gonna be sorry when we bomb him and his little island to shit."

The group hear-heared and raised their sake cups in salute to their collective insightfulness. Jessica felt her stomach lurch with claustrophobia and decided she wasn't hungry. She excused herself to the ladies room.

Jessica was shaking when she splashed water on her face. She chalked it up to the Prolert. *I just need to acclimate again. Tonight I'll take a lower dose.* She had spent most of the night thinking about Stone and his data plank. Stone had always seemed level-headed. He was a Leftie, but not the paranoid type. And even if his story were true, why would he bring this information to a person he admitted knowing was an agent of the OCD?

Jessica looked in the mirror and felt another wave of dizziness.

Cut to: Reflection with blue lips. A long high-pitched beep.

Cut to: Wrists. Bound. Trying to escape.

Cut to: Darkness. Someone is stroking her hair.

She leaned over and vomited bile into the sink just as the bathroom door opened admitting two elderly ladies who looked as though they'd known each other since the beginning of time.

"Oh, dear! Are you all right, Miss?" Jessica felt the woman's tendonous fingers rest on her upper arm, stabilizing her. Her concerned face closed in on Jessica's. She smelled of honeysuckle and moisturizing lotion. It was suffocating.

"Yes, I'm fine." Jessica gasped. "Really. I just need some fresh air."

The old lady patted Jessica on the back. Jessica stood and wiped her mouth on a damp paper towel. She saw the old lady's friend standing in the corner of the room looking at her pitifully, holding her hands up to the base of her neck and fingering a small silver cross. Jessica gave the ladies a tense smile.

"Thank you," she said and patted the old lady's hand. She saw the dark blue veins pulsing underneath the lady's thin skin and pictured it punctured by IV needles and bruising. Jessica hurried from the room.

Just before the door closed she heard the old lady's friend comment, "These kids and their Pollies. It's so sad they can't be happy without them."

Jessica turned the corner into the dining room and almost ran into the table of a young man who looked familiar.

Cut to: His mouth on her throat.

Cut to: Dedos flying over a console.

Jessica's hand flew to her forehead shading her eyes from the fluorescent lights. The man's eyes followed her desperate exodus to the door.

Delph watched Jessica leave. *The tracers are becoming more powerful. There's not much time. I have to move now.* He powered down his Belt Mate and pocketed it before walking to the front and bleeping the bill.

Freedom Park, New York, New York

As Jessica reached the entrance to Freedom Park, she could feel the oppressive heat leaving her head. She slowed her pace as she passed through the gate into the flower-lined paths. She breathed in deeply to the smell of lilacs—her favorite. She remembered swinging in her backyard when she was a child. There was a lilac bush...*where?* Swinging. Her father was pushing her. She could almost feel the gentle jolting of his hands against her shoulder blades before pitching forward again, higher this time. *The lilac bush was...Wait a minute! There was no lilac bush in our yard.* How could there be a lilac bush in cookie-cutter Air Force Base housing in South Central California. She'd been lucky to see a lonely cactus growing tall among the desert scrub.

Jessica looked around herself at the flowers and the path and the trees. In the distance, there was a group of children playing soccer under the watchful eyes of their parents. A cyclist hummed past her on his ultra-light Halo-ped. The park was full of life. There were families, pets, daylilies and oaks, but one thing was certain. There were no lilac bushes in sight.

I'm going out of my mind. Jessica thought. *Jesus!* Suddenly, she wanted very much to be at the edge of the pond in the middle of the park. There was no apparent reason, only urgency. Damning appearances to hell, she ran as fast as she could.

The Chilling Zone: Boston, Massachusetts

The EMG needles pulsed away at 135 micros, toning Subject M-43's arms and legs to a fine athletic contour. The Governess bent over him like Michelangelo refining the details of her David. She dripped fine lines of collagen-laced hydrochloric acid across the temporal-occipital juncture, sweeping up toward the neural interface with the precision of a machine, which surprisingly, she was not.

She lifted her short tweezers off of the palate and selected a nerve cell of the right length from the Dexter dish next to her elbow. Maximizing the magnification on her floaters, she massaged the cell into a collagen tracing she had drawn earlier. She covered the small tweezer marks with half-millimeter sized drops of a synthetic version of the neural protein called myelin. She repeated the process several times in order to complete the connection between the subject's superior temporal gyrus to the suprasegmental gyrus and back down to the interface's nexus.

The Governess inspected her work closely and decided it was good. She centered the blue Kerry light above the site of juncture and set the timer for twenty minutes.

In the negative pressure chamber, she ripped off her mask, looked at the Subject and smiled lifting her hands like a B-movie witch making an incantation and wiggled her fingers toward the Subject.

"Poof!"

She showered in the locker room and slithered into her well-pressed calf-length navy blue skirt and understated pink silk scoop-neck blouse. She checked the mirror and rearranged several stray hairs. Then the Governess strode confidently into the plushly accented office area. Several low-level engineers averted their eyes in deference and made way for her as she passed them. She loved it when they did that.

Freedom Park: Yew York, New York

Jessica finally settled on the edge of the man-made pond in Freedom Park north of Central Assembly Square. The water swirled around her bare feet as she spread and flexed her toes. Her hallucinations of lilacs had been replaced by the very real smell of freshly cut grass. She knew this was real because she could see the park Scrubbie gliding back and forth in rows with his bulging pack of clippings. Jessica felt a little silly about her panic before. She briefly considered throwing Stone's data plank into the pond, but thought better of it. *Could make a good story some time—on a slow news day. Mystery chip found in fallen Senator's head. Details at eleven.*

Even in her current distracted state, Jessica felt Delph's presence before she saw his shadow rise over her own. Her guard sprang up, instantaneously. "What do you want? Why are you following me?" She maintained a facade of calm by continuing to twirl her feet in the cold water of the central pond.

Delph's heart sank. "You really don't remember, do you?"

Jessica twisted her body to face him and cocked her head. Her sunglasses glinted orange-red in the setting sun. He looked familiar, but she still couldn't place him. It made her unreasonably angry. "Remember what?"

"Face to face, I thought I could break through." He sat in the grass facing her.

Suddenly Jessica remembered where she'd seen him. She snatched her feet out from the water and curled them under her so she could face him directly. "You're the guy from the ship!" She said accusingly. "What do you want from me?"

Delph instinctively recoiled backward. "I have information you need." He paused. Jessica looked at him blandly. Frustrated, Delph decided to take a different approach. "I know everything you don't know about yourself. I know you're an undercover OCD agent. I know why you're having tracers. And I know what happened here, at Freedom Park, a month ago."

Panic raced down the center of her body in a burning line. Jessica stood up quickly. "Shhh!" She ripped off her sunglasses looked around and paced back and forth. Then she roughly pulled Delph to a standing position by his jacket collar. She held him up so he stood barely on his toes. She was trembling slightly but from fear, not fatigue. Delph reminded himself of Jessica's raw physical power, especially when she felt backed into a corner. How her current condition impacted this was an unknown variable to him.

She looked around and saw a man across the pond, quietly reading a book. She moved her grip to appear to be caressing the back of his neck and whispered. "Just…shhh! You've got my attention. Now, I repeat. What do you want with me?"

Delph decided to take a chance. He quickly wrapped his hands around her wrists and flipped her grip upside down, forcing her to release him. Jessica wound up to hit him, but he grabbed her arms and crossed them around her, pressing her back close to him as if in an intimate embrace. He lowered them both to their knees. "I'm here to help you. You need to know the truth."

Jessica struggled against him briefly, but Delph's lean stature belied his strength. His gamble had paid off. She was not yet at her full strength. The man across the pond reached into a small bag next to him and pulled out a handful of potato chips.

"Come on, Jessica," he whispered seductively in her ear. "You're inches away. Let it come to you." He tightened his arms around her. She sensed his interest in her was more than informational. He traced a line down her neck with his cheek, and brought his mouth back up to her ear. She didn't feel him extract one hand to reach into his pocket. "My name is Delph Crane. Jessica Butler, this is your life." He tapped the Uplink command into his Belt Mate.

Jessica saw stars. She stiffened against him. He placed a hand over her mouth to stifle her scream.

Cut to: the hotel. Delph manipulating the Wolf.

Cut to: her view out the window at the demonstration

Cut to: condoms on the ground, graffiti on a granite wall.

Cut to: planting a micro detonation charge

Cut to: Marcelo on stage

Cut to: Explosion.

Cut to: Running. Running. Running.

"Delph! Something's wrong! Pack up! Run!"

Jessica flailed her arms blindly. Her kicking feet dug up patches of grass with the sides of her shoes. The reading man looked up, briefly concerned then returned to his book.

"Shh. Everything's going to be all right now" Delph said, stroking her head gently. She collapsed against him. He lowered her to the ground as Jessica regained her senses. She crawled out of his arms and turned to look at him suspiciously and curled into a ball like an injured animal. A confusing montage of partial memories crisscrossed her mind. *I have trusted this man with my life. If I could just remember!*

Delph closed his eyes with something close to pain when she reached out to touch his cheek.

"I want to remember."

"It won't be easy for you, Jess, but you need to know."

"Tell me."

"I'll show you." He pulled a small box out of a jacket pocket. Carefully arranged in a padding of static-proof foam lay three 2CM data planks. Jessica looked at him questioningly. "Your past. Are you ready to see?"

"I have to be."

"Come with me."

Delph picked up Jessica's sunglasses from where she had dropped them and handed them back to her. Then he stood and reached his hand down to help her to her feet. She hesitated before taking it and pulling herself up beside him. Delph was not used to seeing uncertainty in her eyes. In this state, he could almost fool himself into thinking she was an innocent needing care and protection, but he knew better. Once Jessica was oriented to her new situation, he had no doubt she would adapt. Not knowing where he would fit into her new worldview, he needed to stay on guard. For right now, he would pretend.

Jessica straightened her shirt and raked the grass clippings out of her hair, while Delph clapped the debris off of her pants. When his fingers wrapped around hers, she thought to herself that her hand fit nicely in his. So, she cautiously left it there as he led her to a gate on the South side of the park.

Delph Crane's Condominium – Spire 2 West 75th Street: New York, New York

Delph Crane's apartment could have been home to any typical tech-head. It was sparse in its décor and neat. He asked that she take off her shoes. The furniture was basic—one sofa, one chair, coffee table, end table and neuro-diode console—but it was constructed of the finest synthete leathers and chromes. The only concession to fashion was a brightly colored throw rug that filled most of the conversational cluster and extended to the edge of the massive projection pad. It was unfathomably soft. Jessica squished her toes through it. This Delph person seemed to have known her for quite some time, but she was certain she had never been here before.

Delph tossed his keys on a table by the door. "I'm going to set up. Make yourself at home. There's some sandwich stuff in the fridge, if you're so inclined."

She poked her head into the kitchen. To her surprise, she saw what looked like every cooking implement known to man, carefully arranged to be convenient to the main prep areas. She inspected one particularly large iron pan. It was freshly oiled. The copper bottoms of the pots and pans hanging from overhead sparkled bright orange. There was no dust coating the tops or insides. He actually used this stuff. Jessica considered the last time she had attempted to cook anything but eggs… *Did I used to know that he cooked?*

She wandered back into the living room and looked out the large windows. Through a window in the building across the way, just below the man-sized parade of stock figures, she watched a mother strapping her toddler into a stroller. The child was squirming fiercely in an attempt to assert his independence to walk by himself. A piece of the mother's hair fell out of her French twist and into her face. It migrated into the corner of her mouth and became damp as she continued pulling on the seat's belts while in all probability issuing some kind of rational explanation to the child as to the importance of staying safe.

"We're all set. Come into the office."

Jessica started at the sound of Delph's voice. She turned away from the window. "All set for what?"

Delph looked at her with tired compassion. "Come on." He turned and went into the office. Having come this far, Jessica followed.

The home office was the nexus of a tech-head's existence. Jessica found the assumptions she made about Delph's apartment based on her introduction to the living room, carried over into the sanctuary in which she now found herself. There were two VR stations, complete with lightweight dedos, various floaters for specialized work, and pressure-sensitive Formalant chairs to accommodate lengthy sessions of research and trouble-shooting. A full-wall projection console was positioned opposite the stations. Most of the computer hardware resided in what appeared to be custom cabinets at the periphery of the room. The armrests of the stations were equipped with elaborate switchers for accessing one system or another.

Delph had adjusted the lighting to a dim amber glow that in other circumstances could be considered romantic. He gestured Jessica toward one of the stations. She settled in and felt the chair sense her pressure points, gently adjusting to her anatomy. While she slipped on the rest of her equipment, Delph jumped into the companion station and began accessing files. By the time Jessica had her floaters in place, an enormous file directory was floating in space in front of her. She saw the decryption signature at the bottom left of her field of vision and knew these were government files and that they were not legally obtained. One subdirectory centered itself: SUBJECT-JESSICA BUTLER:/ARCHIVE/UNFILTERED-MARKED.

Despite the doubts and suspicions nagging at her since her release from the hospital, looking at the archive file's clinical label she wasn't sure if she should re-learn the truth. Memory filtering itself was partly an attempt to stem the tide of military suicides and post-traumatic stress disorder. *Maybe there are some things we're better off not remembering.* "What is this, Delph? What are you showing me?"

"Associative filtering is a process of wiping the memory of specific events. This technique has been used for the past twenty years in the common practice of psychology, particularly in cases of Post-Traumatic Stress Disorder and abuse. But it has been in use by the government for longer than that to control witnesses and compromised agents."

"I know all of this."

"Stick with me. The process works based on the fact that memories are represented by the increased potential for certain sequences of neurons to fire in a particular pattern that is unique to the pattern that was initially fired when the event actually took place. Filtering wipes out these potentials, reducing the likelihood of firing to a random probability." Delph paused.

"And the random probability often leads the individual to experience random filtered memories that we call tracers. I know this. And I've pretty much figured out by now that I've been filtered."

"Imagine if there were some way to eliminate tracers all together; if there were some way to prevent the brain from recognizing a pattern, even if the neurons fired in that pattern again. Imagine if we could take only those memories we wanted to preserve and introduce them to a new brain, a clean slate, so to speak."

"A new brain? What? Are we talking Frankenstein here?"

"You'll have to decide that for yourself," Delph responded cryptically. "I have some memories here that you will find very interesting."

Delph opened the directory and selected a file. The office disappeared. Threads of light flashed from the center of her vision to the periphery in random succession. Jessica felt herself blinking uncontrollably. The light shifted from white to red to purple before blending with the background.

Cut to: She is kneeling next to a man. He is sleeping. She brings her hand up. It is holding a syringe. She jabs the syringe into the sleeping man's neck. He opens his eyes quickly in surprise. She pushes down the plunger. He falls back into sleep.

Cut to: the man is lying on a gurney in a very sterile-looking room. He has been tied down at all four limbs. His head has been shaved. She is wearing a suit that crinkles. It is hot and sweaty. A woman with short dark hair and onyx eyes approaches the man with a bone drill. Jessica watches, transfixed, as the woman carefully drills twelve holes into the man's skull. Into each hole, the woman carefully places a string of electrodes. She arranges each to pick up on a specific site. The woman speaks.

"Once the fox wires are in place, we can begin extracting specific memory elements. They are compiled in a central database. Desired memories are extracted and transferred to the clone as discrete data bundles."

Clone? Jessica scans the room. She sees an identical copy of the man she brought to the laboratory, also asleep, on a table six feet away. A similar arrangement of electrodes are attached to his head, although his head is not shaven. Both sets of electrodes are attached by a slender cable to a small box in the corner of the room. Blue lights blink in rapid succession on the box as the woman began the transfer.

The man jerks and opens his eyes again. He yells. Jessica wants to cover her ears and turn away, but the figure that was her continues watching. She hears herself ask, "It seems like the subject is experiencing some pain. Isn't there something we can do to make the process less gruesome?"

"Unfortunately, any kind of sedative would contaminate the memory data. The information we want would begin to blur with the information we don't want and we'd risk losing important data or creating a risk of tracers."

"I see." Jessica's digital form turns placidly toward the writhing man again. "Perhaps a paralytic?"

In the real world, Jessica pulled off her floaters and leaped out of the chair. Her still tethered dedos snapped tight against their wires as she paced away from the console.

"That's not me! What are you trying to pull here?" Jessica ripped the dedos off to lose the claustrophobia of being tied down to the VR chair.

"It is. It was. That is a real day in the life of Jessica Butler. That is what you did. You were a somewhat well-known specialist in that area. I was your tech support."

"So, so...someone would make a clone, and...what?"

"When the OCD determines that a particular individual presents a clear and present danger to national security, the Executive Director authorizes a clone to be grown. The clone is created and brought to current life age over three months through a cellular acceleration process. At that point, the clone is fitted with a neural interface that will serve as both an input device and later as a tracking and control device. The clone with its filtered memories, which we call the Convert, is reintroduced to the life that was being led by the Primary and no one knows that anything has changed."

"Except that whatever it was that made the person a security risk has been erased." Jessica guessed.

"And when necessary the Convert's views and opinions are manipulated so that he or she behaves as the government wants them to."

"So, he might appear to espouse views opposite to his original views?"

"Yes."

"And this neural interface. Comes in the form of a data plank?"

"Part of it. Until recently, the system was imperfect. None of the Converts survived."

"So that man..."

"Disposed of by more traditional means."

"Sudden death. Suicide...blah, blah," Jessica filled in the blanks

Delph nodded.

Jessica stared for a moment at her feet. "The OCD went to such lengths that they filtered me to keep this information from me. Why are you risking your position by showing this to me? Why do I need to know this?"

"You need to be prepared."

"Prepared for what?"

Delph averted his eyes and turned his back on her. *She's not ready to know yet. I have to be careful.* He paced a few steps, coughed and turned back. When he did, his eyes burned into the back of her skull. "We have reason to believe that they have succeeded in creating their first functional Convert, with more to follow. You need to help stop them from continuing."

Jessica knew there was more. Delph was fidgeting with the contacts of his dedo sensors. If any more information was accessible, it was in the database Delph uploaded to his VR console. She had no reason to trust him, but she did. "Show me more."

Cut to: Jessica walking down a half-lit hallway pushing a cleaning cart. She stops in front of a door and pulls out a ring of keys, eying them to see which is the most likely fit for this door. She succeeds on her second try. The door opens to a wood paneled office with oriental carpeting. She pushes the cart into the room and closes the door behind her. There is a door on the right leading to an inner office. She swings it open and reaches in. The alarm box is where the plans said it would be. She keys in the code by feel to ensure all the cameras are dead before stepping into the doorway.

In the office, she sees pictures on the wall. The British Prime Minister with President Hara Makako of the Pan Asian

Alliance. The British Prime Minister with Sister Anne Paul the popular nun serving in Ghana. The British Prime Minister with his wife and children. She turns to the desk. One side is very clean; every pen in its holder, every paperclip in its jar. The other side is a chaos of contracts, invitations, and legislation in progress. *Interesting.* She feels herself think.

She moves behind the Prime Minister's desk and wipes her hands across the corners of the chair back. The soft velvet lining clings to her skin as she drags her hands along it. She looks down at the chair back with interest and inspects it closely. One, two, three,...*strands of hair.* She reaches into her pocket and pulls out a baggy and some tweezers. Gently, she plucks the hairs off of the back of the chair and slips them into the baggy. She seals it and puts it back into her pocket.

She closes the door far enough so she can just slip her arm in to re-initiate the alarm and shut it behind her. On her way back to the hall, she picks up a wastebasket and dumps its contents into the barrel on her cleaning cart. *Wouldn't want anyone to think I'm slacking, now would I?*

Cut to: She shoves the baggy deeper into her pocket as she climbs in her porter and drives away.

Cut to: Jessica pulls the baggy out of her pocket. She looks at the three strands of hair. She hands the baggy to Tripp Thompson. Tripp smiles. "Good work, Jessica. You're an asset to your country."

"Thanks, Tripp. I always wondered if you cared."

Tripp smiles.

Jessica pulled off the floaters. The room had gone long with shadows. *How long have I been at this?* The last of the light was leaving the sky as Jessica contemplated the implications of the memories she had just retrieved. She felt disconnected from the actions she had witnessed. It was as though they happened in another lifetime, but the karmic stink unnerved her. Clearly, she was an excellent agent, but that excellence was built on a foundation of dissociation. The insight carried by these retrieved memories was that she never cared about what she was doing to any particular individual. She only cared about the mission. If one or another person had to die or suffer in the process. She sublimated that to the mission agenda and never considered it. She shivered to think of her own wickedness and in the next moment shook her head wondering why it bothered her now. *What's changed? Is this just what happens to people after a near-death experience?*

Exasperated, Jessica tossed the dedos onto the chair and wandered into the bathroom. As she washed her hands and splashed water on her face, she looked in the mirror. She felt like a stranger to herself. The DNA packets, the excuses about needing to root out potential terrorist organizations was a lie. She was a part of an organization whose purpose was to assassinate political dissidents and replace them with more agreeable clone-machines of themselves. That her knowledge was considered so top secret that it needed to be erased completely, told her her what a monster she had been.

The water continued running down the drain while Jessica followed her train of thought. *If I delivered a package of DNA for the British Prime Minister before my accident, that means...*She was shocked by sudden clarity. "Delph!" Jessica shoved at the faucet to turn it off and vaulted into the living room. It was empty. She looked in the kitchen and the bedroom, "Delph?" Back in the living room again, she spun herself around wondering what kind of rabbit hole she'd been tossed into.

She spotted the note taped to the front door. *Jessica, I had to go to work. Can't raise suspicions. Stay as long as you like. Delph.* For the first time, Jessica looked at the clock. It was six-thirty in the morning. The sun wasn't setting, it was rising. "Shit."

She threw on her jacket and turned to leave. Before she did, she eyed an unattended table of scraps and notes that stood by the door. She sifted through the piles looking for anything that might reveal more about her mysterious new friend. She still didn't know whether or not she could believe memories that were retrieved by a tech-head who had half his attention on getting her into bed.

A flash of color peeked from under a shifted pile of Post-It notes. Jessica wiped the pile away to reveal a printed color photograph of Delph smiling into the camera. His arm was draped around a woman who was clearly herself, but the mercenary stare terrified her. *I've changed,* she thought. *But how?* She buried the photo again before hurrying out of the building to her own house to change.

NYPD Unit 6 – 4th Avenue: New York, New York

"Captain Seres, please." Jessica stuffed her thumbs casually into the pockets of her jeans and leaned her hip casually against the counter. She turned on her I'm-better-than-you conceit staring straight at the desk officer.

"Who's asking?" Challenged the skinny sergeant, meeting her eyes with suspicion.

Jessica whipped out her OCD identification and tossed it onto the stack of reports the sergeant was studying with a flip of her wrist. "Office of Civilian Defense. I'd like to speak with Captain Seres. Now." Jessica put on her best imitation of the expression she'd seen in the photograph.

A wave of fear briefly fled across the sergeant's face and he stood to attention. "One moment please."

Ten minutes later, Jessica sat in the parking garage staring into space. Cajoling Seres into running a DNA analysis on the chip was easy enough. It remained to be seen how easy it would be to cover her tracks, if the shit really hit the fan. She punched the starter on her porter and felt the suspension kick in. *What is that plank going to tell me? Even if the DNA is cloned, what does that really tell me? What if I'm playing right into the fantasy of some conspiracy theorist whack job? What if my cover has been blown?*

Jessica's Mate beeped three times. She looked at the ident screen. It was Tripp. She punched "Ignore" and sped out of the garage toward the TWNS offices.

TWNS Newswire 08 | 03 | 2062 | 11:22:56

In other news today, Integrationist Candidate for Senate, Mark Brimmer, has pulled out of the race and declared his support for the ongoing presidency of Home Trust Party leader Andrew Fein. Mr. Brimmer made a statement from the steps of the county registrar's office immediately after officially changing his registration from the Integrationist to the Home Trust Party.

"I had a long discussion with President Fein last week. His passion for enhancing the safety of the American people was inspiring. It was completely obvious that he cares about the welfare of everyone in this country. The terrible plagues which have descended upon us in the past fifty years—the never-ending recession, the ire of the international community, the unpredictability of terrorism—makes this a crucial time in our history. I recognize now that we cannot change course at this critical juncture. Continuity is the best chance we have as a country to overcome these challenges. That is why I have decided to whole-heartedly support President Fein in his quest for unity, prosperity and safety. God bless America!" (audio: smattering of applause.)

Mr. Brimmer's conversion to a presidential supporter is a tremendous blow to the Integrationist Party he founded thirty years ago on the principle of consensus-building and political moderation. As the core of the Integrationist party searches their ranks for new leadership, large numbers of their constituency have already begun to fill county registrars to change their party affiliation.

(Video: people lined up holding NIC cards and registration forms.)

Man-on-the-street: "I would follow Brimmer off a cliff, if he thought it was the right thing to do. He is a brilliant man and cares about our welfare more than any other politician I've seen. So, if he truly believes the Fein presidency is best for the country, I'm going to back him."

Conspiracy theorists are already filling web channels with charges that this sudden change of view is related to the unannounced vacation he took last week. It is charged that during that time, government agents sequestered him and threatened him and his family until he relented. The propagators of this theory have not advanced any evidence to support their claims, but insist that it will be forthcoming as soon as it is available. Brimmer's pull-out from the race leaves only Home Trust Party candidate Mark Alexander on the ballot in New York for election to the Central Senate. This is Paul Roberts, Total Wire New Service.

Total Wire News Service – Manhattan Bureau: New York, New York

Jessica smoothed her shirt and slowed to a casual stroll as she approached the doors of the Bureau. The revolving doors swooshed softly as they brushed her into the cool lobby. She paused for a moment to watch the bustling reporters, pages and informants blend into a foaming mass. Her sense of belonging in this place was suddenly unstable. Instead of feeling energized, she was suspicious of everyone who passed.

A tall man in a brown suit walked toward the security desk and reached his hand into his pocket. Jessica focused on the shape of his fingers as he manipulated a small rectangular Belt Mate. He tapped it to answer its persistent bleating. A woman cut past Jessica carrying a metal suitcase. Suddenly, Jessica was bumped from behind. The security camera swiveled in its mount and focused its glass eye firmly on her. She had stayed in one place too long.

"Look out, lady. You're right in the door." Other than his snide remark, the smartly dressed man didn't spare her a glance as he power walked to the elevator and leapt in just before the doors closed.

Jessica wandered toward the same bank of elevators, scanning the crowd like a predator. She breathed slowly and deeply, tuning her senses to detect the slightest essence of fear or excitement. Instead of feeling subtle, it was everywhere. Scores of people bustled across the smoky marble floor, shoulders rounded, faces cast to the ground. Eye contact was quickly broken and ended with the observed individual scurrying away embarrassed, like a teenager caught having sex in the library stacks. For the first time, Jessica noticed the pursed lips and pinched foreheads. It was as if everyone were afraid their thoughts could be open to public inspection. So, they held them tightly closed.

The dozen or so other people she shared the elevator with all kept their gazes trained to the ever-changing holographic advertisement displayed in front of the doors, thus sustaining the illusion for each person that they were alone in their own space. The holo-ad changed to display a serene view of a beach with happy, relaxed people sunning and rubbing themselves with sunscreen. This picture of paradise was sold as an accessible escape for every deserving American. Jessica scanned the crowd and recognized that few of these people would ever have the opportunity to experience a week of such luxurious pleasure. It was only the wealthy and well-connected who had the time and money to spend on themselves in such ways—people like Tripp, people like herself, though she never took advantage of the opportunity. The doors opened to the 25th floor and Jessica shook herself out of the mix of shoulders and briefcases.

The tone in the Bureau was more subdued than the lobby. Even Carry Ann was encapsulated in her cubby with a cup of coffee and a pair of floaters. Murmurs and snatches of conversations drifted to her ears from distant meeting rooms, mixing with the swooshing and clicking of dedos running across input controllers. Jessica wound her way toward her control room without a good morning to or from a single soul.

As she passed Tripp's office, the door opened and he unwittingly propelled himself into her chest. "Jessica! There you are. I was wondering when you were going to show." He leaned into her conspiratorially. "I have something for you. Come in here for a minute."

Jessica followed him into his office silently. Tripp thumbed a keypad on a locked cabinet near the window. "These came in last night from a contact of mine in Peru. I thought you'd appreciate them." He pulled out a small wooden crate and looked at her with excitement. "Wait 'til you see this." As he flipped open the latch on the cover of the case, he noticed Jessica's melancholy demeanor. "You okay? You're not wiping yourself out are you?" His face was indecipherable.

Can I trust him? Jessica thought as she formulated her answer. *Does he know?* She forced a smile. "Late night. That's all. A few too many Pollies and a handsome man. You know how it is."

Tripp smiled tightly. "Of course. Right."

Jealousy? She wondered how much she'd been missing with her mission-focused slant on life.

"Yeah, well don't party yourself into an early grave, okay? Some of us would rather have you around."

Jessica reciprocated the smile and shrugged, but felt empty.

"So," Tripp recovered. "Here's what I've got for you." He opened the top of the crate to show her a small pile of oranges, individually wrapped in thin Styrofoam sleeves. "They're all natural, non-GMO stock and they're sweeter than anything I've ever tasted. Have some." He handed her three oranges.

Jessica eyed them suspiciously. *Is this a test?*

"Who's going to know?" He countered.

She relaxed a little and chuckled. *No,* she thought. *He's just taking advantage of the advantages. Like anyone would.*

He snapped the case shut and stowed it back in the drawer and looked at her with a smirk. "You'd better log in and get some work done before I have to count you absent."

"Hmmp." She laughed. "Just you try." She challenged, staring him down. His eyes were questioning. He was trying to figure something out and she knew it would be best that she leave before he did. "I'm off. Thanks for the oranges." She spun on her heels and left the office.

Jessica had just finished uploading a report about the migration of the polar ice caps and was enjoying her first bite of orange when her Mate beeped three times.

"Jessica Butler."

"Good afternoon, Ms. Butler. This is Captain Seres from District 1 Central Command."

Jessica swiveled around and quickly flipped the lock on her door. "Yes?"

"Your theory was correct, Ms. Butler. It looks like the DNA sample is degraded. Probably only one or two generations. Ninety-nine percent chance the guy you're looking for is a clone. Are you sure you don't want some department support on this? We've got lots of guys specialized in clone ID and tracking. I'm sure we could nail this guy for you."

"That won't be necessary commander."

"I'm just surprised the OCD is troubling itself with petty crimes now…You trying to put us all out of work or something?" He laughed nervously and cleared his throat.

"Thank you for your help." Jessica ran her fingers through her hair.

"What would you like me to do with the sample and report?"

"Destroy it."

"Wha…"

"Destroy it. And forget you ever saw me." Jessica stood and started pacing.

There was a pause on the other end of the line. "As you wish."

"Thank you Captain. You're an asset to your country." She closed out the connection before he had a chance to reply. Jessica spun herself in circles, then sat herself hard into the cradle chair and called up a secure connection on her station. She cycled through three nuclei that were the usual haunts of Rene Stone. "Come on. Shit! Where are you?" Pulling herself out of secure mode, she pinged his personal address. *Is it worth the risk? Too late now…*No answer. Finally she gave up. She'd never failed to find Stone when she needed him. *Where the hell could he be?* Breathe, breathe. *Calm down,* she told herself. *He's probably just in the shower or something.* "Damn it!"

Jessica looked at the clock. It was three thirty. If she didn't hurry she was going to miss her interview with the British Prime Minister. This was her chance to finally feel him out about his supposed evidence of human rights abuses and his connection to leftist terrorist organizations. Unfortunately, now she wasn't sure she wanted to hear what he had to say. And if she did, she wasn't sure she would be able to honestly report the answer.

"Fuck it! What's started is started." She pulled open the door to her workstation so quickly it startled the rookie reporter whose cubby was nearby. She glanced at him distractedly. "Sorry."

"Umm..." He was too late to reply. Jessica was already halfway to the elevator before his thoughts assembled. *She talked to me!*

British Consulate – 3rd Avenue: New York, New York

"The Prime Minister will see you now." Grey's personal secretary was a sleek older woman who wore a flowing silver pantsuit and long painted nails. Jessica arranged her hair behind her ears and followed the secretary down the hall of the well-appointed British Consulate – the last of its kind in New York. Suddenly, she felt somewhat under-dressed.

Despite the apparent animosity of the British Prime Minister toward the Fein administration, he insisted on maintaining the consulate citing "the spirit of negotiation." Conversely, President Fein tried to use the presence of the British in the country as an example of the hospitality of the United States toward the international community.

"Good afternoon, Ms. Butler. It's a pleasure to meet you." Tyler Grey stood from behind his cherry desk and crossed stealthily toward Jessica with his hand extended. She shook it. His grip was firm but not crushing. His smile was sincere and filled his eyes with an aura of calm joviality. "Diana, would you bring us some tea, please?"

"Certainly, Minister Grey." Diana gave Jessica a sideways glance before departing.

Tyler Grey gestured Jessica toward a chair. "I'm rather surprised you contacted me. Total Wire is, shall we say, the pinnacle of corporate news in the United States. I haven't found there to be much interest in hearing opinions that differ from government or lobbyist lines."

"I'm working on an op-ed piece." She lied easily.

Grey wandered over to his desk to retrieve a manila envelop from a desk drawer. Jessica slid her gaze up and down his lean form. He wasn't wearing a jacket. His crisp custom Italian shirt draped neatly around his waist and shoulders. He returned to the sitting area carrying the envelope. As he passed, she could faintly smell his cologne. He sat and looked her straight in the eyes. "So, why are you really here?"

Jessica hesitated. She was not used to such directness from a politician. At that moment, Diana returned carrying a tray of tea and scones. The cream was pure white, not tinted tan like the pasteurized GMO stock she was used to. *On British soil in the Consulate*. She thought and looked forward to the savory delight.

Diana arranged the cups and plates for the two of them and offered Jessica a box with a selection of fine teas imported from India. It had been a long time since she'd had access to such treasure. Scanning the box with the large eyes of a child, she chose a fragrant Darjeeling. Grey handed her the plate of scones. Her hand brushed his fingertips as she took it from him. She selected a cinnamon scone and placed it on the small plate before her. When Diana had distributed the napkins, she retired once again to the reception area, closing the door behind her.

There was silence punctuated with the sound of glass clinking and spoons stirring while Grey and Jessica steeped their tea and added the requisite cream and sugar. Jessica closed her eyes when she took her first sip. The strong flavor captured her like none of the stale manufactured replica teas ever could. The cream coated her mouth luxuriously. She sighed quietly.

Grey tapped his spoon against the top of his cup and placed it in the saucer. The noise aroused Jessica back to the business at hand. She opened her eyes. Grey sat reclined confidently in his chair his eyes piercing hers over the top of his cup as he took a sip. "So. Here we are."

Jessica straightened and set down her cup. The scone was calling to her from the plate. *I'll bet it's made with real butter.* She tapped into her Mate and opened a new segment for the interview. She hovered her uni-dedo covered pinky over the controls. "Well, Minister Grey, you have made some hefty allegations against the United States over the past couple of years, but have provided no evidence to support them. In addition, there is growing concern regarding your potential connection to leftist terrorist organizations in the United States."

Grey laughed. "Terrorist organizations? Where do you get your information, Ms. Butler? President Fein's spin room?"

"It's not far-fetched."

"If you knew me, it would be."

"So, tell me about yourself."

"It wouldn't matter. Not now. I can see this interview is just another ruse to get b-roll for more American rhetoric." Grey placed his cup on the tray and broke off a bite of his scone.

"I know you were at the gathering of Integrationist cronies on a nomadic gambling yacht last month."

Grey stopped chewing.

"I was there." Jessica stated, calmly

Grey swallowed. "It wasn't what it looked like."

"So, you admit to being there."

"If you don't have footage already, you'll make some."

Jessica pursed her lips to suppress a smile and made eye contact again with the scone.

"I don't know what they're planning, if that's what you're here for. They're a necessary evil. I allied myself with them to finish collecting the evidence the Free International Organization is demanding." Grey took another sip of his tea. "Honestly, I don't believe they are a threat to you or your precious President Fein. Most of them are just kids trying get a better shot in life than they have. They want good jobs and a family. They want to exercise control over their own life decisions. It's no different than anyone else in the world. It's all about control. They don't have any and they want some."

"Well they can't go about seizing control by bombing parks and office towers." Jessica countered. She stabbed at the portable with the uni-dedo distractedly.

Minister Grey reversed the cross of his legs and spread his arms over the back of the wide back cushions. "I often wonder that the contradictions of this country's rhetoric don't make every last one of you go mad. You grow up spoon-fed on promises of freedom and liberty. Then you get the bait and switch by the time you grow up. You've lost your right to privacy. You've lost your freedom of assembly. You can't even grow a vegetable garden because you've all been sold on the idea that natural food is, what, dangerous? Come on. How daft are you people? Try the scone. I promise. It won't kill you."

Jessica obliged. The sweet bread crumbled in her mouth. There was a depth and complexity to the taste that she hadn't experienced since she was a child.

"Do you even want to know the truth?"

Jessica paused and took another sip of tea. "What truth is that?"

"Do you want to know the truth about wealth and power in the United States of America?"

Jessica was silent. Grey appraised her carefully before continuing. *Does he know I'm OCD?* "What's in the envelope, Minister Grey?"

Grey looked at the envelope in his lap and back at Jessica. He stood up and walked to a control panel on the wall. He tapped a command and a calm electronic woman's voice stated, "Entering silent mode". The room's security cameras retracted into the walls with a soft whirring sound. A glowing blue beam swept the room for listening devices. Two beeps signaled the all clear. When this was finished, Grey walked to behind where Jessica was sitting. He leaned over and snatched her Belt Mate from the table.

"Hey!"

He leaned across her and stroked his fingers along her hand, peeling the uni-dedo off as he did. Before standing straight again, he turned his head to Jessica's ear and whispered, "For your eyes only". Then he dropped the manila package into her lap.

Jessica watched Grey make his way around the table to his seat. "Three years ago, my office received an asylum request from an American clone. At first I thought it was just a typical civil liberties case about the general state of disenfranchisement of the clone workforce. Reading his request, I realized I was in error. To begin with, this clone could read and write with great facility and he expressed himself with a clarity that would not be possible using typical drone generation techniques."

Jessica fingered the envelope in her hands. Grey took another bite of his scone and continued. "This clone told me about massive clone farms where the wealthy and connected go to generate a store of spare parts to forestall their old age. He told me about the horror of having portions of his liver removed multiple times to cure and re-cure his primary of the Hepatitis C he got on a sex trip to Central America. Others had lost limbs and hearts and kidneys and lived their lives immobilized in bed hooked to artificial life support systems."

"If this is true," Jessica interrupted, "why would they allow the clones to maintain such high level thinking capacity? Hell, why not just grow clones without any brain at all?"

"Wouldn't you want to recover from an inoperable brain tumor, if you could? How about Multiple Sclerosis? Parkinson's Disease? Despite our best attempts, the brain continues to elude us with its mysterious disease processes. The only thing standing in the way of accessing the power of a new brain is the inability to transfer all of the information from the Primary into the clone mind. But my young asylum-seeker felt they were close to being able to make such a transfer. He feared for his life because doctors had recently discovered an adrenal tumor in his Primary's brain." Grey stood and paced to the window. "Imagine having that kind of technology. That kind of power! To be able to take an entire life lived and transfer it to another individual. My God, imagine what horrors humankind could inflict on itself, if that were possible. Can you imagine such a thing?"

There was a lump in Jessica's stomach where the scone had landed. She stood quickly, dumping both her napkin and the envelope to the floor. "Minister Grey, I believe you are in serious need of some psychological counseling. If you think I am going to believe…"

Grey crossed the distance between them in two paces. "It's here. It's all right here." He picked up the envelope and pressed it to her chest. "And this copy is my gift to you. The original is making its way to the FIO Council on Human Rights as we speak—anonymously and under heavy cover. I agreed to this interview because it doesn't matter any more. It doesn't matter what happens to me. The evidence is in place and the world needs to know. The American people need to know."

Jessica tore open the envelope and dumped a small plank into her hand. She looked at Grey questioningly. His face was set in anticipation, just inches from hers. "What do you say, Ms. Butler?" His lips pressed against each other forming a thin, white line and released again.

He really cares about this. God, Jessica, stop it! She grabbed her Belt Mate from him and turned away. "I'll take it under advisement, Minister Grey." She whirled across the room and out the door.

Able McGable's Diner – Broadway and 57th Street: New York, New York

Jessica sat forward in the ice cream parlor-style chair, leaning her elbows on the bumpy glass surface of the table, looking intensely into Boo's eyes. Cheery '50s rock and roll poured out of the vintage jukebox. The walls were covered with candy stripes of red and white. A woman sitting at the table closest to the door giggled obsequiously at her date's apparently brilliant comedy. Leftover ice cream melted around the spoon in the glass sitting in front of her. Jessica kneaded her face with her hands and sighed.

"So, he just hands you this plank and says take it? What if you run off with it? Then what will he do?" Boo asked gravely.

"Well, he implied that this one isn't the original."

"Where is the original?" Boo cut in.

"I don't know. Isn't that terrible though? Can you imagine just laying around waiting to be carved up like a pork roast? It would be awful."

"Hey, chill out, girlfriend. It's only clones, you know. It's not like they're doing it to people, you know? Jeez."

Jessica looked at Boo and felt like she was looking at a stranger. *Is this really my best friend? Maybe almost dying has changed me.* She sighed.

A red and white clad waitress with retro horn-rimmed glasses danced up to their table. "Can I get you anything else?" She asked, without stopping her bouncing.

Jessica put her head in her hands. Boo replied. "Just the check, please."

"Sure thing!" The waitress' teeth glowed from a wide smile as she prepped the sum and scanned Boo's EAS. "Come back soon!" She called over her shoulder as she boogied away.

"You need to relax." Boo stated matter-of-factly. "Ever since you were in the hospital you've been a little, I don't know, edgy."

"I guess you're right." Jessica tapped her fingers on the café table. The sound was lost in the din of customers around them. "I shouldn't be talking about this in public any way. Not to you. Not to anyone."

Boo leaned in conspiratorially. "Come on. Let's get wired!"

Jessica shook her head rapidly to clear her thoughts, and pushed the sundae cup away from her. "Sounds good."

Pinz 'n' Needlz at Battery Park: New York, New York

Boo took Jessica to a new club by the water. Pinz 'n' Needlz had the biggest dance floor in New York and a harbor view.

Boo always knew where to find action in the city. It was early enough that the dance floor was only half full. The lighting was blue and purple with sporadic black lights to add an otherworldly glow to the edges of the bar and the objects d'art scattered between the couches. A group of young ladies had deliberately worn bright white bras underneath black mesh tops to entice drinks out of the single men, however, none of them were quite physically fit enough to be viewed so intimately. Jessica was glad they all wore solid skirts. She didn't want to imagine the state of their thongs.

Waitresses were circulating freely with trays of straight up Pollie, vodka and tonic water. This barely-legal mixture was first concocted somewhere in Seattle and had been responsible for the overdose deaths of three University of Washington freshmen before the state government recognized the danger. By then, it was too late. Recipes for the drink had been posted to the web with instructions for reducing the reactivity of the Pollie using common household products like glycerin soap and mouthwash in preparation for mixing with alcohol. Some states put a higher legal drinking age on the new drinks. Others set limits on the amount of Pollie that could be served in a single glass and imposed a tax on each drink sold. It didn't affect Jessica either way. She was plenty old enough by any standard and had enough cash to buy as many as she could tolerate. Jessica lifted two of the baseless vials from the waitress' tray and handed one to Boo. She bleeped her payment and tip and raised her glass. They clinked.

The world began to spin just as the tempo of the music began to rise. She felt herself slipping into a comfortable haze, bumping and grinding with the growing crowd en masse. She felt someone's hands around her waist. They danced and turned. Her mystery partner brushed his face against hers and she felt the roughness of his five o'clock shadow run up and down her cheek. They swayed and gyrated with the music, hypnotized by the lights, the Pollies, and each other. He bought her another drink and she turned toward him, nodding her head into his shoulder. He held her gently. He could have tried anything that he wanted, but he didn't. She felt safe and warm and sliding, sliding into oblivion. Beat, beat, beat of the music. Beat, beat, beat of his heart.

Beep, beep beep of Mabel's alert system?

Jessica Butler's Condominium – Amsterdam and 61st Street: New York, New York

"Yes. Jessica. You get up now. Yes?"

"Hmmmph?" Jessica's face was planted deep in her pillow. And her nose was running.

"Yes. Jessica. There is an important call for you. Yes? I will get your Mate."

Jessica opened her eyes, then reduced to a squint. Everything in the room had strange glowing, fuzzy edges. Her mouth felt like her teeth had taken up knitting. Jessica managed to pull herself into a sitting position just as Mabel returned. *Wasn't it right next to my bed?*

"Important call. Yes?"

The Mate almost slipped out of her fumbling hands as she tapped in. "Hello, this is Jessica Butler."

Instead of the greeting she expected, the Mate began squealing and squeaking at an appalling volume. Jessica was momentarily frozen in shock. Suddenly, her limbs went slack and she slumped to the floor.

"Yes. Jessica. It is time to get up. You look sad on the floor. Yes? I will make you some eggs and sausage. Wake up. I will cut some fresh strawberries and…"

"I don't need strawberries!"

"Maybe you would like…"

"Stop it. Just go away!"

"I will get your clothes."

"No!"

"I will get your bathrobe."

"No! Stop!"

"Yes!" Mabel screeched.

Jessica stared at Mabel, surprised. If a robot could be said to have a will, Mabel asserted hers over Jessica. *What the fuck?*

"I will get your clothes. Yes?" Mabel repeated placidly this time.

"Yes." Jessica assented.

After she was dressed, Jessica wandered to the living room her mind in a haze. *Wow, I really overdid it last night. I really have to stop.* She paused in front of her projection platform. *What was I working on? Italy. Wasn't there some story in Italy?*

Mabel was buzzing around the apartment dusting and vacuuming at a pace that surpassed the most manic routines programmed for when Jessica was expecting sudden guests. She couldn't take it any more. She needed to get out of the house. Circumventing Mabel as she made her fifth pass across the living room floor, she reached the door.

Once outside, her head began to clear, but she still couldn't remember what she had been planning on doing that day. *Damn! It's like an itch I can't scratch.* She pocketed her Mate and heard it clink against something in the bottom of her pocket. She pulled it out and found the plank. "See, this should mean something to me, right?"

She walked down the winding road in her complex to a grassy spot where there was a bench and a stand of flowers. She sat and loaded the plank into the Mate's auxiliary port and performed a nanoscan before accessing it.

An assortment of files was available to her. She opened one of the spreadsheets and found a list of names. Each was paired and labeled "Primary" and "Clone age". Various body parts were listed in columns under the rubric "Harvested". Dates were scattered throughout these columns spanning time from the present back about ten or twenty years, at first glance. Jessica knew this was important, but she wasn't sure why.

She closed the file and opened another labeled "Chambers". This was a scanned schematic drawing showing what looked similar to a standard hospital room. Extensive centralized equipment for life support and enteral feeding had been added, however, giving Jessica the impression that she had stumbled into Dracula's castle. Notes in the margins throughout the page referred to the need for easy access and portable surgical equipment. She scrolled down the document. Other floors of the facility were represented here. At this point it became clear that the other rooms had been underground. The designs for these rooms were open and airy with plenty of window space. Furniture was represented throughout the space and notes referred to safes for patient valuables and easy to digest colors for the walls and upholstery. *Why do I have this?*

As she opened a third file, a man jogged by wearing shorts with the Union Jack on the butt. The back of his t-shirt displayed a tasteless cartoon disparagement of the British Prime Minister. *The British Prime Minister...*She turned her gaze toward the document she had just opened and her eyes glazed over in terror. She remembered everything.

The pictures on the screen depicted gruesome scenes of people tied in beds hooked up to machinery. They were minimally clothed. Feeding tubes ran from their guts to a centralized tap in the wall. Catheters snaked out from between their legs and to the floor where they emptied into a central drain. Most of the unfortunate souls displayed large scars and wounds that were poorly healed. One man had clearly been stripped of most of the skin off of his right thigh. A thin gauze of cheesecloth-like material covered the site. Jessica felt herself retch as the bile rose up from her stomach. *I don't believe it. I don't believe it.* She repeated to herself over and over. *It can't be true.*

She flipped through the pictures furiously looking for any sign of doctoring, but the data seals were all intact. The last picture stopped her cold. In the bed, was a dead-ringer of Tripp Thompson. It's right hand was missing, the carelessly stapled, scarred stump rested on the sheet at its side. Jessica recalled the thin filament of scar around Tripp's right wrist. She tapped the screen to blank, doubled over and vomited into the flowers.

She didn't know where to run, but she decided to go back to her condo and put together a multi-purpose gig bag while she thought about it. When she opened the door, Mabel was on her almost immediately.

"Yes. I will make your lunch."

"No, Mabel. Not now."

"Sit. Yes? I will make your lunch."

"Mabel, stop."

"Sit. Yes?"

"End program!" Mabel went silent. "Charge. Maintenance program 2" Mabel rolled off to her charging cubby. Jessica heard the system beep to alert her that it had been engaged.

Jessica shook her head and turned her attention to her preparations. She opened her desk drawer, pulled out the jumble of note pads and pens that were piled inside and flipped open the false bottom panel. Quickly, she gathered her most universally useful gear. She pulled out the microcell charges first, along with several magnetic pulse charges, a lock pick kit, and particle mask. Then she clicked the panel back in place and covered it again with the office supplies. Turning to her closet, she dug behind her largely unused skirts and pulled a few lengths of scaling rope from their hooks on the wall and grounding clamps--just in case.

Spinning toward her nightstand, Jessica almost tripped on her pile of clothes from the night before. *Strange that Mabel didn't catch this.* She grabbed a velvet bag out of the top drawer and slid a four by two amplified palm Taser into her hand. The finger rings rattled against themselves. She pushed the two white buttons at the diagonal corners. Fully charged. Thread wire and several pairs of specialized floaters and dedos completed the set. She arranged everything expertly on her person to avoid raising suspicion that she was armed. The larger items she organized into her favorite black shoulder pack and strapped it on.

Jessica looked around the room completing a mental checklist. Backtracking to the desk, she collected a square, padded storage wallet from beside her console. She opened it to check the contents: two hack planks, one standard US Government issued to all OCD, FBI and CIA agents, the other a Brazilian cello tab designed to build a virtually undetectable ferret interface into any system capitalizing on the weaknesses of their maintenance protocols. Strictly illegal. She plucked the plank from its soft casing. *What information did I need this badly?* She dumped the storage wallet containing the planks into her vest pocket.

She was about to go to the hall closet to look for a sturdier pair of shoes when she heard the error message coming from Mabel's cubby. "Hermit line detected. Remote host contact attempted. Abort?"

Jessica turned slowly.

"Hermit line detected. Remote host contact attempted. Abort?"

She walked slowly across the living room toward the kitchen.

"Hermit line detected. Remote host contact attempted. Abort?"

She stopped in front of Mabel's charging cubby and scanned the screen full of data as it scrolled by. It appeared that Mabel's programming had been infiltrated with a virus to allow remote operation and execution of commands with visual and auditory feedback to whoever had planted it.

"Hermit line detected. Remote host contact attempted. Abort?"

"Abort."

"System aborting. Remote host disconnected. Deleting code. Reset to last known safe programming date?"

"Yes."

"Resetting to last known safe programming date. June 25, 2062. Command complete. Please wait."

But Jessica did not wait. She grabbed her gun, silencer and ammo from the drawer next to the refrigerator, bolted to her porter and shot down the highway determined to find out who was playing with her mind and why.

West Side Highway: New York, New York

It was fully dark before Jessica stopped driving in circles around the city. Instinct told her hours before where to look for the information she needed, but utter disgust had kept her away. Her hands were cold and slippery. She could intellectually acknowledge that the betrayal she felt was unreasonable. She had, until recently, been a part of this conspiracy. Though the confirmation of spare parts farms seemed to be new information to her, she had been a high level operative in terms of supporting the infrastructure that allowed such places to thrive. Given what she'd seen in Delph's retrieved memories, she was not convinced she would have previously cared, even if she did know about the farms. In all likelihood, she would have negotiated a clone for herself in exchange for her silence and called it a day.

Jessica turned around at the next interchange and headed straight for TWNS headquarters.

Total Wire News Service – Manhattan Bureau: New York, New York

The night guard at the front desk was used to seeing Jessica come and go at all hours. She waved her photo ID casually in front of him as she burst past.

"Hot lead?" he asked nonchalantly.

"You could say that." She called back without stopping and ripped her ID through the scanner. The door clicked open and she was gone.

Once inside the secure area, Jessica slowed her pace to a casual businesslike briskness. Most of the offices she passed were dark. The overheads were dimmed to conservation level, turning every shadow into a potential intruder. She swept her eyes back and forth eyeing the security cameras that pried into every corner of the office and corridor. She laid her hand casually on her black shoulder bag as she stepped into the elevator.

Emerging on the twenty-fifth floor, she noted several workstations were in use. She quickly analyzed their relationship to her workspace and Tripp's office. One late-nighter was working at the far end of the floor near the corner window looking out over the hotel next door. Another was smack in the middle of the carousel of cubbies. She could avoid both easily by using the walkway on the edge next to Tripp's office. Avoiding the third would be a little more difficult. It was that rookie who ogled her obsequiously whenever she passed. He was nice enough, but she didn't have time to deal with his questions right now. And she certainly didn't want him to remember she was here. His cubby opened up directly across the aisle from her workstation.

Jessica slipped into the cubby nearest the elevator and took out her ferret clip. In less than a minute she had tapped into the server streams of all three of her colleagues. She entered video mode and keyed in a command to capture visual of the room around each worker. Then she overlaid the visual into their floaters remotely. This was a feature available to help reporters who couldn't concentrate with the visual din of movement in the real world while they were tapping the stream. Few people used it and most of the newbies had no idea that it was an available option.

With the overlays in place, she scurried around the perimeter of the floor. She arrived at her workstation door and tapped it to enter. The door clicked softly.

The rookie turned his head and looked straight at her. "Hello?"

Jessica froze, uncertain if the overlay had failed. Seeing nothing. The rookie shrugged and turned back to his work. She opened the door and closed it quietly. As she did, she looked out the one-way security glass. The rookie turned around again. His brows were furrowed over the top of his floaters. He stood and turned to scan the room. When he saw the 360-degree view didn't change from his sitting position, he took the floaters off and looked at them suspiciously.

"Shit!" Jessica cursed under her breath.

She watched the rookie leave his cubby and start walking around the floor. Jessica knew she didn't have much time. The rookie was young, but he wasn't stupid. She dropped herself into the cradle chair and had barely booted the system before she began punching buttons. The first command cut power to the overhead lights, but not to the workstations where her two colleagues worked happily away. She opened her vest and pulled out the expensive Brazilian cello tab. She opened the console port and slipped the plank in place. She fingered the access code and a broad, colorful control panel opened in front of her. It took her a moment to find the language access that would translate the features from Portuguese to English, but once she did, the program was intuitive.

She traced the fiber connections from her station to Tripp's workstation, using several way stations in Singapore and Iceland. He had a personal firewall with very sensitive trip switches. Jessica's plank program was designed to create back doors using the maintenance loops created to self-correct the system when parts of it became corrupt. The program worked away spitting out convincing, but fake code to tell Tripp's machine that a new virus was coming in over the newswire. She counted down the five seconds it took the workstation to switch into maintenance mode. With the maintenance string initiated, the hack plank slipped in a line of code opening a portal to the outside.

COMMAND: Assign portal – device or port number.

Jessica entered the string to network Tripp's workstation to her Belt Mate.

COMMAND ACCEPTED: Device accepted.

Jessica had only a moment to read the final message as the cello tab released a worm into Tripp's system to devour all evidence of its own presence. Finally, it placed a common easily breakable virus in an obvious place for the maintenance program to find, destroy, and quit.

Jessica smiled. She checked the Mate's menu and saw the icon representing hermit access to all of Tripp's personal files. She stuffed it back in her pocket, removed the cello tab and looked around her workstation room with nostalgia. There was one photograph on the wall. It was a picture of herself and Tripp the first summer after he hired her. They were sitting in an outdoor bar in Cancun. He had his arm draped casually around her shoulder. They both held up obnoxiously large margaritas.

They had just finished shutting down a cell of ex-patriots trying to hack into media outlets in Florida to influence that year's state elections. The prisoners had been rounded up and sent to an undisclosed location in Nevada. Jessica and Tripp stayed an extra week to relax and enjoy the sweat-inducing heat. She felt nostalgic, for those times, for the simplicity. Everything had been one way or another back then. She always knew where she stood, what she wanted and what made her feel good. She was sure she was a servant of the common good. She was sure she was a patriot and a hero. Now, she wasn't sure of anything.

And Tripp, who had been her greatest supporter and mentor...looking into his eyes in the picture, she recognized he had become a predator and a user. Or maybe he always had been. *What else is he hiding from me?* How far would he take her, how much of her health and welfare would he be willing to sacrifice to meet his own ends? *Well, now I'll know. I'll find out everything and take it from there.* An unfamiliar tightness formed in her neck, squeezing her throat. She tore the photograph down from the wall and stuffed it into her pocket. Finally, she turned back to the programming screen and entered a kill code that would destroy all of her personal files on the workstation and reformat the working drive. *Clean start. As if I was never here.*

She secured her gear and slipped the shoulder bag back into place. She peeked out the small window in the center of her office door. The rookie had not returned to his station. She scanned the shadows for signs of activity. He wasn't there. The other two workstations silently hummed away, their controllers fully occupied. She cracked the door open and slipped out into the aisle. Cautiously, she crept around the side toward Tripp's office. Scanning. Scanning. She saw nothing until she passed the workstation where she had left the interface. The rookie's legs stuck out through the doorway and she tripped over them, stifling a grunt.

The rookie stood on his knees and turned toward her. "Jessica! I didn't know you were here. Look what I found. I was just sitting at my workstation, when…"

Her hand moved too quickly for him to see the palm-sized Lightning Bug she had fastened across her fingers. It hit him with 500 milliamps mid-throat and he crumpled to the floor, silenced by his collapsed airway. He never knew it was the woman he adored who killed him. She collected the ferret clip and reassembled the workstation to look untouched. Just in case, she tucked the rookie's legs inside the cubby door.

Jessica emitted a magnetic pulse charge as she exited the elevator. The cameras went black. On hearing her, the security guard looked up and raised his eyebrows in surprise. "That didn't take very long tonight, huh?" She passed him without a word and shot him in the forehead. He lay gracefully over the side of the counter drizzling a stream of dark red. She disappeared into the night.

Wirespace: Delph Crane's Personal Nucleus

Delph was pacing back and forth across the VR grass in the perfect sunlit park he had created for all of his most important decision-making. "They're onto her. They are beginning to realize that the tracers she's throwing are less than benign. Someone is feeding them information. They know they can't trust her any more. We have to bring her in."

Marcelo looked at Delph suspiciously, but his sunglasses hid the full extent of his skepticism. "And how do we know we can trust her? Did you ever think that maybe she *should* be terminated? Maybe she's too much of a loose cannon to be good for anything now." Marcelo leaned back in the padded chaise lounge. Delph continued circling him.

"She's changed. I can't put my finger on it. Something happened in the conversion process that changed things. She's analyzing things in a way she hasn't before. She's seeing connections and consequences."

"That could be a good thing or it could be a bad thing. The bottom line is, we don't know whose side she's on any more." Marcelo dragged his fingertips along the brushed metal of the chaise lounge's armrest. It felt goddamned real. He'd consider jettisoning Delph and his crazy obsession for Jessica Butler, if the guy weren't the best programmer in the country. "In the end, Jessica Butler always plays for her own team, in her own league and everyone else be damned."

Delph stepped into Marcelo's line of sight, just a little close for comfort. "Don't forget. I've got a straight feed. I saw her reaction to the package Grey gave her. She's changed. She's grown a conscience or something. I don't know how and I don't know why, but we need her. She has the training. She has the knowledge."

"Yeah and maybe you can start getting some again."

"I get plenty."

Marcelo raised an eyebrow. "You're thinking with your dick, Crane. Don't forget, this is the woman who was going to kill me. In fact, she thinks I'm dead as we speak. I'd kind of like to leave it that way."

"Hell, *I* was going to kill you that day." He smiled at Marcelo ironically. "And see how well we get along?"

Marcelo picked some stems of grass from the ground and began twisting them in his fingers.

"They're after her, Marcelo. They're going to find her and they're going to kill her. We can use her knowledge and experience on our side. She recognizes that she can't trust them any more. She will come to us and she will help us. I'm sure of it."

"What the hell do you see in this chick?"

Delph stared Marcelo down. "It hardly matters, does it? You know we've really got no choice."

"If she screws us over. I'll kill you, I swear I will. Slowly."

"And I know you don't lie. So, let's go get her."

Marcelo got up and walked toward the tree line. He blinked out of the simulation five steps later, but his voice lingered to have the final word. "If you screw this up, Crane, I swear…" and he was gone.

Jessica Butler's Condominium – Amsterdam and 61st Street: New York, New York

Jessica tore in the front door blindly. She dashed for her Wireman, hooked up her Belt Mate, and started a bulk download. She tossed her shoulder bag onto the bed and was halfway to the closet at the far end of the living room before she noticed Boo sitting calmly on the sofa. "What's up, chica?"

Jessica stopped in her tracks and turned abruptly. Words tumbled from her mouth in general confusion. "Boo! What the hell are you doing…I can't talk. You have to get out of here. You, we, aren't safe any more. Just go."

"Woh, calm down, Sister. Start from the beginning. What's going on?" Boo remained calmly reclined with her legs tucked underneath her.

"Something's happened to me, Boo. I'm not the same person I was before I was hurt in that attack. If I could just remember…"

"What's past is past, Jess. Let it go. Let's go for some coffee." Boo cooed languidly.

"This is serious, Boo. Someone knocked me out this morning with some kind of electronic pulse through my phone. I woke up; it was like I'd been mentally raped. There were more holes in my memory. Something's going on here and I have to leave."

"Why don't you talk to your boss about it? Maybe he can track down whoever is doing this to you."

"No. I can't." Jessica stated simply. She grabbed a duffle bag from the closet and jogged back to her bedroom. She ejected the Mate and entered a kill code on the workstation, which then began devouring itself.

Jessica was throwing clothing and toiletries ad hoc into the duffle bag when Boo flopped herself onto the bed near the bag. "Will you at least tell me where you're going?" She asked with tense concern.

"I don't know. I'll probably check in at the Super 8 up on 180th street for now, and take it from there." She zipped up the duffle, throwing it and her shoulder bag around her. She looked up at Boo, who was picking at her nails distractedly.

"Well, keep in touch, okay?"

"Yes? Jessica. You are home. Friend is waiting. You would like to eat something. Yes?" Mabel stood in the doorway expectantly.

Jessica looked at Boo. "Take care of Mabel for me?"

"Sure." Boo paused, "Jessica..." but it was too late. Jessica had pushed past Mabel and was closing the door behind her.

"Yes? Friend. You would like something to eat. Yes?"

"Yes, Mabel. I'll have a sandwich. How about egg salad?"

"Yes. Friend likes egg salad. Enter name?"

"Name. Boo."

"Yes. Friend. Boo. Egg salad." Mabel ambled away contentedly.

Boo tapped into her Mate with a rarely-accessed connection code.

Highway 9A North: New York, New York

Jessica sped along the crossroad and merged with the traffic on Route 9A. She called up an audio connection to Rene Stone's personal line. Nothing. Not even a message center. She decided to take a risk and called the main number of his front operation in Westchester. "Stone Construction. How may I help you?"

"Rene Stone, please."

"I'm sorry. He's not in today. Would you like to leave a message?"

Jessica's thoughts were racing. "This is...his Aunt Jessica from...Houston. We haven't spoken for some time, but I have to reach him about...some urgent family business."

There was a pause on the other end of the line. "I'm sorry to have to tell you this, m'am, but Mr. Stone is in the hospital with encephalitis."

"What? No! Oh, God." Jessica squeezed her temples between two fingers and flipped the porter into auto drive. "It can't be true."

"I'm sorry. I would have thought someone would have told you by now."

"Where is he staying?"

"I'm sorry. We haven't been told. Apparently the strain is highly infectious. We should know more by the end of the week, if you'd like to call back."

"I...I have to go." Jessica cut off the connection before the secretary could reply.

She initiated a search in her Mate for CRANE, DELPH. Nothing. *Think. Think.* Her eyes narrowed. She swapped over to the hidden core drive and activated the hermit line into Tripp's workstation. She searched again.

CRANE, DELPH – (960) 5864-5783. *Well, well, well, Mr. Crane. How deep are you in the mud?* Jessica drilled down through the search results.

AGENT PROFILE - Activated May 13, 2055. Specialty: information technology, licit and illicit research capabilities, decryption expert, programming of custom applications. T-Col project team: designed and operates fishhook access to Convert homing devices. Tier 3 Security Clearance.

Jessica scanned the information again. She would have to consider this very carefully. She pulled the porter off into the parking lot of the Super 8. She needed a good night's sleep and some time to think about her next move.

An Undisclosed Location: A Secure Communication Line

"She's on the run," the Observer stated. "She's become a liability. We have to bring her in."

"You're going to terminate her." Delph answered definitively.

"There's no choice now."

"Come on, Tripp."

"Don't use my name here."

Delph wiped his palm over his eyes. "You know you don't want to do this. She's your girl." Delph guessed it was fruitless to play the nostalgia card, but he had to try. "You brought her to your inner circle. Mentored her."

Tripp Thompson took a measured breath in and out. "There's too much at stake and you know it. We've got to take her out."

Shit! "Maybe we could…"

"Just send the kill signal. I'll assemble a retrieval team." Tripp waited silently for confirmation.

"Yes sir." Delph conceded. The connection terminated without further comment from the Observer. "Well, here we go." Delph said to himself.

He turned his attention to his virtual private network and began sending snakes into the main control system to copy every bit of information. He downloaded the most recent kill codes into his folio and pocketed it. Through his private nucleus, he sent a tracer to locate her. Within two minutes, he was out the door and on the highway.

Super 8 Motel – 180th Street: New York, New York

Jessica reclined on the bed wearing form-fitting sweatpants and a spandex top. The room smelled like mothballs, but it was clean. She carefully lifted the last few chopsticks of soba to her mouth and slurped up the rest of the broth. She watched the television incredulously. TWNS was broadcasting a news story on the activities of Mark Brimmer. He was currently standing on a stage somewhere in Des Moines with his arm around President Fein. Several thousand supporters, including many former Intergrationist leaders were cheering and raising their arms.

TWNS Newswire: 08 | 06 | 2062 | 18:31:22

Three thousand supporters turned out in Iowa to celebrate the newly reformulated administration of Fein and Brimmer. After an initial rivalry that ended in a heartfelt speech of support, Mark Brimmer, founder of the Integrationist Party has accepted President Fein's request that he join him in Washington as Vice President.

Mr. Brimmer had this to say about his new position: "I'm so proud to be a part of this country's turn toward unity, prosperity and safety. The President has compiled a comprehensive package of security enhancement measures and technologies that are transferable to industry. It's an exciting time to be an American."

President Fein was left with the difficult task of finding a replacement Veep after current Vice President, decorated war hero General Winston Duke decided to retire after a forty-year career in politics. More on General Duke's retirement speech in the next hour.

Super 8 Motel – 180th Street: New York, New York

In his porter in the parking lot of the Super 8 Motel, Delph's fingers flew through the air above his lap as he prepared a transfer sequence to move Jessica's remote programming from the OCD mainframe to his hidden VPN. At best, he knew he had five minutes until Tripp's men discovered her hiding place. After that, OCD cleaners would be crawling all over the hotel—inside and out. The system monitor bleeped "ready". Delph checked the assigned preferences one more time.

Inside the hotel, Jessica muted the television and lay on her back staring at the ceiling. She couldn't remember a time when she felt so overwhelmed and alone. Without any family to call her own, she had thrown herself into her work. Tripp became her friend and confidante, the one person she thought she could trust. He trained her to be strong and resilient. She was no more than a tool to him.

Then there was Boo. Even her best friend from grade school was acting strangely. There was something about Boo's surprise visit earlier that disturbed her. It wasn't that it was so unusual to see Boo sitting in her living room when she got home. She was accustomed to Mabel letting Tripp and Boo in when they arrived. *Friend. Hold on.* She thought to herself. *Mabel called Boo "friend". Why would she do that? As my best friend, Mabel should already know Boo by name. If she didn't, why would Mabel let an unnamed "friend" enter the house?* Jessica knew that her security protocols were tighter than that.

Then Jessica remembered the malfunction and having to reset. She remembered the attempted encroachment of the "remote host". *Last known safe date? When would that have been?* Finally, she remembered. She performed a complete diagnostic, optimization and back up three days before the incident in Freedom Park. It had been her birthday and it was the only way to keep Mabel from trying to throw her a party. *But if Mabel didn't know Boo before I went to the hospital, when did she meet her? Where the hell did Boo come from?*

In the far corner of the parking lot, Delph clicked on a shimmering red icon labeled "kill connection". He leapt out of his porter and ran for the cover of the motel fire exit.

Jessica wilted against the scratchy orange comforter. All of the borders between objects in the room began to blend together and swirl. *Now what?* She thought as she blacked out again.

Delph connected the passkey emulator to the archaic security panel to the right of the door and heard a light click. The panel's status light turned green. He slipped into the stairwell and pulled the door shut behind him, keeping his head turned and the brim of his hat low in case of security cameras. He left the stairwell at the first floor and crossed toward the elevators. He picked up a complementary bag of Pollie-laced crackers on his way through the lobby and blended with the other guests on his way to the fourth floor.

As Delph exited the elevator on Jessica's floor, three black vans pulled into the the the motel parking lot. Several heavily armed commandos emerged from each. Using hand signals to communicate, they fanned out toward the motel's various exits.

Jessica was passed out cold in the bed when Delph opened the door to her room. She was wearing plain black sweatpants and a dark purple tee shirt. He quickly pulled the edges of the thin bedspread around Jessica and rolled her up like a giant burrito.

Delph slipped into a service hallway to avoid meeting anyone and having to explain the human-sized bundle that was slung over his shoulder. In a stroke of luck, the service elevator stood open and empty when Delph approached. Just as he reached the street level exit, a light clicking sounded from the other side of the door. He saw the exit alarm light flicker off. "Shit!" he hissed under his breath. *How did they get here so quickly?* He turned the corner and ran down the stairs to the basement. He leaned against the wall under the final flight of stairs in order to take some of the weight off of his now throbbing shoulder.

Moments later, the door opened and a team of six men in recon gear slid discreetly up the stairs toward Jessica's room. When they passed, Delph dashed up the stairs toward the door, trying to contain the effortful stridor of his gasps. He was halfway to his waiting porter before the OCD operatives even realized that Jessica was gone. Delph flopped her into the passenger seat arranging her like a napping weary traveler. He had just turned from the parking lot onto the roadway when the men came bursting out of the exit door again.

Integrationist Headquarters – Townhouse on 160th Street: New York, New York

The small, windowless room made Jessica feel claustrophobic. She sat with her back to the wall and her knees to her chest. The thin springs of the cheap cot mattress pressed uncomfortably against her thighs and the soles of her feet. She was dressed in a baggy t-shirt and cargo pants that smelled vaguely of gasoline. She didn't even want to consider where the underwear came from. Delph Crane sat across from her, frustrated that he kept losing her attention. But there was so much to think about.

After the initial shock of waking up *again* not remembering how she passed out, Jessica became angry. This hole looked more like an interrogation chamber than a guest room. She couldn't explain the blackouts and they terrified her. If what Delph was telling her was true, he pulled her out of the motel moments before she would have been taken captive by OCD black ops. They couldn't filter her again. That never turned out well. So, there was only one reason for them to be after her. To make her disappear. Staying ahead of them would be impossible if she didn't have control over her mental faculties.

As Delph explained her knowledge of and supposed role in this T-Col operation, Jessica alternately rejected what she was hearing and clung to the hope that she might remember and feel whole again.

"In the beginning, even some moderate Integrationists thought the development of the Transformation Protocol technology would provide us with a much-needed tool against terrorist organizations. Several Senators and OCD sub-directors climbed on board telling themselves it was preferable to assassination, since there was a living being to take up the life of the Primary that was lost. They justified it out of desperation, really.

"As you know, our decades-long war against terrorism backfired when the followers of assassinated leaders organized and further radicalized. Logic dictated that if cell leaders could be manipulated rather than killed, we would have a better chance of winning the rhetorical war, thus lowering the threat by attrition. The principle and theory of the T-Col project was accepted under that philosophy long before it could become a practical reality and long before our government began classifying its own citizens as terrorists. No one believed--no one wanted to believe--that our government would turn this weapon against its own people."

Jessica shook her head vigorously. "And how many DNA packets did I hand over to the Office for the manufacture of these host clones? How many have been converted?"

"That's the thing." Delph turned to look at her straight on. "All of the conversions were failures, until recently. Most of your packets were used for straight up evidential proof of crimes."

Jessica looked at him skeptically.

"Okay, not always so straight up, but only a few made their way to the Chilling Zone."

Jessica stood suddenly and launched herself from the cot to pace the floor. "War is war. It sucks, but what are you gonna do? *Not* kill the guy who's trying to blow up the White House? But creating puppets from the remnants of people's minds? That's Frankenstein! That's...no! It's not possible!"

Delph stood and faced her. "It is possible and we have it on good authority it's been successfully accomplished."

"Stop it!" Jessica held her head at the ears and paced the room. "Why should I believe you? I don't even know who you are. All I know is you're an agent of the Office of Civilian Defense hiding out here with me instead of turning me in. You probably created all of those memories yourself with your technologic wizardry. Why should I trust you?"

Delph tried to swallow his frustration. "We were partners for three years, Jessica."

"That's impossible. I would remember you. At least glimpses. Something."

"The...manipulation of your brain has wiped it away. They didn't plan on having us work together again. They told me you were dead. I only realized when..." Delph caught himself before revealing the whole truth to her. Clearly, she wasn't ready for that. *If I tell her too soon, I might lose her for good.*

"I was there. I was your tech at Freedom Park. I saw them take you away." Jessica crossed her arms. "I couldn't stop them. And I had to protect the mission data." Delph paused and lowered his head. "You were on the floor bleeding. When I knew I couldn't save you I escaped out the back window. Part of me hoped they would leave you there and follow me. But the data wasn't what they were after."

"It was protocol. You did the right thing." Jessica snapped. "I would have done the same."

"You would have done me the service of putting a bullet into my head before letting them take me. I folded."

He looked earnest, but Jessica couldn't take that leap into trust. She hesitated.

Delph continued. "Somewhere inside you've known all along, Jessica. Even if you couldn't understand why." He stepped closer. "Your heart knows me." He touched her cheek. "Your body knows me."

Jessica shoved him away with disgust and he fell sideways over the end of the cot, narrowly missing slamming his head on it's edge. More than his forwardness, what bothered her was that he was right. "Is that what this is about? You're on some stalker trip over me? So, you figure you can convince me we're lovers and...and what? Do you want intelligence? Are you on some private vendetta? What do you want?"

Back on his feet, Delph stepped into Jessica's circle of defense again and wrapped his arms forcefully around her torso, pinning her arms at her sides. He pulled her against him and kissed her. His breath flowed gently across her cheek. He smelled like a combination of peppermint and an uncommonly sweet aftershave.

CUT TO: Nighttime. Lying in bed on her right side. City traffic noise, honking. People chattering about looking for a fix. Cradled in someone's arms. A scent of something sweet.

Jessica bit his lip and broke away before the memory could complete its formation. "Why? Why show me pieces of who I was and leave holes the size of a universe for me to figure out on my own?"

Delph patted his lip and checked for blood. "We weren't sure if we could trust you."

"Who the hell is we?"

"The resistance."

Jessica broke into hysterical laughter. "Ooh. The resistance!" She laughed again. "What is this, *Les Misérables*?"

Delph raked his hand through his ample hair, leaving the ends askew. "There is a small group of us, from many different backgrounds, who have decided the Office has gone too far."

Jessica leaned her head against the wall, continuing to chuckle. "So, now that I've passed your little test, do I get to learn the secret handshake and password?"

Delph focused on her with concern. "You haven't passed anything, Jessica. There are still significant factions in the organization who would rather see you dead."

Jessica was serious again. "Now there are factions in the factions? So, why tell me any of this? Why not wait until you're sure." She stepped toward him with a gesture of aggression. "I could still betray you all."

Delph stood his ground. "I believe you won't betray us. You've got enough questions and doubts to keep you from turning us in. At least until you have more information. Furthermore, I believe that the information to be had will bring you to our side. There was no time left. I had to make a decision quickly. So here we are."

"The Office still has it out for me, then?"

"That's not important right now. Knowledge of the success of T-Col has snaked its way into every level of the government, and some international circles as well. No one is safe. Now that T-Col has gone live, world leaders and freedom fighters alike will be hunted and converted with abandon. It will be impossible to tell who's real."

Jessica paced to the opposite wall and rocked briefly from foot to foot. "*If* this is true, I'm pretty sure Senator Marks was swapped out." Jessica stated flatly. Delph blanched, but waited for her to continue. "I had this informant I used for the Network and other shall we say 'off label' uses. His name was Stone. The last time I saw him, he handed me a chip that had been retrieved from Senator Marks' brain after he was assassinated. I don't think he understood the implications of what he'd found."

"So…"

"I had the chip analyzed. There were traces of degenerated DNA all over the thing—clone."

Delph considered this for a moment. "And Marks ultimately turned against his supporters."

"Now Prime Minister Grey has discovered spare parts farms operating out of seemingly legitimate gene therapy labs in Boston." Jessica's stomach tightened. She started making mental connections. "They're going to replace him and it's my fault."

"Jessica…"

"It is! I delivered the DNA packet. His clone is probably almost complete." She paced the room. "I have to stop them."

Delph smiled. "I was hoping you'd say that. All we need now is a reliable, invisible line into the OCD systems for a little reconnaissance. I'll…"

"I've got a tap on Tripp Thompson's workstation. Cello tab."

Delph's mouth hung open for a moment, void of its original verbiage. He snapped it shut and raised his eyebrows. "Well that was easy enough."

An image of the rookie reporter lying on the floor with blood trickling out of his nose flirted with Jessica's mind. *Yeah, easy.* She frowned imperceptibly and walked back to the cot hugging herself. *There are still so many missing pieces.* She wasn't sure she could trust Delph completely, but she knew her options were slim. She resolved to remain vigilant.

Delph walked up behind her and tentatively placed his hands on her shoulders. She breathed in deeply and searched her mind. He was so familiar—his scent; his touch. She wished she could be certain. She tilted her head down to run her cheek along the top of his hand, then recoiled against the tender feelings the gesture invoked. "We'd better get to work then." Then she turned abruptly and walked into the hall.

Surveillance Footage: Masterman Gene Therapy Clinic and Surgicenter: Boston, Massachusetts

Somewhere in the Longwood area of Boston, two patients lay opposite each other, similarly draped for sterile fields. On the left, one man possessed a full head of dark brown hair, with only a hint of gray at the temples. The man on the right was bald. The man on the left sported manicured nails, a simple gold wedding band, and a small scar surrounding his right wrist that he usually covered with a wristwatch. The man on the right had nails that were somewhat overgrown. He was not married. Nor was he in possession of a right hand. The man on the left had ice blue eyes, like an angora cat. The man on the right had diagonal slashes, anastomosed where his eyes should have been—by all rights.

Two ARIels attended each man, monitoring vital signs, verifying levels of unconsciousness. The ARIels on the left dowsed the man's abdomen with antiseptic and ran the ionic shower over the area. The ARIels on the right ran a scalpel across the other man's belly, exposing the bulk of his digestive system. ARIel number one located the liver. ARIel number two identified the incision lines. The surgeon walked in just as the ARIels turned toward the left with the half liver in a large specimen pan. The man on the right was stapled shut up and wheeled back to his unit. Meanwhile, the surgeon carefully dissected the cirrhosed liver from the abdomen of the remaining patient. The transplant would take the rest of the afternoon.

Integrationist Headquarters – Townhouse on 160th Street: New York, New York

Jessica tossed the floaters onto the table in disgust. She thought she had seen it all. *Maybe I have seen it, only don't remember now.* Her new memory of witnessing the failed T-Col procedure had not yet settled. This surveillance footage was too much. The sight of the mutilated clone had wiped any thoughts of dinner from her mind. "Jesus, he didn't even have a real doctor."

"Gotta keep costs down. The wealthy don't like paying more than they have to." Delph said sarcastically. He was leafing through files on an old-fashioned wall screen. "Look at this. They can perform gene therapy on the clones while they're developing, and remove genetic risk factors. So, some guy who gets macular degeneration can take the eyes from his clone because he knows the clone doesn't have the gene for it."

"Bonus. Sign me up." Jessica rolled her eyes. The easy banter between them and the way they seemed to know exactly what the other would be looking for, was beginning to convince Jessica that they had, in fact, worked together before.

"Wait! Here's something." Delph gestured Jessica over to the console where he was running relevance algorithms on Tripp's private files. The file he had accessed was a large spreadsheet with what looked like GPS coordinates down one side. Additional columns with labels such as "donor load", "primary requests Q1", "primary requests Q2", "# new fertilizations".

"Looks like a treasure map!" he commented.

"Look at all of those sites. Do you really think every one represents a spare parts farm?"

"Hey, if the primary's in really bad shape, gotta be sure the remedy's close by."

The markers indicated there were centers in nearly every major city. "They've been right under our noses.

"Rip that one for me."

"I'm way ahead of you on that one." She heard her Mate beep as it received the data. Jessica was surprised at how well they worked together. All evening, he had known exactly what she was thinking before she knew what she was going to ask for next.

"I think we've mined this drive dry, Delph. What do you say we come back tomorrow and see if there are any snake holes to remote sites or links to the OCD mainframe? Right now, I need some sleep."

"How about eight?"

Jessica was about to nod her assent, but paused. "Let's make it one. I have…an errand to run in the morning."

Delph took a deep breath and played with the edges of his dedo sensors. She realized for the first time he wasn't sure he could trust her either. Somehow that put her more at ease. "I need to visit an old friend." Delph dipped his head in a conciliatory gesture. Jessica wanted to reassure him, without revealing the purpose of her sojourn. "I think my visit will be very informative."

"Cool." He shrugged, trying to act casual. "That's cool. See you tomorrow then." He dipped his head down and up on his way out the door.

Jessica watched him leave. *How much does he have riding on trusting me?* She was thankful that he did.

Washington Square Fountain: New York, New York

Boo scanned the crowd for twenty minutes before considering going home. It was unusually hot, even for July. Both children and their parents were taking full advantage of the cool spray of Washington Fountain. Waiting on the surrounding cement was brutal, even in short shorts and a tank top. Finally, she saw Jessica scurrying toward her from the right. She looked more tightly wound than usual and was strangely dressed. She would have to keep it light today. *At least she's still in the city.* Boo stood, waved and smiled. "Jess!"

Jessica put on her game face. "Boo, sorry to drag you from work."

"Don't worry about it, chica. Where have you been? I was worried about you. The Super 8 didn't have any record of you having been there. What's going on?"

"I...I can't talk here. Can we cross to those trees over there?"

Boo darted her eyes over to the dense glen to her left. *Generally visible, but still deserted.* She hesitated. "Sure, Jess."

Leaving the paved circle of the fountain, Jessica headed purposefully into the center of the small woods. The crunch of dead leaves under her feet brought back memories of building tree forts and tee pees after school with Boo in her grandmother's back yard. *Fake! All phoney!* The hell of this mind manipulation was that she mourned the loss of a best friend the same as if it were real. She didn't know what Boo's part was in all of this, but she was determined to find out.

Once she felt sufficiently isolated, Jessica took a sharp turn to the left and sprang behind a large tree trunk. Boo followed tentatively. "Jess? What's going on?"

Jessica spun her around, pressing Boo against the tree with her knee and forearm. "Why don't you tell me, Boo? Who are you really? OCD? Corporate interest?"

"Jessica, I don't know what you're talking about."

"You don't? How about this? A team of OCD cleaners descended on my motel room less than an hour after I told *you* where I was going. No one else knew where I was going, Boo. No one!"

"Maybe you were trailed."

"Trailed? Me? I'm a special operations agent with the Office of Civilian Defense. I trail, I don't get trailed." She pulled Boo toward her by her bra straps and thrust her head against the moss-covered bark. Boo gasped with surprise. "So, tell me, Boo. Who are you really?"

"I swear, I don't know what you're talking about."

"I think you do. And I mean to find out, by any means necessary." She drew her Taser and pressed against the underside of Boo's jaw. Boo could tell by the pitch of the hum that the device was set to full. "It's really easy to fake a suicide from this angle, Boo. So, start talking. Let's start with your name. And listen carefully, because I'm asking you for the last time. Who are you?"

Boo searched Jessica's eyes for any sign of weakness and found none. She was had. "My name is Matilda Stone. I was recruited by Tripp for OCD special operations two years ago, when my brother went underground."

Jessica blinked. "You're Rene Stone's sister?"

Boo looked at the ground. "My brother was misguided."

"And what are you?" Jessica heard the giggling of a group of older children at the edge of the trees. She pressed her palm tightly against Boo's nose and mouth and pushed the Taser deeper into corner between her trachea and her larynx. "Shh…" The children ran back to the fountain, unaware of their proximity to this minor battle.

When they were gone, Jessica continued. "What do you want with me?"

"I can't believe you haven't figured it out yet."

"Why don't you explain it?"

"I was sent to observe you; to make sure you didn't become too much of a liability after…what happened."

"I fail one mission in how many years and Tripp's sending henchmen to off me?"

Boo's eyes widened in disbelief. "You still think this is about the mission? This has nothing to do with the mission. It's about you and what you've become!'

"Cut the cryptic crap, Matilda!" All of Jessica's suppressed anger surged forward mixing with the false memories of a life she never lived. "If you don't tell me what you know I'm going to shut off your airway. Do you hear me? What do you know about human beings being replaced by clone machine hybrids?"

Boo laughed quietly, crying simultaneously. "Jessica, for Christ's sake, you're one of them. You fucked up the mission. They converted you. Now you can't mind your own business."

Jessica's mind reeled. She pressed the Taser harder against Matilda's throat and leaned her weight into Matilda's chest. Pieces of information started sliding into place, but she still resisted what she already knew was true. "Liar!"

Boo struggled to breathe. "Conversion is a perfect tool, Jessica. No loose ends. No tracers. You're just messed up because someone's feeding you information. The Office is working on that little debacle." Boo's eyes softened. "Tripp really wanted to keep you. He's crazy about you. He didn't want it to end this way. He wanted you back."

"You're just trying to buy time."

"Think about it from the Office's perspective. You're a liability, Jessica Butler. It doesn't matter what you do to me. Others will find you and they will terminate you. So, if you're going to kill me, just kill me and get it over with."

"It's not true! It can't be!"

"Why? What's so hard to believe about the Office preparing to convert their own agents first?"

"There's too much...me."

Across Washington Square, a construction worker lost control of a ladder and smashed a pane glassed window. Jessica jumped and turned. Boo ducked and rolled to the side. By the time Jessica had shaken off the scare, Boo was halfway to the fountain, dodging branches and roots all the way.

Jessica stood stunned. She didn't want to believe it. Every cell of her body wanted to deny what Boo had told her and write it off as the cruelty of a cornered animal. She couldn't. Though her mind rebelled, her body knew the truth. Her hands that had never flexed before three weeks ago. The legs that had never run. They knew the truth. Jessica Butler, the Primary Jessica Butler, was dead.

Integrationist Headquarters – Townhouse on 160th Street: New York, New York

Suspicion and disbelief fought each other as Jessica approached the rebel hideout. She walked back to give herself time to think. All the way she tried to rationalize Matilda Stone's revelations. She tried to convince herself that Stone was simply putting up a smoke screen to distract her from the real torture being propagated in secret locations around the country.

In the end, doubt could gain no traction. She knew it was true. It explained everything. In retrospect, she decided she should be kicking herself for not suspecting it sooner. The unpredictable memory losses, the feeling of strangeness she encountered in even the most familiar situations. In fact, feeling at all was not something she was used to having to cope with. Having to weigh every decision in relation to this new conscience was slowing her down. Reconciling her past actions with her current state of mind was painful. For the first time, she was glad some memories were gone for good.

The safe house was comprised of the second and third floors of a townhouse on 160th street. The ground floor unit was abandoned. There was a persistent smell of garlic and onions in the stairwell, which she figured must have steeped into the faded flowered wallpaper through decades of home cooking. No ordinary family lived here now. Instead, a rag-tag group of about three dozen free-thinkers – all thinking in their own free directions – shared space and slept on top of one another in general disarray. During the day, the futons masqueraded as couches, and sleeping bags lay creatively stashed behind lounge chairs and planters. There was a paucity of real furniture. Into the vacuum had fallen a hodge-podge of doors on sawhorses to serve as tables and crates covered in canvas to serve as stools.

Jessica donned an air of confidence she didn't feel as she turned the corner to enter the meeting room. Her eyes darted around the room, resting momentarily on each person's face, searching for deception. She saw none. All she saw was a group of scared, but dedicated individuals, risking their lives to do what they thought was right. Small clusters of people spoke in hushed tones. Delph was nowhere in sight.

Three or four of the group waved, nodded or muttered "Hey" toward her as she surveyed them. Jessica wondered how many of them knew. They seemed to be treating her like anyone else. How would she have responded in their place? *With a gun.* She admitted to herself.

Jessica turned slowly toward the right. She needed to talk to Delph. Then she saw him. Evan Marcelo. This was the man who killed almost one hundred people, while faking his own death sending her career, and in fact her life, into the toilet. Her life... *What the hell is he doing here?*

Marcelo ducked out a door into the hallway. Jessica sprinted through the room, excusing herself as she bumped into a half dozen shoulders. She followed him down the hallway to a small bedroom, pushing the palm of her hand aggressively into the surface of the door as Marcelo closed it. He turned when he felt the resistance and sighed.

"Look who we have here." She snarled and strode past him tossing the door shut behind her. Delph sat in a folding chair in front of a giant map of the city. Now she could picture him secretly planning civilian bombings and assassinations and placing multi-colored pins along the trajectory of his destruction.

"And you." She snapped at Delph. "Trying to convince me that you're all about freedom and civil liberty. You've got me holed up consorting with terrorists. I believed you. Now there's him!"

"Jessica. You don't understand." Delph said simply.

"I understand all I need to know!" Jessica yelled back, grabbing Marcelo by the scruff of his collar and pushing him up against the wall. "This man is a murderer." Marcelo stiffly stood his ground, mounting no counter attack.

Delph stood gingerly, moving toward Jessica as one might approach a rattlesnake. "He's the leader of the civil resistance. We need him."

"And the husbands, wives and children of all those people you killed. Did anyone think about what they need?"

Marcelo twitched to the left, testing Jessica's grip on him. She turned and landed her fist squarely in his jaw. Marcelo grabbed Jessica by the shoulders and sent her flying across the room. She stumbled over a low coffee table and recovered. Her eyes were wide and wild.

"And what about me?" She screamed. "What they've done to me!" She picked up the table and hurled it at Marcelo's head.

Marcelo stepped to the side and ducked, then crossed the room in two steps. Jessica and Marcelo flew at each other, locking arms at the shoulders and pushing into each other in a war of wills. They fell to the ground. Jessica locked her legs around Marcelo's and punched him in the stomach. Marcelo clutched one hand around Jessica's neck and punched his arm under Jessica's crotch. In a swift move he hauled her off of him, overhead and dumped her upside down on the couch behind them. She struggled in the pillows to turn upright.

Delph put his arm across Jessica as she prepared to spring herself on Marcelo again. "Jessica, stop."

Marcelo growled, "You think you're so different from me, Butler, but you're not. You have directly and indirectly killed more people than I've ever met. Your influence has spanned continents."

Delph fell to the side as Jessica launched at Marcelo again. "You blew up innocent followers in a park. You were their leader. They looked to you for safety and you killed them."

Marcelo spun to the side and kicked her knee back as she landed. Jessica fell into the wall. "You poke around in your clever disguise as a legitimate journalist, collecting information, collecting names, and poof. Suddenly a village in Zimbabwe is wiped out. You see your opportunities and you take them. Damn the consequences. Just like me." Jessica roundhouse kicked Marcelo on the left side. He shoved her into the wall again, making her head crack against the paneling. Jessica counter-shoved before he'd regained his center of gravity and they both tumbled to the floor again.

"Jessica! Marcelo! Stop!" Delph yelled as he tried to pry Jessica away. Marcelo rolled over on top of Jessica, knocking Delph onto the floor next to them.

Jessica clawed at Marcelo's arms, twisting back and forth. "The Office of Civilian Defense identifies individual threats and eliminates them. I am not a murderer!"

"One at a time. Ten at a time. What's the difference, Butler? There isn't one. There's only your justification for your participation in a scheme to strip from us our most basic human liberty—our minds."

"Liar!"

Marcelo grabbed her head and stabilized it, looking straight into her eyes. "One strand of hair. One finger sweep of dust. A bristle from your victim's toothbrush. You turn it in to your superiors and someone's life is revoked!"

Marcelo stood, dragging Jessica along beside him. Delph leaped up, attempting to insert his arms between them. "Stop it! Both of you!"

Jessica twirled Marcelo to the right. Her resolve beginning to crumble. Her aching conscience couldn't defend her. "You murdered innocent people to save yourself!"

"And how far would you go to save yourself, Butler? Wouldn't you do it too? This is war. How would you propose to save yourself?"

"I have no self!" Jessica screamed. She feinted to the left, then flipped Marcelo toward the door. He landed heavily on his back.

Delph's heart skipped several beats. *She knows.* Even Marcelo paused seeming to understand this outburst a little more clearly. Delph stepped in front of Jessica before she could launch herself at Marcelo again. "Evan, go. I should have told her myself. I'll take care of this."

Marcelo looked at Delph with an expression that said *We'll talk later.* And quietly left the room.

Delph put his hands on Jessica's shoulders and looked her in the eyes. She could no longer mask her despair. "So, you know." He said softly.

"Tell me it's not true." Jessica pleaded. "Tell me it's not true and I'll believe you. There's got to be a piece of me – the real me. Somewhere?"

Delph stroked Jessica's hair softly. In the three years they'd worked together, he'd never seen her scared and never thought he would until tonight. His long silence told Jessica everything she needed to know. "You should have told me." She growled at a measured pace. "You had plenty of opportunity. Why didn't you tell me?" Her jaw throbbed from the clenching.

"I knew you weren't ready. I thought you might..." he paused, considering the irony, "fly off the handle. I needed to make sure you could handle it."

Jessica stared blindly through Delph. "So, my Primary..."

"Before you gained consciousness."

Jessica leaned into Delph. He felt warm. His heart beat steadily, calming. Her forehead reached his shoulder. *I'm so tired,* she thought. Delph pulled away. He held her at arms length then turned toward the nightstand. He dug around in the drawer for a moment and sat on the bed. He motioned for her to sit next to him. Jessica lay down behind Delph and stared at the ceiling. She heard a fizzing sound and a faint smell of citrus filled the air. Delph turned toward her holding a cup of Mandarin Pollie Seltzer. Jessica leaned up on her elbows and let him give her a sip. She spread the sweet taste around in her mouth before swallowing it. She luxuriated in the warm feeling of the mix as it wound its way to her stomach. Delph took a sip, looked down at Jessica and smiled. "More?" She accepted, eager to delay the necessity for action just a little while longer.

When the cup was drained, Jessica turned onto her side. Delph reclined next to her and cradled her head in his shoulder. She looked up at him. His face was surrounded by fuzzy white edges, like an angel. She touched his face. He leaned down and kissed her. Her stomach turned a somersault. His lips were soft and warm and she wanted him. She was in fact, afraid that she needed him. She turned her head and inhaled across his face to the corner of his neck. His scent was familiar and safe.

Jessica brought her hand up to the side of Delph's head and drew him closer, nipping lightly at his neck, tentatively at first. She felt him jump slightly with surprise. He turned to look deeply into her eyes. In a moment, his questions seemed to resolve and he chuckled as he drew her earlobe into his mouth. Jessica carelessly tossed one leg over Delph's hip. His hand encircled her lower back.

The urgency of his kisses increased as he worked his way down her neck toward her collarbone. Jessica sighed heavily. Her fingers worked the buttons of Delph's shirt. She splayed her fingers across his chest and dragged them lightly toward his stomach. His skin was smoothly textured under her fingertips. She could feel the heat increasing as she moved. She marveled at it. The scent of him mixed with the Pollie increased her intoxication. Jessica's heart leapt in her chest like a grade schooler going on a field trip for the first time.

Delph slid his hand under Jessica's camisole top and along the side of her breast. He rolled her onto her back and used both hands to slide up the front and sides of the flimsy blouse. His fingers easily snapped open the clasp on her bra. He hovered over her for a few seconds, just long enough for Jessica to see the intense passion in his eyes and something else too—complete devotion.

Jessica was surprised by this discovery. He loved her deeply and without reserve. She knew that without question. For the first time, she appreciated the personal risks he had taken in freeing her. He'd risked blowing his cover as a double agent. He'd risked being converted. He'd seen something in her that even she had not been aware of until now.

Jessica reached for Delph's head and brought his lips to hers. She ran her tongue around the inside edges of his lips. He responded with a groan. He brought his hands up and took possession of hers, spreading her arms out to the sides and pinning her by the wrists beneath him.

She was vaguely aware of Delph pulling at the clasp on her jeans and shoving them down to her knees. She kicked them loose as he freed himself from his own bounds. She gasped, surprised to feel a brief pinch and the tightness that reminded her that this body had never been with a man. Delph paused, sensing the tension and gazed into her eyes. He caressed her cheek as if to ask if she were all right.

At that moment something inside Jessica broke free and she allowed herself to give herself to him completely. Instinct took over and their bodies moved in a synchronized rhythm. Jessica felt the fever taking her over and her movements became jerky. Delph came first, stiffening with sustained pressure against Jessica's sensitive groin, sending her into a cascade of ecstasy.

Delph didn't know how long he had been sleeping. The safe house was quiet. A bluish glow emanated from the nightlight near the door. The sheets lay tangled around his legs. *Some things never change,* Delph thought as he held Jessica, who was flopped across his chest like a rag doll. *She still falls asleep right after sex.*

Everything else was different though—everything. It hadn't occurred to him before that this new body would be a virgin. It made sense in hindsight, he simply hadn't thought about it. Apparently neither had she. She had looked so surprised, he thought she was going to toss him across the room. But she hadn't. Instead, she'd looked at him, deeply, as though she'd never really looked at him before and gave herself over to him as if she were as much in love with him as he with her.

That's ridiculous! He chided himself. Don't get carried away, just because she needed to feel human again. But that was the crux of it, wasn't it? Human. He'd never seen Jessica give herself away to anyone, least of all himself, but that was emotion he'd seen in her eyes. He was sure of it. *So, what now?* He thought. *What now? Nothing! That's what.* They still had a job to finish. Later, if they were both in one piece, he could explore this further.

Jessica was awakened by a bang. She opened her eyes just as the walls stopped shuddering. Delph was on his feet, reaching for his clothes and gun before Jessica untangled her feet from the sheets. She grabbed her Belt Mate and her pants in one sweep dressing while scanning her surroundings. *Shit I let my guard down.*

There were voices of panic and concern coming from the hall outside. Gunfire echoed through the main floor, followed by more yelling and thumping. There was a hiss and a clatter. Jessica was sure it was Gopher Gas. Soon the common areas would be impassable. The nightlight was no longer burning. The clocks were out too. Jessica peered out the window around the edge of the curtain. There wasn't a light burning on the whole street.

Delph cautiously approached the door to the hallway and opened it a crack. He listened intently. Jessica looked at him urgently and shrugged her shoulders up in inquisition. Delph held up one hand and froze. He closed the door again, just before a group of heavy boots passed. He made a gesture with one finger across his throat, pointed at Jessica and then pointed to the closet.

What? He couldn't think they'd be safe in there. She thrust her head forward at him quizzically and raised her index finger, spinning it in circles by her temple.

Delph shook his head on his way to the closet door and opened it. He pushed the clothing toward the left and began picking at the cedar wainscoting along the wall. The panel of wood came loose with a crunch. He gestured her toward the opening in the false wall, indicating that she should hurry.

Jessica ducked into the low opening and turned left, her only option. Behind her, Delph was stepping into the narrow space, rearranging clothing as he went and finally clicking the false wall back into place using two cloth straps that had been attached to it like the back of a shield. Then he wedged a horizontal piece of two-by-four into brackets on both sides of the opening.

Jessica could barely discern a narrow stairway heading down, spiraling around what would be the back of the closet and this she could only see due to some dim light at the bottom of it. She was just about to pick her way down to the next platform when Delph grabbed her by the arm and gestured *Shhhh!* The two of them froze, barely daring to breathe.

The door to the room outside the closet burst open and what sounded like a small army tossed the room, looking for signs of inhabitation. The commotion came to a sudden halt when a single pair of heavy shoes entered the room. "Sir, the sheets are still warm," commented an unseen face.

"They can't have gotten far. Keep looking. And remember, I want Jessica alive for now."

Jessica's entire body tensed when she recognized the voice of Tripp Thompson. Had he figured out that she tapped his system? Was he able to retrieve any data off of her imploded workstation?

Her thoughts were interrupted by the sound of the closet door bouncing open. Small slivers of the lights from flashlights wormed their way underneath the seam of the false wall. Jessica held her breath and felt Delph do the same. She heard the agents knocking on the closet walls from all angles. They knocked on the wall of their hiding place, paused and knocked again. Delph raised his gun and held his finger near the safety catch. All of Jessica's muscles tensed, ready to fight for her life.

"Looks solid in here, sir. They must have slipped out before we came upstairs."

"Then what are you doing still standing here, Jenson?" Thompson asked with casual menace.

"Yes, sir!" The sound of the agent's boots grew faint as they jogged down the hall.

One pair of shoes remained. They circumnavigated the room slowly. She heard a steady scrape of sole on hardwood. *Yes, of course he would think to look under the area rug.* Tripp was nothing, if not thorough. The shoes made their way toward the window. She heard his fingers drumming on the windowsill for what seemed like forever. Finally, he paused and walked briskly out of the room.

Both Jessica and Delph sat in suspension for a moment, while they made certain they were truly alone. Then they allowed themselves to breathe again. Delph gestured Jessica down the stairs. Though the walls were clearly insulated, they descended lightly and slowly to avoid making any noise. The passage terminated at the basement level in what looked like a wall of dirt. Jessica almost planted her face in it before she realized it was there.

Stepping back she saw that what little light they had was moonlight shining in from several small slivers cut into the outside wall of the building like gun turrets. As she considered this, Delph lifted the platform at the bottom of the stairs to reveal a cubby with several picks and shovels crowded into it.

He handed Jessica a shovel. She cocked her head inquisitively, but took it. He grabbed a large pick and thrust it swiftly at the wall with the persistence of a coal miner. A chunk of dirt came loose and fell at Delph's feet. Simultaneous with the blow, however, Jessica heard a landslide of stones and pebbles on the other side of the wall. *It must be only a foot or two thick,* she thought, slamming the blade of the shovel into the gut of the dirt wall.

Within minutes, Jessica and Delph had cleared a hole in the dirt wall large enough for them to crawl through. Delph reached back into the cubby in the stairs and pulled out two flashlights. Torch in hand, Jessica could now see that a passageway lay beyond the façade of the dirt wall. It looked like a mining tunnel from a theme park adventure ride. There were dirt walls and a dirt floor outlined with a lattice of landscaping beams. *Creative. Solid?* She hoped so. Delph urged her forward again. Once they were through the opening together she spared no more thought for the tunnel's construction, they ran full out for its entire winding half-mile length.

The tunnel terminated in a short flight of stairs leading to a metal door. Leftover heat from the day radiated from its surface. Delph pulled his gun again and levered the handle. The door swung open toward the outside. Delph peered into the alleyway, gun first, and gestured Jessica forward. The door latched behind them. There was no handle on the outside.

Jessica and Delph now stood in what looked like a common alley, with several doors just like the one from which they had emerged. All of the others led to the kitchens of restaurants and stockrooms of the precious boutiques lining the main road. A few apartments looked out from above, but their shades were all drawn.

Suddenly, Jessica was overwhelmed by rage. She punched the door then shook her fist. "How the hell did they find us?" She paced a few steps back and forth. "Furthermore, why the hell am I so important to them? Why the hell do they want me so badly? I mean, come on! So, I fucked up. I fucked up, okay! Then they swapped me out for my spare, and that didn't work out so well either. Why, in God's name don't they just cut their losses and leave me alone? Buy me out! Pay me off to shut up! Why couldn't they have started there? There are a hell of a lot more important people in terms of breaking up the Integrationist resistance than me."

"Actually, there aren't." Delph had both hands stuffed deeply into his pockets and was staring at the ground.

Jessica drilled into him with her eyes. He pretended not to notice. "Don't tell me…there's more?" she asked him slowly and deliberately.

The Repair Bay of an Abandoned Gas Station: East Harlem, New York, New York

It took the better part of three hours, scurrying from alley to alley, peering around corners and watching their backs to reach the random bus depot locker where Delph sometimes stashed his Wolf. In fact, it was dumb luck he hadn't brought it with him to the safe house – he wanted it to run some maintenance protocols overnight. It wasn't hard to put on their best harried traveler act as Delph slung the messenger bag strap across his chest.

Twenty minutes later, they had hidden in the repair bay of an abandoned gas station. Jessica used old rags to block up the un-boarded up portions of the garage door while Delph used the Wolf to drop into his Parlor. Some of the more advanced features were grayed out because of the poor quality of the neighboring motel interface he was hijacking for this activity.

While she waited, Jessica soccer-kicked old screws toward a tipped over coffee can in the corner of the room. She was angry – at Delph, at Tripp, at the OCD. She was angry with herself, for being had in the first place. Ignorance really would have been bliss. In the conversion, they could have set her future up any way they wanted to. *Look how easily they inserted Boo into my life.* They could have had her wake up as a country housewife or a narced out druggie. Hell, they could have just let her be an average every day reporter. Why did they go to all of the trouble of conversion and then reintroduce her to everything they wanted to be gone?

And now? She tried hard to convince herself that her having a new body in some way expunged the guilt for what she had done in her prior life, but she was unsuccessful. *Why didn't they just leave me out of it?* She remembered that Converts were supposed to be reborn as more manageable versions of themselves. *They didn't count on me.*

"That oughtta do it," Delph said from his seat at the portable keypad. "Are you sure you're ready for this? I didn't show you this before, because there was no way to parse the memories before I had to compress them. And…"

"Just give it to me raw," she said morbidly. She sat down in an old lounge chair that the previous owner probably kept on hand for those slow periods between servicing carbon-based cars as his business shriveled and died. She pictured him shaking the hand of the last customer who just told him he'd purchased a new porter. Delph was watching her funny. She closed her eyes.

Delph pressed "enter". "It should be easier this time," he said, his voice echoing into a comet's tail. The reflections in Delph's floaters flashed a running commentary on its executed commands.

"Engaging fish hook"

"Active"

"Sending tracer stimulus."

"Downloading."

Jessica's eyes rolled up into the back of her head and her eyelids twitched continuously as the network tapped into the neural matrix in her brain. Images arose in front of her—no, she was in the images. Reality shifted around her. She was breathing heavy. She was running. She was calling Delph.

"...they got here before us. We've been compromised."

She could hear him reply, "The Office has been mobilized, Jessica. Get out of there, now!"

"I'm on my way."

She could hear the helicopters approaching, feel her muscles working, bringing her closer to the relative safety of the tree line. She was almost to the gate, when movement caught her eye, from the right. She turned just in time to see a man with a gun kill two of the President's Secret Service men. *The President was here somewhere? Why? He should be at the summit.*

The man with the gun stood near another well-dressed political type. The second man turned to the gunman in shock—it was Senate Majority Leader Marks, the man whose chip had revealed clone DNA. *My God! He's going to...*before she could finish her thought, the gunman raised his other hand and stuck Marks in the neck with what looked like a hypodermic needle. He crushed the plunger down, even as Marks struggled to break free. The pair spun around and the murderer's eyes met hers just as she finished crossing the distance to the gate. She knew him. It was President Fein. *No! This is absurd...*

There was a short gap in the tracer stream. When it continued, she opened the door to the hotel room. Delph turned.

CUT TO: Bright lights. Foggy can't see. Like gauze over eyes. Arms and legs pinned to a...cold metal table. Head numb. A sound—grinding—vibration. *My head! They're cutting open my head!* Struggling. Vice grip. Can't break free. Pressure. Skull cap falls to table below.

Drizzle. Drip. Drip. Liquid hitting the surface of a metal pan. *Why can't I speak?* More pressure. Mushy sounds. Shadows of hands moving overhead.

CUT TO: A warm day in February. She and Tripp Thompson are sitting on the open-air deck of the TWNS employee cafeteria. She grabs her napkin as it is almost set loose by the wind. No one else has ventured beyond the heated interior. Tripp explained, "The Primary is prepped for transfer with an open craniotomy. Once the skull is removed, over one thousand single-strand electrodes are inserted into individually targeted parts of the brain. The process takes approximately five hours.

Five hours? Oh, no, no...

"The last to be inserted are the lines to the brainstem, because at that point, the Primary's autonomic system becomes unstable."

CUT TO: Cold. Voices. "That should just about do it. Let's bring the medulla online."

Pressure. Pain. Pain! Lights!

Dark.

Jessica could feel herself hyperventilating before she could move. Delph's shoes made a sandy scraping sound as he walked over to her chair, but the sound was still muffled. Soon she was able to regulate her breathing, but the air was stale. She began to cough.

"Jessica! It's over. It's over. Come out of it!" Delph's voice was close to her ear.

"They want that memory, Delph. That's got to be it. He knows I saw him. Something must have gone wrong, they must have reason to believe there was a tracer. But there wasn't. If they'd just left me alone!" Jessica's fervor was escalating again.

Delph shook her by the shoulders. "Come on, Jessica. Get a grip. We can't let anyone hear you. Come on."

Jessica clenched her jaw and forced herself to breathe evenly. As she did, Delph stood up and looked at her cautiously. She looked a little green. Jessica leaped from the chair and rushed to a corner to vomit. When she returned, she paced in small circles spitting. Delph looked regretful. "You needed to know. If I could have divided the streams of the tracers I would have, but there was something strangely corrupted about that particular data packet. It wasn't just corrupted, but fused. I've never seen anything like that before."

"How did you know?" Jessica looked at Delph fiercely. "How did you know what I saw? You were up in the hotel room the whole time. Or were you?"

"Yes, I was. The truth is I didn't know until I had processed all of the data packages available to me. As you can imagine, I had to take what I could get and run." Jessica started kicking screws again. "I wanted to find out as much as you did why the Office was willing to expend so many resources on a washed up agent. In particular, why were they so obsessed with retrieving you. Not knowing where this memory could end up? That would do it." With the potential for triggering this kind of tracer, they couldn't take the chance. I'm sorry you had to relive the..."

"It's okay." She held her hand up in a stop gesture.

"I'll figure out how to...."

"It's fine!" she barked and headed for the back door. "I need some air." She paused before leaving. "Don't wait up." Jessica left the bay quietly, clicking the rickety wooden door shut behind her.

Walking at night always made Jessica feel like she had more room to move. There were no crowds, no pressure for social interaction. No one needed to make excuses for lack of eye contact. Most of the people on the street this late at night preferred not to be seen as well. They were engrossed in the process of wrestling their own inner demons. The air was cleaner at night too. She coughed up some of the moldy dust from the repair bay and spit on the sidewalk.

There were too many open questions nagging at Jessica for her to find any real relief in the quiet darkness. She wandered the city in a zigzag path, periodically reminding herself to stay vigilant. As the sun rose, she found herself wandering into Penn Station and buying a ticket up to Westchester. She hobbled over to the ladies room to straighten herself out a bit while she waited. There was one question she needed answered right now. She suspected she didn't want to know the answer, but at least one thing would be settled.

The Offices of Stone Construction: White Plains, New York

Rush hour was in full swing by the time Jessica reached the cozy offices of Stone Construction. She had never been here before. The nature of her contacts with her erstwhile contractor turned informant had always precluded such open interactions. She had expected the place to look more like a warehouse, with a tin roof and boxy exterior--maybe a few trailers off to the side. This building looked more like a pharmaceutical office, with its beige walls and ash wood furnishing.

On the phone, Stone's secretary had told her he had encephalitis. It was possible, sure. Happens all the time. Still, she had to know for sure. She pulled on the sizeable cylindrical door handle, entered the hushed lobby and walked casually toward the reception desk.

"May I help you?" A plump woman with fire engine red hair, asked briskly.

"Rene Stone, please." Jessica replied officiously, stifling her anticipation.

"Do you have an appointment?"

"No, I don't, but my business is…"

At that moment, Rene Stone burst in jovially from the inner hallway. "Jessica! My love!" He looked fit in his khakis and maroon *Stone Construction* imprinted polo shirt.

Jessica paused suspiciously. Stone had never been so vocal greeting her, even in wirespace. "Stone. It's good to see you. I was concerned about your recent…illness. How are you feeling?" She shook his hand, his palm was soft and warm.

"Never better. And how many times do I have to tell you? It's Rene to you. Don't forget it. Come on in, sweet pea!"

Sweet…what? Oh never mind. "Sure. I've got a few minutes." Jessica followed Stone into his office, where he sat enthusiastically behind his desk. He motioned for her to take the seat in front of him. She chose to pace instead. "Okay, you can drop the long-lost cousin act. I've been trying to reach you for weeks."

Stone smiled and spun his chair toward the window. He placidly watched a dump truck full of gravel pull out of the driveway. "Have you ever had a near-death experience?" Jessica turned away and started pacing again. "It changes you," he said, thoughtfully.

Sure does, she agreed.

"Encephalitis. Man! I always thought, if I was gonna go, it'd be from a crane falling on my head or something, not my brain catching on fire."

"You gave me a plank. You said the DNA was degraded." Jessica started, carefully.

"Did I?" Stone folded his hands on his desk in front of him, looking mildly concerned.

Jessica continued. "You told me I needed to investigate…"

"Oh! That!" Stone acknowledged.

"Yes. That." Jessica stated. "I looked into it and…"

Stone interrupted. "I'm sorry about all of that. I got a little paranoid right before I got sick." Jessica was stunned to silence. "They said you can have 'walking encephalitis' for a while, before it takes you down."

Jessica raised an eyebrow...*walking encephalitis? Right.* Her stomach balled up. She changed her tack. "You must have lost a little time while you were at the hospital; forgotten some things. They say that happens sometimes."

Stone shook his head. "Yeah, I don't remember most of my hospital stay. Otherwise, I seem okay now."

Jessica angled for a tracer. "Did you hear about Senator Marks? He died. He had encephalitis too." She lied, giving him the "official" version of the Senator's death.

"Really?" Stone looked surprised. "Must be an epidemic. I guess I'm lucky to be alive, then." He looked at the picture of his wife and daughter that was sitting on a shelf overlooking his desk.

Jessica searched Stone's face for any sign that he was hiding recognition of the events surrounding the death of the Central Senate Majority Leader. She saw nothing, only the relieved face of a simple man, who was happy to be alive to see his family again. Comparing the face in front of her with the one in the picture, she could see subtle differences now. There were fewer smile lines around his eyes. His teeth were whiter when he smiled. And he had just a little more hair.

Looking at the picture of Stone's family and seeing the loving smile it brought to his face, Jessica decided she couldn't drag him back into this. She was full of regret enough for both of them and she knew now she could get along without him. She would leave him to his peace.

"Well, I've taken up enough of your time. I'm glad to see you're feeling well again." Jessica stood to go. She'd never been so sorry to be right. This man she barely knew, she mourned him. After all, no one else could.

"Jessica," he said, before she'd reached the door. "I know I've been a little intense over the years. What with my conspiracy theories and all." He shrugged and bobbed his head apologetically. "You've been very patient."

Jessica looked him straight in the eye. Compassion and jealousy washed over her in competing tides. "A good reporter is always on the lookout for a lead." She turned away. "Let me

know if you crank out any more good ones." She walked out
before she could hear his reply.

An Apartment on West 72nd Street: New York, New York

On her way back from White Plains, Jessica received a
communication containing the location of a new safe house on
the first floor of a run down townhouse near the 72nd street
boat basin. Conveniently, one of the younger members of the
group inherited the property from her grandmother two years
before. It needed so many repairs, including plumbing and
electric, that the girl hadn't known what to do with it – until
now. In order to avoid raising the suspicion of the tenants
upstairs, Marcelo and Delph posed as contractors during the
day. It was almost midnight before Jessica arrived. When she
slipped in under the crisscrossed "caution" tape, she thought
they were doing a good job with their front. The hallway was
cluttered with tools and drop cloths. Wallpaper samples were
stuck to the wall by the living room door with masking tape.
With most of the group temporarily in hiding around the city,
this place seemed too quiet to be the stronghold of an
insurgent movement. Everything looked so ordinary. *Unlike I
feel.* Jessica pushed through the swinging door between the
hallway and the kitchen. It was empty there as well.

She had delayed coming to the safe house after arriving
back at Penn Station. After her discouraging meeting with
Stone, Jessica hadn't wanted to speak with anyone. What she
needed to do was think. She popped into a consignment shop
and swapped out her clothes, adding a floppy hat and new
sunglasses for extra protection. Then she started walking again.

Weaving around the streets of the city, Jessica became
philosophical. She recognized that her recent "woe-is-me"
attitude wasn't helping her out any. However her current form
came into being, all she could be now was Jessica Butler, with
all her baggage and all her rage. Any alternate past she might
have lived was erased with the conversion. There was power

though in knowing that *she* actually *didn't* commit crimes against humanity. The woman who did all of those things was dead. All that was left of her were tracers. *All that's left is me. All that's left is now.*

What she could benefit from, however, was all of the high level military and espionage training they had given her. She maintained someone else's memories, but she had her own mind and she could turn this weapon against its creator. But how? *There isn't enough time. We need a plan. We need the real Jessica Butler.* Falling into despair again, she continued walking until there was no place left to go but the safe house.

There was no food in the refrigerator. So, Jessica decided to look for Delph in the basement. She thought he said something about setting up some cots down there. Before she reached the door, Marcelo lunged at her seemingly out of nowhere and cornered her next to the oven. "You should have let us know where you were going and when you'd be back."

"What's it to you?" Jessica answered defensively.

"You think this is summer camp, Butler?"

"Excuse me?" Jessica nested her fists into her waist.

Marcelo hissed at her. "Our information tells us we have less than two weeks until Grey is going to be targeted. We don't have time to fuck around with fallen OCD henchmen who don't know which side they're on."

"In case you haven't noticed, Marcelo, I've been helping you."

"What have you brought to us that we didn't have already? A link to Thompson's computer system? Delph would have figured that one out soon enough. Or maybe you're talking about taking off right after an OCD raid on our headquarters? How did they trace you there, Jessica? How did they find out where we were?"

"I don't know!" The question had occurred to her more than once on her little sojourn. Her chest was burning with anxiety. Her neck and shoulders locked into a single unit. She turned to stalk across the room, but Marcelo blocked her way.

"Who did you go to see today, Butler, and what did you tell them about our operation?"

The dam broke on Jessica's frustration and isolation. "Nothing! I didn't tell anything to anyone!" She pushed Marcelo in the chest and he stumbled heavily a few steps backward. Then she began circumnavigating the kitchen island to give them some distance. "I went to see an old informant. Yes, Marcelo, I had informants. It goes both ways you know. He'd been missing for weeks. His secretary told me he had encephalitis." She flicked her fingers into air quotes. "Thanks to all of you though, I knew better. I thought I knew anyway." She stopped walking and propped herself on the island with her arms locked at the elbows. "The guy wasn't my friend, but he helped me, you know? I wanted to check on him." She looked down. "I was right."

She remembered the picture of Stone and his family on his office shelf and the subtle differences between the husband and father they knew and the man who now came home to them at night. Would they ever sense that something had changed? Would it be for the better? *He didn't have to die.*

A knot tightened in Jessica's throat. She could feel her pulse in her teeth. The first tear shone brightly in her left eye and wormed its way to her chin. It was followed by others and more that crowded the turnstiles at the gates of her eyelashes. She could not restrain the sob that followed. "He was happy. The damn bastard was happy. He doesn't have the beginning of a clue what's happened to him. And he doesn't remember anything—about the killing of Senator Marks, about the chip, and the DNA. He remembers nothing. The Office did it's dirty business and set him free. And then there's me. Why?" She swept her arms across the island, spilling several dirty plates, knives and a jar of peanut butter to the floor. "Why do I know what I know? Why don't I get to forget too? Why!" Finally, she collapsed on herself, folding carelessly across the crumbs and cried.

Marcelo stepped deliberately to her side and bent down to her ear. "You want to forget," he whispered. "I could put a bullet in your brain." Jessica hiccupped and froze. Marcelo paused for effect and put his hand firmly on her shoulder. "Or..." he continued, "you can pull yourself together and use what you know to keep the Prime Minister alive until he's in the clear."

Marcelo stood and walked calmly to the hallway door. "The choice is up to you." He turned, pulled out a gun and pointed it at her head. Jessica tilted her face up from the counter to look at him when she heard the safety release. "So, tell me. Do you really want to forget?"

Looking into the open barrel of Marcelo's gun brought Jessica back to focus. The last thread attaching her to her dream of normalcy broke and her resolve hardened. *Jessica made this mess. Jessica needs to clean it up.* She wiped her face and dried her hands on her pants, standing tall and facing Marcelo directly. His weapon remained steady. "No, Marcelo. I'm going to stay."

Marcelo quickly pulled the gun up, re-engaged the safety and stuck it back into his jacket. "That's the spirit." He walked away from her, whistling tunelessly.

TWNS Newswire 08 | 10 | 2062 | 05:32:01

The final preparations are underway for a gala reception to follow the historic summit meeting between President Fein and British Prime Minister Tyler Grey at the United States Capital Building. It is hoped that these talks will draw the United States into a broader conversation about the merits of the Two Points treaty, which has the potential to loosen the international trade embargo against the United States.

One of the precepts of this treaty is the allowance of inspections to prove that the United States is in compliance with the Human Dignity clause of the International Accord on Human Cloning, which was signed by the United States during the previous administration in 2041. Advisors to the President are resisting the FIO call for inspections, stating that the accusations are unfounded. The Fein administration is demanding immediate disclosure of all evidence relating to violations of the Human Dignity clause. These requests have so far been stalled by FIO, which cites international security concerns regarding some of the evidential documents.

The talks between President Fein and Prime Minister Grey are expected to generate a great deal of controversy regarding the relationship between the United States and the international community. Credible threats to the wellbeing of the British Prime Minister have been verified, but details are not being released at this time. In a press conference, President Fein stated, "The full force of the United States military will be on hand and in control of all security within fifty miles of Washington, D.C. until the talks are completed and the Prime Minister is home safely."

Some civil liberties organizations are accusing President Fein of using the Prime Minister's visit as an excuse for establishing martial law in the Capital region. More on this story as developments occur.

Travelink Northeast Rail: En Route Between New York and Washington, DC

Jessica shifted in the cheap Sensi-föm seat. There was a sharp crackling sound as the material semi-successfully remolded itself to her new configuration. She rolled her head to loosen her stiff neck and sighed. She understood that the SpeedRail with its recliners and curiously attentive staff would have been too exposed, but she was having a hard time convincing her aching back that this cheap and slow shuttle ride was worth the pain. *Man, how do people commute like this every day?*

Mock stretching, Jessica kicked her heel back to be sure her gig bag remained where she left it underneath her seat. She stuffed her light jacket behind her lower back and settled in again. The train hit a bump in the track and she rocked with the movement, willing her eyes to stay open. Trains always made her somnolent, but between the lack of sleep and the intensity of concentration over the two weeks while planning their mission, Jessica's body was dragging her toward unconsciousness. She fought it, not trusting she would wake at the right stop; not trusting the man in the seat across from her to not kill her in her sleep.

The landscape rolling by alternated between trees and open meadows. They were nearing Delaware by now. It was almost game time and Jessica felt ready. She had channeled all of her energy into saving the British Prime Minister. Saving him was like having the chance to hit a giant "Unfuck" button that would begin to unravel all of the atrocities and all of the cover-ups she had been a party to. Saving Minister Grey was the beginning of her own salvation too. She knew she wouldn't stop there, but she couldn't think about that now.

Every stage of their plan had been covered with contingencies and plan B's. The raid on Marcelo's safe house had spooked him and increased his general paranoia. A little paranoia wasn't a bad thing, however, considering who they were up against and what they needed to accomplish. If the OCD could find their main hiding place, who knew what other information they had gathered. The suicide switch for the main nucleus branch had been activated the moment the group was aware of the raid. That meant the most sensitive information should be safe. Still, Jessica knew more had to be done to keep from being tracked. Hopefully their new precautions would be enough.

Jessica tossed on a pair of cheap-looking blue plastic floaters and tapped into her Mate. She eyed the man across from her. He appeared to be absorbed in The New York Times crossword puzzle. His nose twitched up and to the right as he snorted through some congestion. He followed it up with a raspy throat clear. Jessica wished a private compartment had been available, but that would have looked too well-heeled for her current cover. She looked casually around the off-white plastic walled compartment and found the security camera. It was near the ceiling above the compartment door. Jessica slumped in her seat diagonally like a college student heading on break and turned a movie on in her floaters.

On another channel, Jessica pulled up a map of Washington, DC and confirmed the distance between her hotel and the Ritz-Carlton where the closing ceremony gala was to be held. She traced her route again and downloaded the latest satellite information about traffic closures and detours. This activity was all redundant, but she didn't know how else to pass the time until her next scheduled rendezvous. She tapped into the photo bank of their supporting operatives again. *Don't want to mistake who's who.*

Jessica tapped her foot and looked at the time in the corner of the floaters. Ten-fifteen a.m. The man across from her folded his flexible Mate screen and stood suddenly. Jessica started. He looked at her and offered a friendly smile. "Excuse me." He stepped over her foot and left the compartment. Jessica sat dumbly looking after him.

An Undisclosed Location: A Secure Communication Line

The Voice was angry again. Tripp Thompson tread lightly with his words, trying to assuage him. "Sir, we couldn't predict they would have such an elaborate escape route. What with their central location and…"

"Why wouldn't they? These people aren't stupid. You failed."

"Jessica was our best site scout in this division. With her offline, I did the best I could, sir."

The Voice was quiet for a moment. Tripp knew that wasn't good. "Yes. Offline." Tripp could hear the Voice fidgeting with a pen on the other end of the line. "Or should we say, off of *our* line. You had an Integrationist mole working under you for three years and didn't know it."

"Crane gave me no reason to suspect his loyalty. He completed every mission I sent him on. He never questioned anything."

"He was waiting for the right opportunity, that's all. This is all bad, Thompson. I can't afford any more screw ups like this."

"I know, sir." Tripp's palms were beginning to sweat. He fidgeted with his antique fountain pen. A drop of ink made a splat mark on his fingertip like black blood.

"It's taken us weeks to figure out how to get Butler back online."

"Yes, sir." Tripp thought he heard footsteps outside of his front door. He turned but saw nothing.

"Terminate her." The Voice said definitively.

"I'll take care of it as soon as she's brought in, sir." Tripp said eager to diffuse the Voice's anger.

"You're done too, Thompson."

"Excuse me?"

"We have no need for your services any more."

Tripp saw a shadow out of the corner of his eyes, coming from the direction of the kitchen. "Sir?"

"But we can't simply have the bureau chief of Total Wire News Service go missing, now can we?"

Suddenly, Tripp understood the terms of his dismissal. "No! Wait!" He stood and backed away from the table, right into someone solid. A Kevlar-wrapped arm surrounded him from the left "You can't do this! I can fix this! I can fix it all! Just give me a chance!"

"Calm down, Thompson, it will only hurt for a minute."

At that moment, Tripp felt a needle pierce the right side of his neck, near his collarbone. His head and arms went limp first. "I can fix it," he repeated weakly. *Please don't.* This last was just a thought that floated lightly in all directions like dandelion seed as he fell unconscious.

Travelink Northeast Rail: En Route Between New York and Washington, DC

Jessica had to turn sideways to wedge herself around the mass of the woman standing in the aisle of economy coach leading to the café car. The woman was gripping a coffee in one hand and a donut in the other. A small smudge of powder nestled in the wrinkle leading down from her lip.

Once past this obstacle, Jessica continued to the end of the car and slapped the door release. *Come on, come on.* The door slid open and she walked casually into the next car, scanning the crowd for a woman with a pink shopping bag and green tennis shoes. There were two. *How on earth?* She thought. Her eyes swung back and forth between them. Finally, one of the women seemed to pick up on her hesitation.

"Linda?"

Jessica locked her gaze with the woman who had spoken.

"Linda, it is you! It's been forever." The woman leaped up, with her arms extended and gave Jessica a big hug. "Are you getting some food?"

Ummm. "No, there's a line at the bathroom in our car. I thought I'd have better luck down here."

The woman nodded slightly and pointed to the opposite end of the café car. "That car's almost empty. I'll bet there's no line there." The woman's eyes never strayed from Jessica's. She took Jessica's hand and held it between both of her own. "It was so nice to see you again. Say hello to your mother, will you?"

Jessica felt the flat plastic pouch, bearing the small rigid square she was looking for being pressed into her hand. A small amount of security returned to her. "Yes, I will. It was good to see you." Jessica folded her hand around the baggy as the woman withdrew her hands, then turned and walked evenly toward the door at the far end of the car. She activated the door latch and stepped into the next car, which was also coach class. Her vendor hadn't been kidding. Jessica could see only three heads scattered around the periphery of this car. One of them she recognized as a newbie to their organization. He didn't turn to look at her as she slipped into the lavatory.

The bathroom was dimly lit by round, yellow overheads. The shade was drawn. The vanity surrounding the sink was spotted with dried water and soap scum. A few paper towels threatened to fall from the dispenser on the wall and join the half dozen or so that had already succumbed into a pile by her feet. A vent fan made a buzzing sound from somewhere behind the wall near the toilet, which smelled like ammonia.

Jessica swiveled her shoulder bag around to the front and opened it, pulling out a sealed sterile blue mat and spread it on the vanity. She placed a shot glass sized container of alcohol on the mat, opened it and dumped the contents of her "friend's" baggie into it. She looked over the small silicone patch. The entire casing was no bigger than a breadcrumb and contained three microscopic strands of engineered DNA suspended in five drops of saline. These tiny devices could store all of the personal details of their owners: demographic information, family tree, criminal records, education, financial history, account and payment information, their social contacts, and their entire medical record. Some people even used them to keep their wills and other confidential documents. She wondered what new ailments she would be registered as having now and how many bankruptcies were supposedly plaguing her. Those who sold their EASy chips on the black market usually really needed the money. Those who bought them usually really needed to hide. A small, neatly lettered note in the bag said "Linda Bullard. Credits US$ß10,000." *Should be enough to get by.*

Putting the cup down gently, Jessica reached into her bag again and pulled out a razor blade, a pair of tweezers, and a book of matches. She held the tools over two lit matches until the edges had blackened, then dipped them into the alcohol basin. She lay two opened sterile gauze pads on the vanity liner. She searched her left forearm for the small line indicating where her own EASy chip had been inserted three years ago. She ran her finger along the faint ridge to delineate the beginning and end. *Bleep myself in...*She pressed the razor blade to the line and made a small cut following its course, biting back a string of curses as she did. *...not so EASy.*

Spreading the skin lightly with her fingers, Jessica felt her vein roll to the side under the pressure. She could not quite see the old patch buried in its hiding place. She used the edge of the razor to dig around a little bit and finally heard it tap quietly on something solid. She spread the cut open again and saw a glint of gold metal. Sticking the corner of the razor against the edge of the chip, she popped it out of place and carefully dropped it onto the sterile pad, which was quickly being stained with blood.

Using the tweezers, she extracted the new chip from the cup of alcohol and pushed it into place where the previous chip had been. The alcohol burned a trail up her arm as it drizzled into the open cut and was pushed into the bare muscle tissue beneath the chip. She grit her teeth and closed her throat against the pain. Jessica dipped the gauze pads into the alcohol and used them to wipe her arm of the residual blood. Then she pulled some antibacterial surgical glue from her bag and flipped it open with her thumb. Tracing the edges of the primitive incision, she carefully lay down a line of the glue. Then she pressed the edges of the opening together as neatly as possible and held it firm for one minute.

There was a knock on the door. "Hey lady, you okay in there?"

"I'll be out in a minute." Jessica called.

Now, for the final touch. Jessica dipped into her bag one more time and pulled out a small square of Permaskin. Using the tweezers, she pulled the rubbery synthetic skin off of its backing and gently laid it over the sealed incision. Working from the center, toward the edges, she gently pressed the dressing to her arm. The area tingled as the fine coating of acid and antibiotics were stimulated to action, bonding the material to her natural skin. With the side of her pinky, Jessica carefully feathered the edges lightly.

When she was done, Jessica inspected her work and decided that it was passable for an EASy chip placed two to three months ago. Since not everyone had immediately climbed on board the "Big Brother" train, she knew that it would not appear suspicious to anyone.

Jessica rolled the vanity pad up tightly, tying the ends around each other and stuffed it deep into the trash. Then she reached around the side of the blind and opened the window a crack to toss the alcohol and her own electronic identity out the window and hopefully under the wheels of the rest of the lengthy train. Cup in the garbage. Jessica inspected herself in the mirror before leaving the room. She nodded contritely to the man waiting outside the door and picked her way back down the train.

TappedIn Inn – K Street NW: Washington, DC

The taxicab rolled quietly up to the door of the TappedIn Inn. A uniformed attendant in a navy blue jacket with buckle-like silver clasps opened Jessica's door with a smile. She stepped onto the carpeted sidewalk, while the cab driver retrieved her luggage. "Welcome to the TappedIn Inn." The attendant meticulously transferred the bags onto the baggage trolley.

The cab driver tapped Jessica on the shoulder. "That'll be ten fifty."

Jessica hesitated momentarily. *No time like the present.* "I'll bleep it."

"Sounds good." The driver unclipped his scanner from his belt loop and held it out to her. Jessica swept her arm over the reader's pad and waited. The machine made its characteristic beep as it processed the information from the chip. The screen flickered and the word "Approved" appeared. Jessica entered a tip and swept her arm across again to accept the charge.

"Beep." A receipt printed out at the bottom of the machine.

The driver detached the receipt and handed it to her. "Thank you Ms. Bullard. Have a nice afternoon."

"You too." Relief spread through her. The chip worked. Now she only had to stay undetected until ten p.m. and this would all be over.

The bathtub was carved out of an enormous hollowed out block of pink marble raised on an artistically jagged platform of granite. The top rim was formed into a series of shallow petals, which created cubbies that were the perfect size for one person to snuggle into. The faucet and drains were solid brass. A skylight opened up directly over the tub. Within reach, a brass towel rack held two of the thickest towels Jessica had ever laid her hands on. She squeezed her toes together on the spongy chocolate colored bathmat and leaned down to touch the dark granite step. It was warm. *Heaven!*

Jessica stashed her bags in the corner of the room and was thankful that old Linda Bullard's credits were enough to afford a five-star hotel close to her destination. Her new anonymity allowed her to briefly relax a little. She browsed the room service menu. *Bleep! It's so EASy.*

After ordering a duck salad with goat cheese and sautéed mushrooms and a flavored seltzer, she slipped into a hotel bathrobe and began running a tub full of hot water. Warmth spread through the soles of her feet as she stood on the granite platform testing the temperature. *Ahhh...* There was an assortment of bath crystals, beads and bubbles laid out on the vanity. Jessica chose an aromatic citrus ball that felt like limestone in her hands. As she tossed it into the water roiling beneath the faucet, she considered that this would likely be the last luxury she would enjoy for some time. Even if they were successful, there was no way she could go back to New York. And there was still the matter of the spare parts farms. Marcelo was right. With her collection of knowledge and skills, she could do more to ensure the survival of democracy than almost anyone. The weight of her karmic debt to society was grave. She needed to find those farms and destroy them.

Jessica let the bathrobe fall to the granite warmer and slipped her left leg into the now fizzing water. Heat seared up to her knee, stinging just enough to be pleasant. She felt the muscles in her release, then repeated the process on the other side. Jessica closed her eyes as she reclined against curved surface of the tub. She stretched her legs out and resolved for forget everything for one hour.

An Undisclosed Location: A Secure Communication Line

The Voice smiled when the agent on the other end of the line finished speaking. Butler had taken the bait. Linda Bullard's EAS had been used twice, both times in Washington, DC. It was concerning to him that she was there so quickly, but he did not feel unprepared. The agent cleared his throat. "Sir, are you still there?"

"Of course."

"Shall we bring her in, sir?"

The Voice considered this for a moment. "No, lieutenant, I believe she will come to us instead. And she'll bring friends."

"Sir?"

"Put your best men in the ballroom."

"It's done, sir."

"Good. Now, just stay on your toes."

"Yes, sir. Of course, we're doing all we can to…"

The Voice cut the connection abruptly. He didn't need any obsequious speeches, not today. *If you want to get something done right. Do it yourself.* He smiled smugly, linked his hands behind his head and arched his back, sighing. Then he tapped the intercom. "Susan, how about getting some Turkish coffee in here."

"Certainly, sir."

The Voice looked around the shape of his office, breathed in and let out a soft, extended "Ooooooooo". He looked at the focal point on the other end of the oval and thought about the trail of the sound waves all focusing on that one point in space. That a whisper spoken from behind his desk could be heard with clarity across the room, just like a word spoken or a signature written could be felt clearly across the world. He liked that.

Ritz-Carlton – 22nd Street, NW: Washington, DC

Tyler Grey buttoned his cufflinks and took a sip from the teacup sitting on the tiny decorative pedestal that passed for a tea table. There was a knock at the door. Through the peephole, he saw the innocuous young porter he'd been assigned standing by his door holding a small box. He opened the door. The porter straightened self-consciously. "There's a delivery for you, sir." He held the package out to the Prime Minister, who took a barely perceptible step backwards. The porter pulled the box back toward himself and looked at the Prime Minister quizzically.

"Who is it from?" Grey asked.

"I'm not sure, sir. It came by Federal courier."

Grey continued eyeing the package suspiciously. "What's your name again?"

"Brian Douglas, sir. I'm a senior at Georgetown University. I…"

"Step in for a moment, Brian."

Brian stepped in and allowed the Prime Minister to close the door behind him, but he stood stiffly in the foyer of the suite. Grey walked across the room to the mirror and pretended to continue dressing by fiddling with his tie. "Have a seat."

Brian padded to the overstuffed sofa in the living room. He meant to sit on the edge, but instead sunk in deeply, rolling backwards and found himself folded sharply into the cushions. He shifted, attempting to hold himself erect with his abdominal muscles, which quickly began shaking. He waited for the Prime Minister to speak again.

Grey didn't know what to think of Brian. Either, he had something to hide or he had serious issues with authority figures. Someone at a hotel this size, in Washington, DC should be used to interacting with men of his stature. *This boy's nervous.* He eyed Brian through the mirror and felt badly for him. He couldn't be more than twenty. He seemed earnest enough.

Brian watched as the Prime Minister moved smoothly to the point in the room that was furthest from the sofa he was sitting in. He was beginning to fear that whatever was in this box was something to be concerned about. Brian shook it discreetly in his hands and tipped his head slightly toward it. Something scraped around on the inside. *At least it's not ticking.* He thought grimly.

Grey feigned busy-ness with a lint brush "Why don't you have a look inside that box for me."

Brian's eyes darted over to the Prime Minister. "Oh, but sir, the delivery person said it was for your eyes only. I couldn't."

Grey kept his back to Brian and pushed the corners of his lips together. "I trust you."

Brian worried his eyebrows and placed his left hand on the seal holding the top and bottom halves of the box together. Not that such a simple precaution would save him if this box were a "suspicious package". Brian silently prayed. *Hail Mary, full of grace.* Grey tightened his shoulders. *The Lord is with thee.* Brian squeezed his eyes shut and flipped the box open. *Blessed are thou amongst women.*

Nothing.

Brian opened his eyes. Grey approached peered over Brian's shoulder. "What is it?"

"It appears to be a piece of jewelry, sir." Brian pulled a two-inch gold charm out of the box and saw a small slip of paper resting beneath it. He handed this to the Prime Minister.

The paper contained three words. *Look. Remember. Follow.*

Grey was unsure of the meaning of the message, but it chilled him. He reached for Brian's tip pad and credited him US$ß30. "Thank you, Brian. You've been very helpful."

Brian visibly relaxed and smiled. "Thank you, sir." Then he spun around and left Grey to his own thoughts. Grey turned the charm around in his hand and examined its features. In it, a hunter was fearlessly battling an attacking lion. The angle of the lion made it almost appear to be crouching to attack whoever held the charm. *Curious.* Another image caught his attention. A woman, descending from the sky? *What could this possibly mean?* He debated whether he should keep the charm in sight throughout the event that evening. Perhaps a new Integrationist leader was trying to make contact with him. He decided, however, that whoever was looking for him would probably be able to identify him on sight, without the charm. *Is that a bad thing or a good thing?* He slipped the charm into his pants pocket, patted the front to see that is was secure and surveyed himself once more in the mirror.

TappedIn Inn – K Street NW: Washington, DC

Down the street, Jessica also examined herself in a mirror. She needed to look sufficiently formal for the party, which necessitated a form of slinky eveningwear, but there was practicality to be considered as well. She admired her new Silverfish under-garment tool net in her reflection. It hugged her body like veneer and wore just as smoothly. When she used it the first time, she had expected it to be itchy, but it wasn't. Now it was her favorite underlayer whenever she needed to forego her full combat gear. She performed a few crouch and roll maneuvers in the ample space between the sofa and the television. The net flexed and stretched in all the right places, like skin.

The implements of Jessica's gig bag were spread on the bed. She considered them carefully. She would have to economize, given her packing limitations. The mission-critical items were several miscellaneous sizes of metal tubing, some thread wire, an awl and hand drill and a chewing gum-sized wad of polarized-ion putty. She carefully arranged these items into the webbing of the Silverfish, which snapped them firmly to her skin. Next, Jessica considered the precautions she should take. She slipped two particle masks under the sides of the Silverfish just beneath her armpits. It made her feel like she was wearing a padded bra. She shifted it toward the back to maintain full range of motion in her arms. The palm Taser, two magnetic pulse charges, a wireless earpiece, and her gun with extra ammunition completed the ensemble.

Jessica chuckled at the vaguely robo-woman look that the filled toolnet created. She pulled the scoop-necked flowing gown over her head and arranged the edges of the netting to fit its contour. She spun herself around looking for any odd spikes or lumps that would give her away and decided the look was satisfactory. The length of the gown hid the fact that she was wearing heels that were stouter than would ordinarily be expected at an event such as this. She stepped in for a close-up and inspected her mascara.

Now for the finishing touch. Jessica walked back to the bed and lifted the heavy gold necklace from its blue velvet box. She examined the two-inch pendant hanging off the chain. A lion stared fiercely out at her. It was hovering over a small hunter carrying a spear. Above and off to the right, a woman extended from the clouds. In her delicate fingers, she held the end of a leash that tightly held the lion back from eviscerating the small man. The woman had a benevolent smile on her face.

Jessica stared at her intently. *Am I the goddess floating down from the sky to smite the forces of evil?* She wasn't too sure of that. She felt more like the soul of Lucifer in pursuit of redemption. *Am I the lion?* Wouldn't it be easier to simply leave here, disappear and have nothing more to do with this dirty business? As far as she knew, this was the last frayed end of the karmic thread of her own actions. Or was it? *How many packages have I delivered and forgotten thanks to my own conversion? How many Converts have yet to "go live"?* If Marks and Stone were indicative of T-Col's efficiency, it had advanced from a failed experiment to a factory. She brushed her thumb over the golden image that lay in her hand. Ducking her head, she slipped the chain over her head and arranged the pendant just above the neckline of her dress.

Ritz-Carlton – 22nd Street, NW: Washington, DC

A long line of limousines discharged their passengers at the front of the Ritz Carlton in the heart of the power district of Washington, DC. They stood two and three thick in the softly lit entry archway. The cluster of transports looked like a Maine river log jam. Jessica walked casually from the around the corner, brushing softly around the side of one of the cars as though she had just alighted from it. She refreshed her lip gloss as she glided toward the entrance, where she presented the Secret Service agent with her counterfeit ticket. He looked at her carefully and scanned both the holographic stamp on the invitation and Jessica's EASy chip. "Welcome Ms. Bullard. Please progress to the next security station. Aisle two."

Jessica followed in the direction the Agent indicated and entered a bull-pen leading to six thermo-graphic inspection stations. *Did this Silverfish come with a warrantee?* Reviewing her tool inventory in her head, Jessica tried to recall if she had completely tucked all of the ends of the tools into the fabric and sealed each one. She stepped up to the inspection station in aisle two. She was greeted by an officious female agent, who towered above Jessica at about five-ten, she guessed. "Please open your purse and lay it on the table."

Jessica complied.

"Are you carrying anything metal or hazardous on your person?" The agent asked while sifting through the few contents of Jessica's clutch bag.

Jessica considered the polarized-ion putty lodged between her breasts. *Hazardous? What qualifies as hazardous?* she mused silently. "Nope." she replied out loud.

Apparently satisfied with the handbag, the agent pointed toward the thermo-graphic scanner. "Please step into the scanner, m'am."

Breathing evenly to control her heart rate, she stepped forward. The machine released a series of clicks and taps. Finally, a green light flashed on the control screen. The agent smiled at Jessica and handed her clutch back to her. "The ballroom is straight back and to the left, after the Palm Garden."

"Thank you. And where is the ladies room?"

"Past registration and to the right."

Jessica tipped her head slightly and smiled at the woman as she stepped past her. Once inside the ladies room, she looked around to make sure she was alone and headed down the row of stalls. She smiled at her good fortune. Each stall was a room unto itself with full walls and full doors sporting brushed chrome ivy-shaped handles. She locked herself into the one closest to the far wall.

Pulling the awl from her right hip holster, Jessica gently scraped away the grout between two of the tiles near the base of the wall separating the ladies room from the main security office. She pulled the tile out from its nest and laid it on the floor next to her. She replaced the awl in the netting and pulled out the tiny hand drill. She drilled an eighth inch hole through the bedding of tile glue and plaster. She felt the drill jerk as it met the open space between the walls and hit the opposite side.

The point of entry into the security room should be out of view underneath the main video console. Nonetheless, she needed to proceed quietly. Jessica felt the drill bit cut into the wallboard on the other side. She pushed into the resistance she felt. Finally, she felt the bit break through on the other side. She pulled the tool back out of the hole, detached the drill bit and put it away. Next, she inserted a length of thread wire through a small metal shaft and stuck it through the hole she made. It fit snugly just to plan. Digging into the cleft between her breasts, she pulled out the polarized-ion putty and attached it to the inner end of the wire being careful not to squeeze the center too thin or let her fingernails pierce it. *That'd be a hell of a way to ruin the surprise.*

The door to the bathroom opened and Jessica heard two women click across the tile to the vanity. She attended carefully to the sounds of their voices, in case she needed to find them later.

"What was that thing Connie Wilberts had around her neck?" High Nasal Voice asked. "I thought they gave up road kill fashion in the 50's." Both women laughed.

"You can't blame a person for their upbringing." Low Voice replied, "Senator Wilberts rarely brings her up here. She's just stuck in Oklahoma with their dusty constituents."

Jessica wished she could pop out and head butt them into each other just to shut them up. At least they were so self-absorbed and loud she wouldn't have to worry about being discovered. She pressed the tile back into place, smoothed her dress and spread the tile dust around with the toe of her shoe. She flushed for effect and walked to the bank of sinks.

Low Voice sashayed around Jessica on her way from the mirror to a stall, while High Nasal Voice hunched across the vanity attending to her fire engine red lipstick. Her attempts at restoration were doomed to failure, as some of the bright gel had already bled into her spreading smoker's lip wrinkles.

Jessica shook her hands lightly after washing them and picked up one of the delicately embroidered linen towels that had been specially created for tonight's fete. In it the British and American flags were intertwined on gold flagpoles. Jessica noticed that the corner of the American flag was wrapped up around the bottom of the British flag like it was ready to devour it from below. She dropped the towel into the basket next to the window and faced the wall. She palmed a small nail file and brought it to her ear, sticking it gently inside—deeper—click. She turned on the transmitter in her in-ear device.

"Jessica, you're on." Delph acknowledged. Jessica, cleared her throat softly, their sign that she couldn't talk right now. She slid the nail file back into her purse as Low Voice flushed and exited the bathroom with her friend without washing her hands.

Jessica arranged her hair with her fingers once more before exiting to the hallway again, blending in with the clusters of guests making their way to the ballroom.

"There's something you need to know, Jess." Delph warned across the hermit line. "Tripp Thompson's gone missing. I think he became a liability somehow. We're going to be dealing with a new commander here and I have no idea what you'll be facing."

Jessica turned the corner into the ballroom and scanned the crowd thoughtfully. A flash of silver caught her eye near the podium. "We have another problem." She replied as she watched. Her eyes were firmly gripped on Boo, who stood wearing a rhinestone-studded gown in the middle of a circle of gentlemen. She was gesticulating widely and otherwise being her usual charming self. Boo rotated in the crowd. As she did her right leg slid through the ample slit up the side of her dress. At the top of the opening, Jessica could barely discern a corner of silver netting like her own. Anyone else would have mistaken it for flashy lingerie.

"Boo's here and she's armed."

"With what?"

"Don't know yet." Boo turned again, this time she saw Jessica. Her smile wavered for a moment and then re-established. "She saw me."

"Stay calm."

"I'm going to need some damage control."

Boo gently excused herself from her retinue. Jessica walked diagonally across the room to intercept Boo. She reached her hands out, grabbed Boo by the shoulders and pulled her into a service hallway. The metal door clicked loudly shut behind them. Boo began reaching her arm toward her right thigh. Jessica smiled brightly. "Boo? Is that you? It's been ages!" She hugged Boo firmly until she felt Boo's arms tentatively wrap around her back, palms flat—and empty. "Wow, you look great!" Jessica continued. "Did you do something with your hair?"

Boo's expression carried the flatness of the uncertain. "Highlights. That's all."

"Well, it really brings out the gray in your eyes. I was going to get some highlights last week, but I chickened out." Jessica giggled lightly.

A hint of boldness crossed Boo's face. "I'm sorry, Jessica, it's just the last time I saw you, you were trying to kill me. So…"

"God!" Jessica said rolling her eyes. "I am so sorry about that! You know, the next day I came down with a nasty case of encephalitis. Worst thing I've ever had. They tell me I was a little violent at first." Jessica paused for effect. "I didn't hurt you did I?"

Boo's eyebrows shot up and she donned a small grin. "Oh no, no. Nothing like that." Boo looked past Jessica down the hallway. "So, how are you feeling?"

"Great now. Never better. Buckets of energy." Boo turned to face Jessica again. Jessica locked stares with Boo. "I don't know what they did to me in there. But it must have been really something!"

Jessica grabbed hold of the service door, flung it open and glided back into the swirl of tuxes and ball gowns. Boo leaned thoughtfully against the wall next to the door.

Jessica stayed close to the wall surveying the room for more OCD operatives.

"That was brilliant! " Delph cackled in her ear. "I'm gonna nominate you for an Oscar!"

"Great, just what I need. And I've got nothing to wear. Now where's our guest of honor?" She turned and hid her face in a potted palm tree.

"Motorcade got held up on the Northwest Beltway. They should be here soon."

"You don't think they're gonna do him out there, do you?"

"My intelligence has everything coming down here. By the way, watch out for the foliage." Jessica retracted her head and examined her small tree sanctuary. "If things get tough they're gonna blow."

Jessica looked carefully at the small white Christmas lights that glimmered in the center of the leaves. Attached to the tip of each light was a small drop of putty. Jessica walked casually toward the center of the room. "Okay…"

Boo was standing by the podium again, eyeing Jessica suspiciously. Jessica made a big show of waving naïvely to her and smiling. Boo turned abruptly away and looked up at the enormous American and British flags hanging on the curtains behind her.

Just then, a string of Secret Service agents filed into the ballroom all wearing wrist-mounted "crowd pleasers", the rounds of ammo running up their forearms. The energy in the room made a swift change in direction. *It's showtime!* Jessica thought. The rabble began to organize themselves into rows, eyeing the severe expressions of the agents as they spread across the front of the room. All present uniformly faced the podium as the lights focused around it.

Mark Brimmer crossed the small stage, looking more portly and well-tailored than he ever had as the leader of the Integrationists. Enthusiastic applause punctuated his approach toward the podium. He held out his hands, palms down and invited the audience to silence. "This week's summit between President Fein and British Prime Minister Grey Tyler was the most productive meeting we have engaged in since the beginning of the International embargo closed our ports to foreign imports and exports."

Jessica dipped her head into her shoulder. "Which way are they brining him in?"

"The motorcade has just come into my view. They're threading their way into Bush Square."

Jessica scanned the room again and noticed that Boo was on the move. Brimmer droned on. Jessica eyed Boo's trajectory. "Boo's heading stage left. What's back there?"

Jessica heard Delph tapping away on his keyboard. "A series of hallways leading to the kitchen, the basement and, yes, that's it. It's a shielded entrance. That's probably where they'll bring him in."

"I'm heading back there." Jessica waited until Boo had turned into the hallway before following. Before she could reach the door, it opened again.

Brimmer continued, "…give you, the President of the United States."

Boo strutted out of the back hallway with Andrew Fein on her arm. Jessica turned her face away, so as not to draw attention and slipped into the hallway before the door closed. "Which way am I going?"

"Straight back. Then your first right." Jessica followed, pulling out the palm Taser on her way. Several of the overhead fluorescents were in need of changing. Their flickering threw green shadows across the cinderblock walls. She turned the corner in time to see the door open. Tyler Grey strode in, followed by his secretary and a circle of Secret Service Agents. Jessica ducked back around the corner before anyone in the group could be alerted of her armed presence.

She fell in line quietly behind a female agent as the group moved toward the ballroom. The door opened to a burst of excited cheering and applause from the crowd. No one heard when Jessica connected the armed Taser with the lower back of the agent in front of her. She caught the dead weight of the agent as she fell and tossed the woman easily over her shoulder. The door closed, briefly separating her from Minister Grey. "I need some privacy, Delph. What have we got?"

Tap, tap, tap, whish, tap. "There's a locker room next to the rear elevator. Take your next left and it's the first door on the right."

The unconscious agent's head swung back and forth repeatedly crushing her nose into Jessica's back as she hustled to the locker room. She pushed her way in stripping her gown as soon as she tossed the unconscious agent onto a bench. Then she pulled on the agent's clothing, which was a surprising near-fit. The agent groaned and tried to turn over. Jessica caught her before she rolled to the floor and hoisted her into a nearby locker. She clicked the door shut, but could not remove the key.

"What the…oh, man!" Jessica ran across the room to her discarded handbag and pulled a quarter from her change purse.

She tossed it into the slot, turned and pulled the key just as she heard the first knocking from inside.

"Hey, where the hell am I?" The agent's voice was muted as Jessica hid her clothing and false identification under a pile of dirty towels. The agent continued knocking. "Hey! Is anybody out there? Where are my clothes?"

Putting on her most officious bearing, Jessica headed toward the ballroom. She daisy chained the agent's face-obscuring floaters with her own Mate. This way she could access both her own and Secret Service activity and add an extra layer of anonymity. Just before reentering the ballroom, she reached under the tight collar of the uniform and pulled the pendant out of hiding.

Tyler Grey was just finishing his speech when Jessica took her place in line next to the other Secret Service agents. The man to her right looked at her severely. She straightened her spine and focused herself toward the front of the room. Her scrutinizer eventually did the same.

A second round of applause poured forth as Grey turned collegially to President Fein and shook his hand. He smiled at the crowd before descending the stairs leading to the aisle toward the front of the room. Boo positioned herself to Grey's right and began guiding him away from the stage. The Secret Service agents fanned out in the crowd instructing people to make way. In the interim, Jessica circled around the outside by the wall and intercepted Boo and Grey as they reached the door to the foyer. She placed herself right in his view. "Excuse me, Mr. Prime Minister."

Recognition flashed across Grey's face, with quick uncertainty as to whether she was a friend or enemy. Then he saw the pendant.

Back at the stage, Andrew Fein spoke into a small transmitter hidden in his signet ring.

Jessica reached her hand out to grasp the British Prime Minister's wrist.

Boo turned to look worriedly behind her at President Fein. She turned back—desperate.

Music was playing and the invited guests were beginning to mill about contentedly. Many stood considering their options at the buffet table. They didn't notice the line of Secret Service agents working their way down the center of the room, two-by-two.

Jessica glared at Boo, challenging her to try to stop her.

Boo returned the stare with a devastated glossy-eyed gaze.

Boo's hand moved to her left hip.

Jessica figured out what Boo was going to do a moment before it happened. Turning toward the door, Jessica pulled the British Prime Minister's arm harshly, propelling him toward the side of the stage. She followed this up with a push from behind. "Run!" She could barely discern a high-pitched beep behind her as Boo made one final attempt to fulfill her mission and blew herself up.

Shrapnel flew against their backs and legs as Jessica and Tyler Grey ran through the foyer. Screaming and confusion could be heard in the ballroom as the guests registered danger for the first time.

Jessica banked left down the hallway to the ladies room. "Delph! The security office. Now!"

Another explosion rang out and the door to the ladies room blew off its hinges, hitting the opposite wall and splintering just after they passed. A moment later, Jessica heard soft popping sounds as a line of smoke screens blew. In short order, the entire hallway filled with acrid smoke, sparks and flames. Jessica tore through the Secret Service agent's shirt, reached under her arms and pulled out the two particle masks. She handed one to Grey. They both strapped them on as they turned left toward the catering manager's office. The tinny sound of walkie-talkies floated at them from the direction of the lobby.

Jessica kicked in the glass window next to the door, reached around and flipped the lock. The heavy smoke, as it filtered in after them and through the open hole in the window, made it difficult for her to see. Jessica took hold of Grey's hand and felt her way through the maze of cubicles and recycling bins.

Three more explosions shook the building. *They must be cutting their losses with the witnesses in the ballroom,* Jessica thought. The emergency lighting kicked in. Jessica wasn't sure which was worse, the darkness or the density of the illuminated smoke screen. Finally they reached the back wall. Jessica flattened herself against it and slid right to left, pulling Grey along behind her. Then her hand hit the horizontal bar of the emergency exit. She shoved against it, flinging it hard against the wall on the other side. The door beeped impotently. "We're out!" she called into the earpiece, scanning up and down the alleyway into which they had emerged.

Jessica heard a revving engine and looked left. Marcelo sat in an electric blue Beemer motioning for them to hurry up. Jessica pushed Grey ahead of her and they both ran full tilt toward Marcelo's car. Sirens sounded in the distance, they were the high-pitched two-toned sirens of the Office of Civilian Defense. OCD reinforcements were on their way. Jessica and Grey leaped into the waiting porter and slammed the door. Marcelo pushed zero to sixty in two point five seconds.

"You're going to need this." Jessica said, taking the pendant off from around her neck. "It's got all the paper trails and authenticity-sealed visual data you need to prove your case to the FIO." She handed the pendant to Grey, who put it around his neck and hid it beneath his shirt.

Marcelo banked tightly around another curve. Grey fell across Jessica pushing their chests together. Grey's face came to rest about a centimeter from Jessica's own. He smirked jovially, "Thanks anyway. Maybe some other time."

Marcelo stopped the porter at a small airfield just outside the city. A helicopter stood ready on the small tarmac. Jessica leaned over the seat. "Are you sure this place is secure?"

"You're not the only one who can do their homework, Butler. Let's go Grey." Marcelo got out of the car and opened the Prime Minister's door like a chauffer.

Grey turned to Jessica. "If you ever need a friend. You know who to call." Then he leaned over and kissed her on the cheek. "Thank you." Before she knew it, he was gone, running toward the waiting helicopter with Marcelo by his side. Jessica sighed and ran her hand across her face. The smell of soot, salt, and fear permeated the car. She opened the door, got out and leaned back on the hood. It was hot from its hard ride. She decided to stand.

Marcelo stood and watched the helicopter rise into the night. *From enemy to ally,* she thought and shook her head. *God, I need some Pollie.* The helicopter shrank to a speck as it flew away. Jessica watched as Marcelo turned and headed back toward the car. His arms were loose and supple and he was smiling. It was the first real smile she'd ever seen on his face, involving his mouth, cheeks, and eyes.

Bang!

Jessica heard a shot and saw a piece of Marcelo's skull fly away from his head. His expression didn't even have the opportunity to turn blank before he fell to the pavement.

Bang!

A bullet whizzed through the air, hitting the bumper of the blue Beemer. Jessica scrambled over the hood to the driver's door and slid into the porter. She drew the former agent's piece from its holster as she tossed the porter into reverse.

Bang!

The windshield. Inches from her head. There was one more failsafe. A back up to the back up plan. Jessica flooded the converter and sped toward the river at the side of the clearing. Gunning it a final time, she jumped the gradient and plunged into the water.

Holding her breath, she wrestled herself free of her stolen uniform and slithered through the window, buoyed by the frictionless Silverfish. Flipping herself on her back, she paddled out to the middle of the river where the current was swift. As it began to carry her east, she activated the exit coordinates on the suit's internal GPS. Then Jessica spread her arms like da

Vinci's Vitruvian man and sighed. Pulling out of a curve, the river carried her away.

A Farmhouse in Dry Run, Pennsylvania

Delph lay sleeping contentedly in the big four-poster bed dreaming of the homemade pancakes and waffles the bed and breakfast owners had promised them for the morning. Jessica chuckled at the way his face was smashed into the pillow. She was relieved when the plump, aproned woman did not comment on her state of hygiene at their arrival yesterday. She merely pointed out that she kept special black face cloths for heavy grime and showed her the thick terrycloth robe she kept hanging in the closet.

This robe was what Jessica slipped out of after closing the door to the bathroom and turning on the light. She held out her arm in front of her and picked away at the Perma skin hiding her home surgical procedure from days before. Underneath, the scar was beginning to heal a vibrant pink along its boundaries. Jessica placed the little black cloth under her arm and pulled out her razor.

Twenty minutes later, Jessica was sewn up again and dressed. Linda Bullard's EASy chip sat contentedly at the bottom of the bed and breakfast's septic system. *Flush. Now that's so EASy.* Jessica smirked as she slipped her shoulder bag across her chest and looked at Delph again. She felt bad for leaving him this way, with a coward's exit before dawn, but even if he were awake, she wouldn't know what to say.

Jessica almost crossed to kiss him one last time before leaving, but worried she might wake him. So she just left her key and a simple note on the nightstand before closing the door quietly behind her.

The full moon illuminated the street, but Jessica kept to the edge of the road to avoid unwanted attention. After a little more than an hour, she saw headlights in the distance. Moments later, she stepped into the light, extending her thumb. An 18-wheeler truck pulled up and stopped beside her. "Can I have a ride?"

"Where're ya goin little lady?"

Jessica paused. "Where are you going?"

The truck driver raised his eyebrows. "Boston"

How'bout that. "Perfect."

The driver smiled. "Come on in. Make yourself comfortable." Jessica tossed her bag into the seat between them and hauled the door shut behind her. Then she was nothing more than taillights rolling away on the state highway.

Delph was only half surprised to wake up alone in the morning. Lord knows it had happened enough times before all this started. Why should things be any different now? But he swore things were different. She was different. He rifled his hair and looked at the clock—eight a.m. Then he saw the envelope. He picked it up, opened it and read: *Justice is rarely swift and often painful, but one way or another our debts in this regard must be paid. Please. Do not follow me.*

TWNS Newswire 08 | 18 | 2062 | 08:47:45

In FIO open session this morning, the British Prime Minister, Tyler Grey, finally presented the definitive evidence that had been called for by President Andrew Fein regarding the United States government's involvement in illegal cloning of human beings for spare parts. It is said that the cloned people are kept in abhorrent conditions, living for months and sometimes years missing vital organs and limbs. Subsequent to the power of the evidence presented today, the Free International Organization general assembly has announced that it is dropping plans for continued talks to remove the trade embargo against the United States.

A small contingent of freshman representatives in the Central Senate assembled today at the capitol and announced that there will be a full investigation into the President's alleged involvement in this scandal. Unfortunately, several hours later, the leader of this ad hoc assembly of congressmen was struck down with encephalitis and hospitalized. There is no word yet on the condition of the representative or how soon he is expected to recover.

ABOUT THE AUTHOR

Morgan Duran lives in the Boston area with her husband, daughter and two cats. She is a medical speech language pathologist with a particular interest in voice, neurology and consciousness. Morgan is an enthusiastic geek with a passion for technology, science fiction, *Doctor Who* and anything associated with Joss Whedon. She has been a lifelong reader of Stephen King and she credits him with helping to refine her reflection on the deeper instincts and impulses that drive character choices. His advice in *On Writing* inspired her dedication to the elimination of unnecessary adverbs. Morgan is also a singer and songwriter. Her collection of dance/electronic music *In Hiding* will be released soon.

www.ingramcontent.com/pod-product-compliance
Lightning Source LLC
Chambersburg PA
CBHW061607170626
46811CB00001B/344